Life-Lines

by
Ann Z. Leventhal

MagiCircle PRESS

Library of Congress Catalog No. 86-61825
Copyright © 1987 by Ann Z. Leventhal
Cover photo by Dwora
Cover design by Jo Shields

The characters and situations in this novel are
products of the author's imagination. Any
resemblance to actual people or events is
therefore gratuitous.

Published by Magic Circle Press,
10 Hyde Ridge Rd., Weston, CT 06883
Manufactured in the U.S.

First Edition

This book is dedicated to
Iza S. Erlich and H. David Leventhal
in gratitude for
her psychotherapy and his loving counsel

CONTENTS

Chapter I

READY
• *April, 1976* •

Once Jennifer Weiss would have known what to do. She would have felt comfortable doing it. But this is 1976. If Jenny yells, "Ladies First" now, and sweeps past Aaron and Luke into the elevator, she will be demonstrating that she prefers being taken care of to being treated as an equal. This Jenny does not admit even to herself. But her sons suspect. Grinning back at her, Aaron and Luke are just waiting for their mother to demand her old privileges. Clamping the words tight inside her mouth, Jenny follows Aaron and Luke across the threshold. The elevator door shudders, then shuts behind her.

"What floor?" In the crook of his arm, Aaron holds a Passover sponge cake.

"Nine, meathead." Legs stretched out, Luke leans in a corner.

Jenny steps over his feet. This is progress. They are not fighting over who will press the button; she gets to do it.

Quivering, the elevator starts up. Jenny grips the railing. In cars, supermarkets, department stores, movie theaters, and at parties, she holds tight. It is only at home that Jenny relaxes. Now, above the door, a yellow dot jerks from number to number. After five but before six, the elevator convulses, darkens, and dies. Jenny and her boys are nowhere, trapped inside a box of thick, rusty air.

"Don't move." Her stomach is a lead puddle at her waist.

"Who's moving?" Luke asks.

"Should I push Alarm, or Door Open?" Aaron strikes a match and studies the buttons.

"Blow that out! You want to start a fire in here?" Did he do something to stop the elevator? Is this Aaron's idea of a joke? Jenny gropes in her pocketbook until she touches a hard rectangle. Saul always says he cannot understand why the hell she lugs a bagful of junk everywhere. He should understand. Tucked under Jenny's arm, her bag is a chunk of home.

Jenny takes out a disposable flashlight, points the light around, examines the space like a prospective tenant. Wood walls, steel railing, not much in the way of potential. The light makes a leering jack o'lantern out of Aaron's face. Jenny shifts the beam to the panel of buttons. Door Open might lead to an Abyss.

"Press Alarm," she says.

Aaron does. Nothing happens.

"Okay. Hold onto the rail." Jenny braces herself. "Now try Door Open."

Nothing.

"Great," Luke says. "I always wondered how I was going to die."

"Just hold still. Let me think." She cannot crouch in a corner with her coat over her head in front of them.

"Don't sweat it, Mother. You're not used to thinking," Aaron says.

Jenny stands her flashlight in the middle of the floor. "We can pretend this is our campfire." Or they could be inside King Tut's tomb waiting on this Passover, like their ancestors, to be freed.

"While we're in fakesville, why don't we do it up?" Aaron asks. "Go for the metaphysical and pretend you've given us a ray of hope."

"What if no one realizes we're in here?" Luke asks. "What if they just leave us?"

"They won't." Jenny barks to cover her own rumbling fear. What if this time she really is abandoned and left to die?

"I don't want to be rescued." Balancing his cake on one finger, Aaron weaves a path around his mother and brother. "This scene's got to be better than Aunt Barbara's."

"That's ridiculous." Jenny pretends. "Even a bad Seder is fun." It will give them something to talk about in the car, something to prefer about their own home.

"Yeah. Right." Aaron nods his head up and down, up and down. "It'll be a real blast." His scalp blinks mushroom-white in the dark.

Jenny made them get haircuts so her father would not lecture Aaron and Luke about being hippies. Now, shorn, her sons look as

2

defenseless as new soldiers and, once again, Jenny has sacrificed too much—her sons' beauty— just to please her father.

"Pretty cool, isn't it?" Brushing his palm over his velvetized hair, Aaron grins.

"What makes you think we aren't going to suffocate in here?" Luke clutches the necktie Jenny made him wear.

"Don't worry about it." Sweat drenches Jenny's back, staining the expensive silk blouse she bought because Saul once told her ivory was her color. Ivory is the color of old teeth. All her life Jenny has let men impose their rotten taste on her. For a while, she even liked the off-whites herself. But no more, not after tonight.

"How much oxygen you think we've got?" Stretching his neck, Luke opens and closes his mouth like a fish.

"Plenty." Jenny assumes.

"We better call for help." Luke appeals to her.

"Okay. With me together now, one—two—three—help!" Jenny shouts up to a mirror eye in the corner. "Come on you guys." Three midgets together. "No one will hear just me."

"You kidding?" Aaron asks. "Your voice makes hard rock sound like Mister Rogers."

"Maybe we should all shut up to conserve oxygen." Luke pinches his mouth into a line.

"I got a better idea," Aaron says. "You stop breathing."

"That's not really funny." Luke's voice quavers.

In her mind, Jenny flips through a file of disasters culled from twenty years of *Hartford Courant*s. A five-year-old once suffocated from aspirating toothpaste in Bloomfield. Before the Heimlich maneuver, a Stamford man at his fortieth birthday party, choked to death on a piece of steak. Mounds of dirt occasionally cave in, smothering construction workers or small children who play where they shouldn't. And once, a couple of teenagers died in Simsbury because their exhaust pipe got stuck in a snow bank and they were too busy necking to notice the carbon monoxide. Elevator deaths involve people who get stabbed, are pushed, jump, or fall into the shaft.

"We won't suffocate," she says. "At least, not in here."

"You sure?" Tearing off his tie, Luke unbuttons his collar.

"You're such a wimp." Aaron drops his ski jacket to the floor and sits on it. The light, brightening the underside of his face while shading the upper part, makes of him a swami, about to read the future in his crystal ball.

"Think we should open that, let in some air?" Luke points up toward a trap door.

"I'll do it." Kicking off her shoes, Jenny grabs one. "You get on your hands and knees and let me climb up."

"I'm taller than you." Luke is always calling this to her attention. "Why don't I get on top?"

"She's too weak to hold you," Aaron says.

"Just both of you, do what I say." Jenny will show them. Grasping Aaron's shoulder, she hoists herself up. "There's more to power than mere brawn." But can Jenny be wily enough when she has no son to stand on?

"If you really believed in women's lib, you'd stop needing guys to do your work for you." Aaron darts immediately for his mother's sore spot.

"I do plenty of work. I market and cook." Which, they all know, takes Jenny at most, two hours a day. "Plus I do my art." A couple of hours of cutting and pasting.

"Anyone beside you call that stuff art?" Aaron asks.

"Plenty of people." Wishing this was true, Jenny presses Aaron's shoulder for emphasis, his muscles a hard knot under her palm. Amazing to think he came out of her body. How she would like him back up there! Yanking her hand away, she almost falls off Luke.

"You let Dad support you." Aaron smirks.

"I have my own money." Jenny digs her toes into Luke's haunches and, cautiously, reaches up.

"I thought those were Grandpa's bucks." Aaron persists.

"That money is mine." She opens the trap door on a dark odor, a sooty light.

"Earned how?"

"Never mind." There must be someone out there who would pay Jenny to do something. These days she cannot be like her mother and make a life for herself out of doing nothing.

"Hurry," Luke groans "You weigh a ton."

"Thank you." Jenny grasps Aaron's head as if it were a mossy post and lowers herself to the floor.

"You really accomplished a lot up there, too." Aaron chuckles. Bent double, Jenny's rubber-soled moccasin lifts the door a murky sliver.

"Please—help—I—need—help," Luke gasps. "I—can't—breathe." He flops over and goes limp.

Playing dead is one of Luke's specialties; ignoring a strong impulse to give him mouth-to-mouth is one of Jenny's. She sinks down in a corner. The rug, like pre-war auto-upholstery plush, prickles against her calves. She and Barbara used to fight over who got to sit in front.

"This is an adventure," she says.

Luke lumbers to his feet.

"Where? Where?" Swooping around, he hops over Jenny and around Aaron. "Show me the adventure." The elevator quakes.

"Sit down," Jenny screams. She has heard of elevators falling out of control.

Luke freezes. The elevator holds. Thank God, Jenny thinks, a holdover from the days when she believed in Him. Now she is realistic.

Jenny could go into someone else's file of *Courant* headlines: WIFE AND TWO SONS OF TRINITY PROFESSOR DIE IN FREAK ACCIDENT. Page One. She has always yearned to make the front page.

An elevator crash might even qualify for the wire services, photos of her limp body flashed all across the country. A dramatic death gives its own identity to a life; Jenny would not have to become a great artist. She could be the woman who died in the elevator.

But the boys are too young. And Esther is only nineteen; she still needs a mother from time to time. As for Saul—Jenny imagines him wracked with sobs. And Mimi has been her friend for almost thirty years. Jenny cannot die without telling Mimi good-bye. Jenny cannot die before she has made something significant out of the yards of purple velvet she has been saving. She is not sure her parents could survive her death. And this is her sister's elevator. Barbara would be convinced the accident was all her fault. And of course it would be. Jenny smiles.

Luke sounds a trembling 'Taps' on his harmonica.

"Play something less morbid." Jenny has finished her own riff on dying.

Luke trails off with a gruesome glissando.

"It may be a while before they fix this thing," Jenny says. "Why don't we make our own Seder while we wait?" She is accustomed to killing time with made-up games.

"Great idea, Mother. I don't know how you think of these winners." Aaron rolls his eyes back so his empty sockets gleam.

"Remember how you did that." Once Jenny lets him disgust her there will be no end to it. "In case I want to paint your portrait."

"You got a real good chance I'll sit for you too." Aaron's disdain could just be that of a seventeen-year-old boy for his mother. After all, Esther is a photographer. She ought to know, and Esther says Jenny's collages are wonderful.

Besides, if Jenny knew for a fact that her work would never sell, she would go on doing it. And if she believed she might someday make something great, Jenny would devote herself to art full time. She has never done anything full time.

Now she returns to housekeeping. Pulling a bandanna from her pocket book, Jenny shakes it and spreads it out over the rug.

"So what about this Seder? We have any food other than your cake?" If she ever plunges into the Bohemian World of Art, Jenny will never again have to worry about feeding her family.

"I would've had charoses if you'd let me make it," Aaron says. "Aunt Barbara hasn't figured out yet that only nuts go in, not shells. Last year her charoses almost broke my tooth."

"So you've told me. Many times."

"Then why didn't you let me make the charoses this year?"

"Barbara said she wanted to. You could've called her if you wanted to do it."

"I don't mess with your sister." Ever since he saw his aunt split an apple with her bare hands, Aaron's called her 'Killer.' Takes one to know one. Aaron, Jenny, Barbara, they are all ruthless about getting their way.

"You want this wine for your Seder?" Luke tosses a packet of ketchup onto the bandanna. "And some matzoh?" Three Burger King coupons.

"Just remember, I baked this." Aaron puts down his cake. "I get to give it out."

Jenny hopes they get out of here before anyone has to eat Passover cake. Even Aaron's tastes like an eraser.

"And here's your charoses." Luke drops fishhooks in a plastic bag on top of the cake.

"One of my favorite foods. Only get it once a year." Aaron picks up the hooks. "And you let Aunt Barbara ruin it."

"She means well." This worries Jenny. Her sister has no idea how nutty she is. They could both be like that.

"You'd think a fatty would know how to cook," Aaron says.

"How about bitter herbs?" Luke drops a jew's harp, knocks the flashlight on its side, turns the objects on the floor into brown and gold abstractions under a web of light.

Jenny takes out sketch pad and pencil and copies the geometric pattern. She likes working by feel rather than sight. The results always interest her. Someday they may interest others, once she meets the right people, gets some exposure.

"Earth to Mother. Earth to Mother." Luke has his hands cupped around his mouth. "Thought you said we were going to have a Seder."

"Yes. We will." She sketches a last, quick crescent. "I'll make decorations. You play 'Dayenu' to establish the mood." Jenny rights the flashlight.

"Anyone ever tell you you're crazy?" Aaron asks.

"You know perfectly well they have. What else do you have that we can use for a Seder?"

Aaron takes from his pockets a scissors-handled tweezers, a roll of peppermint Lifesavers. and a book of matches.

"Do you smoke?" When she was in high school, Jenny carried peppermints to disguise her breath.

"Do I look like I smoke?" Aaron asks.

"Yes."

"Bummer. Can I help what I look like?"

"Lung cancer is a horrible way to die. The worst."

"Being bored to death by lung cancer lectures is another downer."

Jenny wants to tell Aaron he must draw the line at death. She wants him to know that people who smoke, like macho men, look silly and scared. She wants to know if he smokes because she didn't hug him when he used to suck his thumb. She wants to talk about the smell, the tartar on his teeth, the cost. Jenny remembers her mother trying to tell her.

"I've got some goodies," she says to show she still has something to contribute.

"Whoop," says Aaron.

Jenny puts down a plastic bottle of contact-lens tears and a tin of imported blackberry candies. Hands dart out. She swats them.

"Prayers first."

"Just one to give us energy?" Luke pleads.

Aaron snatches up the box.

"Give it!" Luke lunges. The elevator wavers.

"Stop!" Jenny yells. "You really think candies and cigarettes are worth dying for, Aaron?"

"What is?" He slides the candy next to his cake.

"Nothing." Except maybe her children. In this stalled elevator they are safe.

"But we're going to die anyway, aren't we?" Aaron insists.

"I've got some salt water." Always. Jenny squirts artificial tears into the top of the candy tin. Like the world that spins in only one direction, always taking them toward death, she keeps her real tears underground. "Do either of you have something for green herbs?"

"I could do with some fresh herb right now." Aaron snickers.

"Are those tweezers for pot?" Jenny wants to know the secrets of every secret club.

"Where did you hear that tweezers have something to do with 'drugs' mother?" Standing next to his brother, Luke blocks off Jenny's light.

"You a head?" Aaron thrusts his face close to hers. "Come on. You can tell us."

"No doubt." Jenny waits, making sure it is Aaron who has to back off. He and Luke can keep their secrets. She picks up her sketchpad. Jenny just needs to know secrets she can use and they have given her one of those. She outlines a pair of candles. Boys gang up when they want to break out. Jenny needs to find someone she can gang up with.

Aaron springs up on the rail and flips the trap door open. "For Elijah." He catches her shoe before it lands on his cake.

Jenny stares up into the gritty light.

"Ready for the old boy, aren't you." Aaron leers down at her from his perch on the rail.

She shrugs. Old boys have not done much for Jenny in the past. Stabbing a fish-hook through her candle sketch she hangs it over a framed license. The elevator was inspected a month ago. Some inspection. If Jenny had charge of the real world, inspections would mean something.

"I'm sick of 'Dayenu.'" Luke slaps his harmonica on the rug. "What else can I do?"

"How about practicing the four questions?" she asks.

"You won't need that." Aaron grabs for the harmonica Luke whips behind his back.

"What'll you give me for it?

"Don't forget, that's my cake and my Lifesavers."

"I don't know if I can ask the four questions without Uncle Marvin here to do his touchie feelies." Luke yields his harmonica.

"What a great excuse!" Jenny's brother-in-law massages people to soothe his nerves. When he rubs her, it is obvious he isn't actually feeling anything. Still, Marvin could be bisexual. Or gay. She could be too. Jenny stops drawing.

She could be a latent lesbian. If she is, she ought to do something about it. Jenny cannot possibly concentrate on art when half the time she's worrying about being gay. Not doing art is a relief.

Her candle picture falls off the hook.

"*Mah nistaneh halilah hazeh . . .*" Luke says.

"How's this for a theme song?" Aaron plays "We All Live in a Yellow Submarine."

"Great." Jenny goes back to her sketching. She would be having a marvelous time if Saul were here but these days he is hardly ever around when she wants him; Jenny should be used to it by now. She draws a ceremonial platter, and, unable to remember exactly what a roast egg, lamb shank, horseradish, parsley, charoses, or matzoh looks like, she makes a series of squiggles. Her sister's ceremonial platter is probably just as bad. Jenny flips to the next page.

When this is over, Saul will be sure to want to know why Jenny did not lead the boys out through the trap door to the next floor. If Saul were here with them, that is what he would do. He would expect Jenny to follow him. And she would. She looks up at the furry dirt in the elevator shaft. Climbing out alone would have been too dangerous she will tell him.

"Why is this night different from all other nights?" Luke asks.

Jenny sketches the three of them, around the flashlight, distorted as they are in the mirror eye.

"What makes you so sure it's different?" Aaron asks.

"Ssh." Jenny thinks she hears someone coming. But it is the elevator itself, creaking, shuddering, working itself loose. The light flickers on. "Lie flat." She flings out her arms and legs. "Like this." Spread out, a mouse can absorb the impact of an enormous fall.

The elevator, swaying like an aged camel, lurches up, rising until its yellow dot, bouncing on six, seven, and eight, lights gently on nine.

It is 6:35. They are hardly even late.

Chapter II

SET

• *The Same Evening* •

As long as she is with her parents, Jenny need not worry about what to do. Like a fly swaddled in silk, she can protest, she can struggle, but barring the miraculous arrival of a stranger who will cut her loose, Jenny is tied to her mother and father, tied to their way of life, her only weapon to detest what is happening to her. And that she does, sneering at everyone who lives by the family rules.

Marvin opens the door to the apartment. "Am I glad to see you!" His eyes shoot behind Jenny to Aaron and Luke. "Come on in." Throwing an arm across her back, he hooks his hand around Jenny's neck. "By the time we realized you were marooned, the outage was just about over." Marvin's fingers are sticky, as if he is the inventor of pre-pasted wallpaper because his body exudes glue. "Look everybody who I've got." He nudges Jenny and the boys into a foyer stuffed with people, possessions, and soft thick heat.

"You made it." Lifting his gin and tonic over the confusion of heads, Saul toasts her. Then he leans, relaxed and elegant as a silver chain, against an etagère.

Jenny stuffs her blouse into her skirt. If she leaned on anything that flimsy, it would break. Only Saul is exempt here from the rules.

"The electricity was off for exactly twenty-four minutes and fifteen seconds." Marvin holds up his watch; illegible in this murky light but heavily gold. "Luckily I have only four electric clocks to reset." Clocks stand between palms, palmettos, ferns, and statues; next to African masks, clocks hang like portholes to nowhere over wallpaper tigers and leopards; Marvin's clocks clack, 'tch, tch,' like a chorus of old people spotting Jenny the critic.

"God be praised. You are here." Her sister bustles over, an apron rattling against her thighs.

"What have you got in there?" Their father is a bulldog on alert. "Bones?"

"No, Daddy." Barbara, who has never claimed her right to privacy, scoops peach pits from her pocket and shows them to him.

"How much do peaches cost this time of year?" Simon stares as if the puckered stones in his daughter's palm are gold nuggets. "I bet close to a dollar apiece."

"I didn't ask." Barbara flips the pits back into her apron pocket. "When the bill comes, Marvin will pay it."

"Must be nice." Nodding, Simon approves.

"What can I give you to drink?" Marvin asks Jenny.

"Drinking time's over. Listen everybody." Barbara smacks her hands, clapping for attention. Gold handcuffs wobble on her wrists. "Listen."

"Do you boys know what you'll be doing this summer?" Simon asks his grandsons.

"I want all of you to meet Pierre El Mahle." Barbara pulls a young man, standing beside a grandfather clock, into the middle of the crowd. "He's a good friend of Emily's." Shoulders hunched, Pierre eyes the Reubens.

Jenny backs into the closet doorknob. Trapped. They are all trapped.

"Hello Aunt Jennifer." Emily flutters for a moment, a downy nestling in Jenny's heart. "I'm glad to see you."

"Me too." Blood rushes into Jenny's face. She is not glad at all. Her affection for this niece is embarrassing, ridiculous. Affection for these relatives ties Jenny to them. The girl is a cow.

"What about your Esther? " Barbara asks. "What's she up to these days?"

"Getting through her exams, I hope." Having no idea what Esther is doing, Jenny forces herself to look at her sister's face.

"My niece plans to make a career of photography." Barbara has lipstick on her teeth.

"Excuse me." Jenny pushes in back of Aaron and Luke.

"What's this?" Aaron snickers. "Peek-a-boo?"

"Just be still." Jenny takes a deep Yoga breath. She is not, as her sister's bloody smirk implies, a coal miner using her daughter for a canary. A good mother encourages children to leave the nest. Jenny just wishes she had someone to encourage her.

"Like my outfit?" Sweeping aside a palm frond, her mother presents herself. "De la Renta, reduced from four-eighty to one-seventy." Anna sways from side to side, her arms spread to show her pink pantsuit, her ruffled purple blouse, her big breasts molded like rockets.

"I'm glad you like it." This goes for her mother's magenta lipstick too.

"Everyone tells me it looks stunning on me." Leaning forward to kiss, Anna engulfs Jenny in a cloud of 'Joy.'

Jenny would so like to keep her mother's cheek—soft and warm as a sun-ripened fig—touching her own. She pulls back. From now on, if Anna wants to love Jenny, she'll also have to love her work.

"Want to see the sketches I did in the elevator?"

"Not right now." Anna never wants to see Jenny's work. "What does Saul think about your drawings?"

"He hasn't seen them yet."

"In general, I mean."

"He encourages me." As long as Jenny makes sure his life is not disrupted.

"I'm surprised." Cocking her head and bunching up her features, Anna looks at her son-in-law. "Your father never permitted me to work. I always thought Saul was just like Simon."

"Well, he isn't." Jenny folds her arms across her ivory silk blouse. She does not want her mother to think Saul is a 'good provider.' She does not want a husband like her father. Jenny married to get away from Simon and Anna who looks, in that ridiculous pink suit, more like a Madame than a Mommy.

"Show your father your drawings." Her mother backs away. "Simon knows what's good and what isn't."

He is boasting to Emily's boyfriend about his pre-fabricated houses. "Between Levitt and I, we built homes for a whole generation of New Yorkers," Simon tells Pierre. Jenny's father put thousands of people in colored boxes. If she lets him, he will lock her in a box too.

"You made walls for my papers, Dad." Slipping his arm around his father-in-law, Marvin appears ready to scratch the bulldog's ears. "Pre-pasting paid for everything in this room."

"Do you really want all the things in this room, Marvin?" Saul peers at his brother-in-law through his distance lenses. "Think about it." Saul's office at the college is a monk's cell with one picture on the wall: a giant cross-section of a brain. "If I were you, I'd get rid of some of these things."

Jenny pushes her hair off her forehead. She is not as dumb as she looks. If Saul wants to get rid of her, Jenny is ready to go off on her own.

"Show your father your drawings," her mother says. "I'd like to hear his opinion."

"Not now. It's after sundown." Apron clacking, Barbara shoves back the dining room doors. "Daddy, you're there." She points Simon toward the table. "Luke, where are you?"

Jenny stuffs her pocketbook and sketchpad into the closet and sags against the door. She would have liked them all to see her sketches; she would have hated for any of them to see her sketches; thanks to her sister, Jenny will never know if her parents like her work.

Across the foyer, Luke grabs his throat, gags, staggers.

"Cute." Jenny shoves herself off the closet door.

"Luke? In here!" Barbara calls out. "You belong up at the other end."

"Check." He saunters to the table.

"Mother, you sit here next to me and Aaron. Saul there. Pierre, you're next to Emily." Barbara clutches Jenny's forearm. "You go up with Marvin." Her sister lets go.

Jenny looks around.

Seated, a fresh gin and tonic in hand, Saul is gazing into a spikey mass of iris, her sister's center-piece. Not daffodils. Or tulips. Iris. Either Saul is captivated by the lavender petals arched over tufted gold hairs, or he is dreaming of the other Iris, Iris the Radical Lesbian Feminist, his student. Saul has never shown this intense interest in flowers before.

"What you waiting for, Princess?" Jenny's father pats the seat beside him.

"Nothing." Jenny slips into the last slot, between Simon and Marvin. Leave it to her sister to choose, out of all her husband's patterns, prison stripes.

"Now I'll go over all the names for you, Pierre." Barbara gloats. "Next to you is my nephew Luke." She uses a celery stalk for a pointer.

Luke waves. Pierre smiles, his teeth as white against his dark skin as sails in sunlight.

"Marvin you know, of course. And that's my sister Jenny."

Barbara's celery stipples Jenny with cool water. Jenny could use more. This place is stifling. "And our father, Simon Reuben."

"Please—" Simon wipes his face. "—a little less exuberance young lady."

Barbara is forty-five.

"My nephew Aaron, my mother Anna, and my brother-in-law Saul." Crunch. Barbara sinks her teeth into her pointer.

Saul reaches behind Emily and offers Pierre his hand.

"Where you from?"

"Rah-bah."

"Exactly where is Rah-bah?" Simon thrusts his body against the table as if only it stops him from springing at the boy.

"Morocco. In Norse Africa."

"Oh yes. Rabat." Simon's teeth bite the 't' and he sits back. "My wife and I were there, and in Casablanca, when was that, Anna?"

"In 1954. The year Jenny started Vassar. Hardly seems possible." Anna shakes her white-blonde head in bewilderment. "It's been more than twenty years."

"I'll never forget the Medina, Casbah, whatever they call it." Simon waves the back of his hand, his diamond pinky ring twinkling fiercely. "Why anyone would want to buy goods from such a filthy place is beyond me."

"I thought you got your living room rug there." Barbara gives her father the frozen attention a bird gives a snake. If it is to be Simon against Pierre—because of the condition of the Casbah or anything else—Daddy must win.

"Piece of crap," says Simon, the arbiter of what is good and what is not.

"I bought two rugs for a song in the Medina." Anna frowns at Simon. "The decorator told me I should've bought two hundred."

"You're lucky, Pierre." Aaron is going to tell a Lucky Pierre joke. Jenny stabs her eyes into him. "My sister Esther isn't here." Aaron winks at his mother. "One less name to memorize."

"God willing—" Barbara lifts her eyes to the ceiling. "—Pierre will have many other occasions to meet your sister."

Across from Jenny, Emily sits with an air of heavy contentment. She has her man. Jenny wonders if he has already ferreted under her niece's gauzy peasant blouse to nuzzle Emily's breasts. Either Emily is wearing a bra, or her nipples are barest pink. Jenny, convinced that normal women do not have such thoughts, blushes.

"Time to start," Barbara announces. "Mother, will you please light the candles?"

"With such pleasure I can't tell you." Anna used to say prayers with Jenny every night after tucking her in. *"Boruch Atto Adonoi . . ."* Now Jenny's mother spins the ritual over the family, the ritual soothing as a lullaby, the ritual rocking like a cradle. Saul riffles pages, reading ahead. Barbara moves her lips around her mother's words. Pierre and Emily squeeze together, their fingers touching along their prayerbook's spine. Luke gestures with his eyebrows to be sure his mother sees Uncle Marvin massaging his shoulder. Aaron stares out the window. And Jenny's father, his nails clicking, taps the table.

". . . who hath commanded us to kindle the festival lights."

Striking a match, Anna nudges a tiny wick. It lies inert, refusing to burn. Jenny's mother pokes at it and flame eats the wooden match, chews toward Anna's thumb. If Jenny is to be an artist, she will have to hurl light between the shadows of past and future. Her mother's hand trembles. Regal in its silver holder, the first candle flares, then the second. Jenny releases her breath.

And stares at the iris. Big deal, a couple of candles. Who cares about that kind of mumbo-jumbo?

"Zu Gesund, zu Leben, zu Naches, und zu Kvellen." Simon lifts a shot glass of whiskey and tosses it back.

"I don't see that part in my book," Aaron says.

"It means to health, life, luck, and—." Jenny has never before thought to ask. "What's *kvellen*?"

"Ecstasy." Simon licks his lips.

Her father? Ecstasy?

"Say the real Kiddush now, Daddy." Barbara frowns. Even the thought of deviation disturbs her.

Jenny too. Except for having three children shoot out of her body alive, she has known very little ecstasy. She wonders if Saul would say the same. Maybe for him, and for all men, ecstasy is part of the routine.

"Boruch atto Adonoi boray pri hagoffen," Simon says. "Praised art thou O Lord Our God, Ruler of the World who hast created the fruit of the vine."

"A-men." Saul drains a glass of sacramental wine. He hates the stuff. He pours himself another.

Jenny glares at him. Saul drinks too much. She glares. He expects it of her.

"Any plans for this summer, Emily?" Simon's eyes slide from his grandaughter's pink cheeks to her strapping body. He used to eye Jenny like that. Now, it is Saul who stirs in Jenny the old pleasure, the old shame.

"Not really." Emily blushes. "I have several possibilities I'm considering." She laughs nervously, her breasts quivering. "Nothing firm."

"Time for the greens." Barbara snatches up the parsley and salt water.

Marvin recites the prayer for herbs and tears, spring and sadness.

"Parsley's full of vitamins." Barbara tosses a bouquet at her daughter. Smiling and bowing like an exhausted ballerina, Emily picks up her tribute. Barbara passes the rest of the parsley and hard-boiled eggs.

"What does one do with these?" Pierre stares at the platter.

"What does the turkey think one does with an egg?" Aaron mutters.

"Ssh." Jenny kicks his foot.

"Take one, dip it in salt water, and eat it. Like this." Marvin's pinky sticks up, polish, like dabs of mucilage, shining on his nails.

"Can't go wrong." Jenny's mother slides an egg between her magenta lips. "Luscious." Anna's rolling eyes and monkey mouth suggest that here is ecstasy, in an egg. Jenny frowns. She too loves food.

Saul turns to Pierre. "The eggs are part of the Slavic, rather than the Hebrew tradition." Saul takes a neat bite out of tradition. "The lamb shank and greenery are also elements in this fertility rite." His lips are yellow with yolk pollen. Licking her own lips, Jenny can taste it. "Indeed, Passover is the Jewish Easter with Moses, rather than Jesus, as the central sex symbol."

"I thought it was about liberation," Jenny says.

"That too." Saul finishes off his egg.

"Honestly, your husband makes everything out to be sexual." Barbara cackles.

As usual, Jenny's sister is wrong. Saul makes sex out to be anything but sexual. Jab, jab, his needle sews Jenny to the mattress most mornings and some nights. Once in a while, she goes with him into his black embroidered fire, but usually Saul, as a lover, is resistible, maybe because, like Jenny's father, he is a man. Only a lesbian would notice Emily's breasts.

"Lo!" Marvin holds up a dish of matzoh. "This is the bread of affliction which our fathers ate in the land of Egypt. Let all who are hungry come and eat. Let all who are in want come and celebrate the Passover with us."

"Please God." Barbara waggles a board of affliction at Pierre.

"I understand you're in medical school here." Anna sits very stiff; a wrong move could rip the line beteen her grandaughter and a doctor.

"I just next month finish my residency," Pierre says.

"What's your specialty?" Jenny likes this French Arab Jew. And, despite herself, she is glad her niece snagged a doctor, a nice doctor.

"Pediatrics." He even has a likeable specialty.

"Pediatricians earn next to nothing compared to radiologists I understand," Simon says.

"Pierre has already been offered a position on the staff of Montefiore." Marvin tugs his cuff, exposing a cuff link like a bale of gold. Marvin's son-in-law need not concern himself with making money.

"He was second in his class at Einstein." Barbara cracks walnuts with her hands. Crack, crack, like so many skulls.

Aaron elbows Jenny to make sure she is noticing Aunt Killer.

"I was telling Pierre about your wart medicine, Grandma." Emily's brown velvet eyes pass slowly from Pierre to Anna. "Do you happen to have any with you?"

"Who has warts, darling?" Anna asks.

"Me, Grandma." Emily snorts prettily.

Anna hooks her fingers over the table edge, her nails magenta seeds on the white cloth. "I'll go fix you some medicine right this minute." She pushes back her chair.

"Sit." Simon commands as if he is the master, his wife the dog. "This is no time for your cock-a-mamey remedies."

Her hair a shimmering crown, Anna rocks her seat from side to side, maneuvering herself back into her place. "Later, Emily honey."

If Saul spoke to Jenny just once like that, she would walk out on him. But Saul does not order Jenny around. No one tells her what to do. Sometimes she wishes some one would. Jenny pours herself another glass of wine.

"I didn't know you had warts." Marvin stares anxiously into his daughter's face.

"They're not that bad." Blushing, Emily glances at Pierre.

The doctor must already know all about Emily's warts. Jenny imagines him licking them. She imagines herself with a few warts for him to lick.

"On my foot," Emily says.

"Well that's certainly a relief." Marvin turns to Jenny. "I don't suppose we have to rush her off to the hospital this minute." He lays his sticky hand on her forearm.

"Nope. Don't suppose you do." If Jenny could only be a cowboy, not just talk like one, right now she could be out riding the range under the full moon.

"I just have to tell you, that Saul of yours, he's a wonder." Marvin must think her arm is made out of bread dough. "He never even breathed hard, but I almost died walking up nine flights." The rims of Marvin's eyes shine. "In only three more weeks, I'll be fifty."

"Congratulations." If a dog looked at Jenny with those wet eyes, she would lavish pets on him. But this dog is Marvin. She freezes.

Removing his hand, Marvin nods at Jenny's mother. "Properly marketed, Mother, we might have something." Marvin's real mother has been dead for years. "Maybe your wart cure should be my next venture."

If Jenny could get at her sketchpad, she would draw the matzoh piled in front of her, show the broken brown bubbles lined up like blasted dreams.

"Hey Ruby!" Jenny was called Ruby before she was married, Aaron knows she hates the name now. "How about some olive action down this way?" He grins at her, his cheeks dimpling like her father's.

"You give up the magic word for Lent?" Jenny glowers at him.

"Please, please Mother, will you pass the olives?" Aaron flips manners at her.

"Here." Jenny shoves him the dish, her son, like Saul and Simon, always getting out of her whatever he wants.

"I forgot people call Jenny Ruby. My friends used to call me Ruby, that is, when they weren't calling me Sheeny or Jewboy," her father says.

"That must've been very hard on you, Simon." Saul says. "Being labelled like that when you were a little boy."

Saul's kindnesses always catch Jenny by surprise and make her feel a rush of love for her husband though, even without that love Saul has too great a hold over her.

"You know—" Simon pauses as if this is the first time he has ever thought about how he felt. "—it really was pretty rough."

Jenny presses her father's hand, passing love through her skin into Simon. Now see what Saul has done; she has not touched her father for years.

"Could we please get to the four questions?" Barbara demands.

Luke clears his throat. *"Mah Nishtaneh Helilah Hazeh . . ."* Behind Luke, high in the black window, the moon's mottled circle is bordered by its own bright echo. At Seders all over the world, under that same moon, youngest children are asking the same four questions tonight, their lips turning up in grape juice corners. Jenny's mouth curves in a matching grin. "Why on this night do we hold this Seder service?"

"We celebrate tonight," Simon answers, "because we were Pharoah's bondsmen in Egypt, and the lord our God delivered us with a mighty hand."

Out of Egypt where Jenny's ancestors built the Great Pyramids, into the Promised Land where the best they could do was a Wailing Wall. But no one mentions that their bondage had its rewards.

"Praised be the Lord, for He is Good." Rising from her seat, Barbara belts out a Hebrew chant. She lifts her arms, gold handcuffs wobbling, hands shaking high over her head. Barbara sways, moving flesh like hula hoops in loose arcs around her.

"Way to go." Aaron claps a beat.

Luke takes out his Jew's harp and plunks an accompaniment.

"You show 'em kid." Simon's fingernails peck at the table.

Saul taps his glass with a knife.

Jenny taps her foot on the rug.

"You're really cooking, Aunt Barbara." Aaron quicken his beat.

"I could dance to a speech." Barbara's peach pits knock like castanets.

"You get that from my mother," Simon says. "Mom danced like a regular whirling dervish."

"I just have to say one thing." Anna glows with mega-kilowatts. "Such joy is beautiful to behold."

Simon is telling Pierre he was four when his mother left Odessa with him, his two sisters, and a trunk full of oranges.

"God be Praised." Barbara drops back into her chair her face, like that of a Mormon, Moonie, Hassidic, Jew for Jesus empty save for joy she dabs at with a napkin.

"Anyone else in here warm?" Marvin gets up to open a window.

By now Jenny is used to the heat.

"Look at that moon." Marvin grasps Pierre's shoulders and twists him around. "Costs me an extra four hundered a month to get that view over the park."

"Money talk." Barbara flings her napkin in her lap. "It's out of order, and the word Seder, let me remind you, means order." Brushing her walnut shells into a pile, she sweeps the pile in with her pits.

"You act like I said something awful," Marvin says. "Like I'm not as anxious as you are for this Seder to be conducted properly."

A cockroach scuttles from under the rim of the ceremonial platter and stops in the light, its feelers quivering in panic or rapture.

"I never even said anything about money," Marvin continues. "I was talking about the moon."

Splat. Clunk. Her cheeks scarlet, Barbara slams her hand and bracelet down on the bug.

"Don't get over-excited," Simon says. "Marvin has every right to be proud of what he makes."

Jenny and Barbara giggle. Like the old days. ("What's all that laughing in there? You two are to go to sleep right this minute.") Her sister slips the cockroach carcass off the table onto the floor.

"Remember what Wallace Stevens said about money." Saul's lips are bruised with wine.

"First, just so we can evaluate his remarks—" Jenny's father leans forward. "—tell me who is this Wallace Stevens?"

"A great poet from Hartford," Saul says.

"I wasn't talking about money," Marvin says. "I was calling Pierre's attention to the moon."

"If he's from Hartford, no wonder nobody ever heard of him." Smirking, Simon drops back in his seat. "So what did this genie-ass have to say on the subject of money?"

"Stevens said, 'Money is a form of poetry.'" Now the smirk is on Saul. He knows what is written in books, knows his purple lips are "heavenly labials in a world of gutterals."

Jenny flushes. Marvin never opened the window. They are all sealed in.

"What form of poetry buys groceries?" Simon asks. "If you ask me, this Stevens sounds *meshugeh*."

"Sounded." Saul's voice thickens. "Wallace Stevens is dead." He pours himself another glass of wine.

"Well I'm not." Jenny glares and this time she means it. "So please stop drinking."

"Try some of this, Dad." Pushing the grape juice, Luke knocks it over, purple racing across the tablecloth to cascade in Pierre's lap. "Oh shit. Sorry about that." Luke's arms flail like a colt's legs.

"Watch your language." Slamming her napkin at the grape juice, Barbara gallops into the kitchen. Dishes clatter. Silverware clashes.

"It's okay. No worry." Pierre stands, his beige gabardine slacks gashed purple.

"You'll have to let me take you to my tailor, have those replaced." Marvin glues his eyes on Pierre's crotch.

The table quakes as Barbara sidles over to her guest. "Jenny, I ought to make you do this." She sponges Pierre, spreading the stain up his thigh.

"Here." Simon yanks out a wad of bills. "Stop embarrassing the poor guy." He peels off four twenties. "Tomorrow he can buy himself new pants." Simon counts the money out on the table. It lies, obscene, next to the matzoh.

"Do me a favor, Aaron. Pour your grandfather some wine," Anna says. "Get him to calm down."

"How about trying some cleaning fluid?" Marvin asks.

"Cleaning fluid!" Barbara screams. "You want to kill us? Stink up the whole apartment? Is that what you want?"

"What a crazy question!" Marvin says.

"I'll talk to you later." Snatching up the cash, Barbara jabs it at her father. "You and your money. Desecration."

"I was just trying to help," Marvin whines.

"Not very effectively," Barbara shouts.

"You shouldn't speak to your husband that way." Anna shakes her glistening head.

"Will you please butt out," Simon yells.

"Could we finish the service?" Jenny begs. "It's almost eight o'clock." The fighting can take hours. "We have a big drive ahead of us."

"Pay no attention to any of this, Pierre." Anna's magenta fingertips sweep the air. "Only talk, that's all it is."

"Now you're a member of the family, Pierre." Smiling as if he has played his part in the scene well, Simon pockets his money. The Reubens have initiated their latest victim. Pierre looks concerned. Barbara's chest heaves as if she has been crying.

"On page twenty-eight—" The book Saul holds up blocks his face. "—will everyone please read in unison?"

"How manifold are the favors which God has conferred upon us." The old fairy tale cannot cover the wound. "Had He divided the sea and not permitted us to cross on dry land—" Contained year after year in this golden cocoon of holiday lights, these people hate each other. "Had He permitted us to cross the sea on dry land, and not sustained us for forty years in the desert—It would have satisfied us." Jenny is almost forty. How long will she keep going back with them into this desert ? "—fed us with manna—" Her sister's once size ten body settles in the chair like a parachute wallowing to earth. "—given us the Torah—" Emily and Pierre bend over their book. Anna beams, the purple ruffles flaring from her neck, wings that do not fly. "Sent us prophets of truth." Aaron turns down his mouth and nods. He, like Jenny, detects the truth

21

under this truth. "—made us a holy people—" Saul pauses to stare into the iris as if they hold his future. "How much more then are we to be grateful—" Her stomach clenched, Jenny reads loud and fast, louder and faster, pressing every one of them until everyone's Egypt, Manna, Sabbath, Torah, Temple, and Satisfieds whirl into Amen.

"Hally loo," she crows since yes, yes, there can be no more backsliding. The Reuben family is terrible enough for Jenny to leave.

Chapter III

ROUND ONE
• *Two Weeks Later* •

At home there is no need for Jenny to change. She lies in her backyard letting the sun leach out of her all the salts of anxiety. Sweat beads her upper lip and runs between her breasts. Here Jenny can be a housewife who dabbles in art. She can forget everything and sun-bathe on this first hot day of the year.

There is really no necessity for her to become independent. On Passover night, the closer the car got to Hartford, the better Jenny felt. The home she established for Saul and the children suits her. Her life is very pleasant.

But she cannot take as much sun as she used to. Jenny's skin smarts. She stands up, her head, for a moment, light.

Those daffodils have had it. Jenny tears off their fragile, withered, slimy heads and throws them at the sodden pile she calls 'humus': gothic branches hung with black sludge and grass clippings, like the dead shaving hairs Saul leaves in the bathroom sink. Obviously she must do something to turn that slop into compost.

Jenny cannot make herself go to the library to get instructions on how to dig a pit, layer it, apply chemicals. She cannot organize all the details from all the articles she has already read.

As it is her tulips are gorgeous, their scarlet petals spread to expose dark, exotic secrets Jenny wishes Saul was here to see. But Saul will not be home before dinner, and by then, the tulips will have closed.

Maybe she should paint them. Jenny can easily imagine those

tulips on the cover of *The New Yorker*. The magazine has often had worse covers than pictures she could do. Dreaming of her first *New Yorker* cover, Jenny goes into the house.

At five o'clock, the sun is still high, and her kitchen warm. Upstairs, the boy's rock and roll thuds while downstairs, Brahms fills Jenny, making her as large as the kitchen itself, glorifying what she is doing.

She is using a bulb baster to suck umber-flecked gold fat in and out, over her roasting chicken's legs and thighs. Again and again, Jenny squeezes, squirting juice over the bulging bird. Smiling, she slowly closes the oven door.

Jenny can hardly wait for Saul. If he is late, her chicken will dry out. He keeps setting up 5:30 conferences with this new protégée" of his, Iris Wilde. Jenny's eyes fill.

Usually she waits for "All Things Considered" but now, in the "Gaudeamus Igitur" part of Brahms' Academic Festival Overture, Jenny switches off the radio. No more rejoicing therefore because she is young. Not at thirty-nine and three quarters.

The phone rings.

She sets the timer for a final basting. The phone rings again.

Why doesn't one of the boys get it? It is probably one of their friends. Or Saul. And they can take the message.

The phone rings.

The dishtowel makes her fingers smell moldy.

The phone won't stop ringing.

"Hello," Jenny says.

"Mom?" It is Esther.

Upstairs a door opens. Electric guitars throb.

"Who is it?" Aaron yells.

"That for me?" Luke wants to know.

"No." Jenny yells. "For me." She drops into a chair and puts her feet up on the table. There is not much to say. She has not run into anyone interesting lately, and Esther has already heard that Jenny sold three out of eight collages she showed at the bank. But it is okay. Ess is doing the talking. Jenny hugs the receiver to her ear.

"Remember I told you about Rick Simons?" Esther asks. Rick Simons must either be the potter from Kalamazoo, or the anthropologist from Brooklyn. "He's from Seattle, going to Georgetown Law next year. Okay if he comes home with me for spring break?"

"Sure."

Georgetown. Either Rick Simons is Catholic, or he is not. The name could go either way.

"He's a vegetarian," Esther says.

"No problem." Jenny lists meals in her mind: Macaroni and Cheese, Eggplant Parmesan, Spaghetti with Mushrooms. "Does he eat fish?"

"I think so."

Jenny adds Shad and Shad Roe to her list while Esther tells about a photography professor's critique of her work.

"He says I have a talent that I can develop in time."

The timer buzzes. Jenny's chicken is almost cooked.

"That's the good news. The bad news is my roommate's driving me up the wall," Esther says.

"I know exactly what you mean." Jenny's roommate is probably at Iris Wilde's house doing what the feminists call role playing: Saul fools around, his wife cooks.

"You wouldn't believe what it's like around here," Esther is saying. "The room reeks of cigarettes even when Caro's out, which she practically never is."

Iris Wilde's room probably reeks of hashish and past orgies, not chicken and cat shit. Iris is the kind to have heirloom mirrors and objets d'art, Jenny thinks, not snapshots and kindergarten paintings curling, like dead skin, off her walls.

"Is it too late to make a change?" Jenny asks. In her case, after twenty years it may be too late not to make a change.

"Actually, the situation's not all that bad," Esther says. "It's just that when I get uptight, I concentrate on Caro's bad points."

"I know the feeling." Jenny may be imagining that Saul is having an affair. If so, it will be marriage as usual, Jenny will sit here, every night in this kitchen, until the day she dies.

"I want to hear exactly what you think of him," Esther says. "Okay?"

"Think of who?"

"Come on, Mom. Rick. I've just been telling you. We'll be there Thursday, driving up in his car, okay?"

"Sure." Jenny's phone has a long cord. Stretching it, she gets up, goes to the sink, and fills the water pistol that hangs there.

"Just one more thing. Mom?" Esther pauses as if she is afraid to say what she wants to. "About when Rick's there—"

"Not to worry. I promise I won't do anything to embarrass you. I'll even vacuum before you come." Jenny shoots the cat who dives off the table.

"It's not that. It's—" Words rush out like cold water. "I want Rick to sleep in my room. With me."

"No." This is probably a test. Like Civil Defense. Jenny is ready. "It's definitely not okay."

"Come off it, Mother. I know you. Basically you're not a hypocrite."

Aaron picks up the extension.

"Hey Ess, how you doing?" Over the music his voice is hard, but not impossible, to hear.

"Great," Esther says. "And you? Any news on the waiting list yet?"

"They say I should hear by June."

"Hang up the phone please, Aaron," Jenny says.

"You'll get in," Esther says.

"At this point, I don't give a shit."

"It gets like that."

"Hang up, Aaron." Jenny aims at the damn cat up on the table again. Scooting down, he knocks a napkin and fork onto the floor. Next fall Aaron will be gone, then Luke. Jenny and the cat will wait, day after day, for Saul to come home. What will she do with all that time? The cat prowls to amuse himself.

"What's up with you and the women these days?" Esther asks Aaron.

"The usual's up." Aaron snickers. "You know how it is at my age." His sexual energy is pungent and palpable as sweat. "I mean I do some partying, but you wouldn't believe the dip shit girls at school."

"When are we going to eat?" Luke bangs into the kitchen. "I've got a Latin quiz tomorrow, and I can't study on an empty stomach."

"At 6:30," Jenny says, "same as we always do."

"Same as you always say, but we never do, you mean." Luke takes a carton of ice cream out of the freezer.

"Don't eat ice cream fifteen minutes before dinner." Jenny clings to the old orders as if, these days, anything could ruin Luke's appetite. Often he saves her the trouble of putting groceries away by eating them right out of the bag.

"What's for dinner?" Luke asks.

"Chicken."

"Might as well eat ice cream then. Your chicken blows wombats." He is shaping a fudge ripple igloo.

"Aaron, will you please hang up?" Jenny speaks into the phone.

"Not so intense," Aaron says. "I'm expecting an important call. You're the one who should hurry up and get off."

"Hang up and I will," Jenny promises.

"If you ask me, the Kingswood boys are the real dip shits," Esther says.

"Who's asking?" Aaron hangs up.

Luke takes his ice cream back upstairs.

"Esther?" Jenny again closets herself in the warm kitchen, quiet now save for the slight snapping of chicken fat, and the cat fooling with something in the sink.

"Yes."

"I want to talk to you about this." A lie. Jenny wants to lie down and suck her thumb. "Maybe to you it means I'm a hypocrite, but I just don't see how you can do it. I don't see how you can do it."

The real trouble is, Jenny sees exactly how Esther and her boyfriend can do it. In the missionary position. Like her father and mother. Saul taught Jenny, he is now teaching Iris. But what is the curriculum?

"Easy. My bed's big enough for two," Esther says.

"You know that's not what I mean. What about the boys? What kind of influence would it be on them?"

Esther will never fall for that lame argument. God damn that Saul. He has got Jenny too mad to think.

"I don't believe you're being so ridiculous, Mother. Aaron and Luke know the facts of life."

The timer is buzzing. Jenny's chicken is done. Where the hell is he? There is no sense being married to a man who is never around. A ribbon of chilly evening air wraps itself around Jenny's shoulders. Esther is telling her how much the boys already know about sex. Jenny shudders, sneezes, gets up, slams and locks the window.

A woman was raped a few blocks from here last year by a man who climbed in a first-floor window. She lived alone.

"So it's a little late for me to be a role model," Esther is saying. But her mother still needs to learn. Jenny is sick to death of innocence. "I know for a fact that Aaron's no virgin."

There are, however, certain things Jenny would rather not know.

"Luke's only twelve," she says. "I don't want him getting ideas."

"No matter what I do, he'll start experimenting soon. He's getting to the age for it." Esther calls screwing around 'experimenting' as if it is a science.

"Are you using birth control?" Jenny is speaking someone else's lines. It is not her daughter who is having sex with this Rick. Esther is not even sure if Rick eats fish.

"Yes," Esther says, "I use a diaphragm."

When Jenny was Esther's age, she was married, but she had never seen a diaphragm. Only heard rumors.

"Going to bed with a man is more complicated than you make it sound." Look where it got Jenny. "It's not just a biological thing you know."

"You're the one who brought up birth control right away, like that's all it's about, not me," Esther says.

The cat scoops the chicken neck out of the disposal and streaks behind the refrigerator with it. Jenny hopes he chokes; no she doesn't. She rouses herself, aims down refrigerator alley, scores a direct hit. The cat flees, leaving the chicken bones back there for her to clean up.

"I'll see what your father thinks," Jenny says. Saul will figure out a way to stop it.

And he can worry about getting in back of the refrigerator too. When Esther went to her first dance, Saul said he hated to think of boys with their sweaty hands on his daughter. After he hears what this Rick is up to he will be glad to work off steam moving the refrigerator around. Or else the bones can just rot back there with everything else.

Jenny wads up paper towel and stuffs it into a hole in the baseboard. Saul was supposed to fix that weeks ago. Maybe the rat has already left this wreck.

"Is Dad home now?" Esther asks.

"No." Over the rattling top of the asparagus pot, the cat knocking a pencil around on the linoleum, and Esther's voice, Jenny waits for Saul's car to pull into the driveway. He deals with college kids every day. Saul will know what to do about this.

"It's like being kosher," Esther says, "before people knew why they got sick from pork and shell-fish."

Two cars drive by, the sound of their wheels like tape being pulled from the pavement. It must have started to rain. Saul and Jenny used to walk in the rain holding hands.

"Only diehards go through all that now, Mom."

"I don't see where being kosher comes in," Jenny says.

A car door slams across the street.

"It's exactly like being a virgin, there's no reason for it any-more." Esther has birth control, antibiotics, abortion. "What do you think Rick and I do here?" In college, Nelly Zelman came into Jenny's room a couple of times and played with her breasts. Jenny is not sure any sex has felt that good since.

"I try very hard not to think," she says, "and until tonight I was good at it." She has roasted the chicken, steamed the asparagus, tossed the lettuce, chilled the wine. Jenny has brought everything to perfection, and still there is no sign of Saul.

If Jenny does not get out of here, she will end up turning off lights to save money. She will turn on TV to keep from hearing night thumps. She will sit shining, in the blue-white glow, like a negative no one will ever print.

"It's six-thirty." Luke slams the swinging door from the dining room against the kitchen wall. That's when you said we'd eat."

"When will you make up your mind? I have to tell Rick tonight," Esther is saying. "If the answer's no, we'll have to make other plans for spring break."

Jenny's only daughter is threatening not to come home unless she can screw some Catholic she hardly knows right in the next room. The cat, now retching, will probably kill himself with a chicken bone. Luke is finishing the last gallon of ice cream. Saul is probably pinned under the car dead, or worse, he is alive.

Aaron picks up the extension.

"Will you girls get off the phone? I told you, I'm expecting a call."

"Hang up," Jenny says.

"I have to know by ten o'clock at the latest."

"What?" Aaron asks.

"I can't make a decision until your father gets home."

"I forgot," Luke says. "Dad called before and said he won't be home until after ten."

"Did he say where he could be reached?" She will call Saul at Iris Wilde's. Know the truth once and for all.

"Just that he had a meeting at the college," Luke says.

Saul will come home and tell Jenny all about his meeting. And, for once, thanks to Esther, Jenny will have something to tell him.

"Tell Rick you'll let him know by eleven."

"What's he want to know?" Aaron asks. "I bet I can fill in the blanks."

Jenny hangs up.

Her children know all about sex. It is time she found out. But how? She could write away to Fredericks of Hollywood, get herself a fringed g-string, go to a fancy restaurant without underpants and the whole time nobody, except her and a guy under the table, would know he was touching her tuppy with his tongue. Jenny is melting down there just thinking about it.

She burns her hand on the pan she slides out of the oven.

"Shit. Oh shit." Even thinking about sex gets her in trouble.

"Hey, that chicken looks great." Aaron comes into the kitchen. "Want me to carve? You always mess up the carving."

"Fine. You carve." Jenny blows her nose in her apron, takes it off, flings it down the basement stairs toward a dishcloth lying like cow flop on the way to the washer. Soon she will have to—Jenny slams the door. "I'll dress the salad."

"Easy on the vinegar. You always overdo," Aaron says.

In this house there is always someone to tell her what she is doing wrong.

"Now you're over-oiling." Reaching around Jenny, Aaron snatches the bowl.

Luke smears butter on his asparagus.

Jenny sits down. Elsewhere there must be people who would appreciate her. The main thing to remember is she is not ugly, she is not stupid. If she puts her mind to it, she will figure out how to get out of this mess. She has gotten herself out of messes before.

Jenny's wine looks at her, yellow and clear as a teddy bear's eye. Behind the refrigerator the cat crunches his bone. Jenny has established that she is not interested in other men; she has already had too many men.

"Your chicken's not as vile as usual." Using a drumstick as a finger, Luke is reaming his gums.

"Wish I could say the same for you." Glad she trained the boys to leave her a thigh, Jenny bites off a blistered chunk and cannot help noticing. It is delicious. A good cook can always lure people to her table.

"We won today, eight to six," Luke says.

"You score?" Aaron asks.

Once Jenny figures out how to make the first move, the rest will be easy.

"No. But I got credit for two assists."

How does Saul do it? He just begins. Jenny would have to have the other person's permission.

"Is there anything besides frozen yogurt for dessert for a change?" Leaning back in his chair, Aaron is already taking a box of cake out of the bread drawer.

"You're obviously capable of seeing for yourself," Jenny says.

Some people are pretty likely to say yes; she just has to figure out who they are.

Jenny shoves back and stares at the carcass on the table. She can feel something like it stuck inside her, something she wants to get out. But what? "Get finished in here, you two." She stacks the dishes. "I've got work to do."

30

"What kind of work?" Handing Luke a coffee cake, Aaron keeps the hot cross buns for himself.

"Art." Those bones remind Jenny in some way of a bridge. "I'm going to make something out of the chicken bones." Or a boat maybe.

Hee-hawing like donkeys, their mouths stuffed with cake, the boys leave. Jenny wishes getting out of here was that easy for her.

Chapter IV

ROUND TWO
• *Later the Same Evening* •

Jenny may have lost her sanctuary—she is not sure what to do any more even in her own home—yet she has not lost her salvation. Art. In her Jewish Mother days she might have turned these chicken bones into broth. Now they mean more to her than stock though exactly what their meaning is, she does not yet know. But Jenny feels in herself a foolish certainty: in this carcass there is beauty to be preserved.

She rubs chicken meat off the bones. She gouges mushy secrets out of the chest cavity. She picks at shreds of flesh. This carcass is, like Jenny's own nose, cartilage and bone; she has somehow to make it solid as marble.

Jenny races upstairs to find her book. Not in the bedroom bookcase, on the night-table, in Saul's study. Where was she the last time she had it? Running into the bathroom, she paws through the hamper. It is there.

She reads the chapter on plastic lamination. Not exactly what she wants but she might be able to adapt the technique. Grabbing her bag of scraps, she goes back to the kitchen.

What she imagines is a coating that will harden like ice on a branch. She clears off the table and dumps everything out of her bags. The whole construction—bones, purple velvet, ribbons, whatever Jenny decides to use—covered in plastic would inevitably look like a huge paperweight. She wonders about wax. Murky drips burying these bones could be the effect she is after.

There cannot be even a speck of membrane on the cartilage. Nothing that will rot. If she scrapes with steel wool, the cartilage will lose definition. Picking up the bones, Jenny gnaws. It is like biting skin around her nails; no matter how much she chews, the edges are ragged.

On television, prompted by a few drops of liquid detergent, food wafts off dishes. Jenny squirts 'Joy' into her kitchen sink and fills it with hot water. She drops the carcass in. Nothing floats off. Instead, bubbles cluster like frog-eggs around the skeleton.

Saul's car door slams. Nine thirty-five. She was hoping for ten. Saul's feet hurry up the back steps. Each of his rubbers slaps, it slaps on the linoleum in the back hall.

The sink, draining, s-s-sucks.

Sweeping into the kitchen, Saul sets his precious briefcase on a chair before he leans over Jenny.

"How are you?" He kisses her.

"Busy." She pushes him away, her lips not his on demand.

"So I see." He eyes the dirty roasting pan, stacked dishes, chicken bones, cloth swatches, ribbons, papers. Why must he make such a point of it? Jenny knows she has no business working on art before she cleans up. "Have a good day?" His hair and skin are glazed with fresh rain. Grownups go out in the dark alone.

"Not very." Drops bead on Jenny's arm, slave arms coated with chicken fat.

"Why don't I help you with this?" Saul shoves his sweater sleeves to his elbows.

"Because I don't want your help." He is not going to make Jenny feel more guilty by cleaning up her mess.

"Boys upstairs?" Saul moves toward the front hall.

"Just wait. Exactly where have you been?" Sharp as an ice pick, Jenny's voice stops him. "I expected you here by 6:30 at the latest."

"I told you I had a Curriculum Committee meeting tonight. Here." Saul's; long thin finger taps the calendar that hangs near the phone. April. Wednesday. 28. Curr. Comm. Mtg. He has her nailed. Tap, tap, tap. "And I called and left word with Luke in case you forgot. What more do you want of me?"

"Nothing." She wants him to get her out of this mess. "My mistake." Grease flecks belt Jenny's sink. If she had drawn that line with a ruler, it could not be more exact. Saul's printing on the calendar grid is equally tight, equally precise. All over this kitchen, lines close in around her like a net.

"You're very uptight tonight." Coming up behind Jenny, Saul massages her neck.

"That's projection." Reluctantly, she shrugs him off. "You're the tense one." What he was doing felt good. "Take it easy, Saul, you'll live longer that way."

"Maybe so." His face, like his hair, is moon-white. Saul is fading, one way or another, on his way out. All the rats are leaving. Only Jenny clings to the damn ship. "I have been feeling a lot of stress lately," Saul says.

"We live in a stressful world." Jenny turns back to the gray heap in the center of the sink. Her bones.

"Any mail?" Saul asks.

"Nothing of any importance." She turns on the faucet. The carcass jerks, like a punching bag, around the sink.

"Where'd you put it?"

"What I really need for this—" Jenny turns off the water. "—is some maggots." Once she buried a swordfish bill and dug it up six months later. Maggots had eaten away every trace of tenacious flesh. Now she wants something else that will work for her like that, something that will not take half a year to eat away what she no longer wants.

"Could you please tell me where the mail is?" Saul never lets up.

"Don't be hostile. I know where it is." Jenny has not lost the mail in years.

"Would you mind, then, telling me?" Saul holds her past against her.

"It's upstairs."

"Where upstairs?"

"Either on my night table, or on top of the toilet." Jenny rubs her bones. Still slimy, the wish-bone is floating loose. Maybe she could use it in a smaller piece, 'Wishful Thinking.'

Above her, Saul clomps around. What is he expecting that is so important? Only bills and junk come here. They used to get invitations, but now that most women work, the only parties are the ones Jenny gives.

"Anyone seen the tongs?" she shouts. If she could hold the bones over a burner, she might be able to sear off the soft tissue. Above her, Saul is talking to the boys. He adores his children; she cannot fault him there. "You guys, who took my tongs?" The kitchen drawer opens part way. Jenny snakes in her hand and feels the tongs, in back of a potato masher wedging the drawer. She has not mashed a potato in fifteen years.

"This what you're looking for?" Aaron comes in with her wire cutters.

"No, but I'll take it." Jenny can do anything with a wire cutter.

34

"How about a reward?" Aaron twirls her pincers just out of her reach.

"Satisfaction. You're returning stolen property." Jenny jerks the drawer. It jams, the noise hard inside her teeth.

"How about something a little more tangible?" Aaron keeps twirling. "Like maybe your car for a couple of hours."

"It's a school night." The drawer jumps open a crack. Worming her hand inside, Jenny can touch the masher but not move it.

"I know, but I told Kim I'd do the bio homework with her." Aaron weaves around the kitchen balancing the wire cutters on a fingertip. "In person if possible."

Jenny slams the drawer. Metal shifts, maybe in the right direction. She tries slow sliding. Slowly, the drawer jams. If she gives Aaron the car, he will not be here to grin at her. He will not be here to remind her he has had sex.

"Be home no later than ten thirty." The minute Jenny has the wire cutter in hand, she feels better.

"It's already quarter to." Aaron lifts her pocketbook off the doorknob, plunges his hand inside. "How about if I'm home by eleven?"

He has her keys. No matter what she says, he will be home no earlier than eleven.

"All right, but not one minute later. And Aaron—" Jenny stares into her son's eyes.

"What?" Aaron raises his brows and stares back.

"You are to do biology with Kim, nothing else. Definitely no anatomy." Jenny is King Canute ordering the tide to stop. "You hear?"

"Anatomy is biology, Mother, and biology is destiny."

"I thought you said the girls at Kingswood are dip shits," Jenny reminds him.

"That was before. This is now," Aaron reminds her.

"I'm too young to be a grandmother." At least Jenny feels too young.

"Not really." Sniggering, Aaron swings out the door.

The cat slinks in.

"Aaron's going to college in the fall." Saul saunters in from the front hall. He does more than jog. Flipping the pates of *Runners World*, he also reads about jogging. "You planning to tape your lectures so he can take them with him?"

"If necessary." Jenny is not letting Saul tell her how to raise her own children. "Will you please unstick this drawer for me?" She stands back.

"Sure." Pinning his magazine under an arm, Saul shifts the drawer from side to side until it opens, fully, smoothly, as Jenny knew it would. For him.

"Thanks." She pulls out the potato masher and pushes it into the trash can. She should have gotten Aaron to take out the trash as part payment for the car.

"What're you doing with that?" Saul asks.

"I don't know." Jenny takes the masher out of the trash. A wet cone bulging with coffee grounds flops to the floor. Jenny wants to flop down next to it. She gets the dustpan and brush, and sweeps up the grounds. Saul goes back to his magazine. She can hardly reach the cabinet over the stove to get it open. He is tall. And reading. Holding her potato masher as if it were a bridal bouquet, Jenny flings. A silver napkin ring with Saul's initials on it dives, hits, pits the white enamel stove making a black spot that will be forever. The masher bounces out and onto the floor.

Jenny drags a chair to the stove and climbs up. Saul chuckles at something he is reading. Nothing funny in the cabinet: napkin rings, a toast rack, a coffee mill, all the bourgeois bricks of this prison Jenny is in.

"I meant, what do you want done with those chicken bones?" Saul points at the carcass floating in the sink. "You want me to get rid of them for you?"

"No." Jenny does not want the lousy Philistine to do anything for her. Slamming the cabinet door, she jumps down. "That carcass is part of an assemblage. I've just got to get the meat off." She hoists her bones out of the water and holds them over a burner. They drip. Flames spit at the burn on her arm. The tongs are getting hot. Any minute now, the skeleton will fall apart. Pieces will get jammed in the gas jet. Why is Jenny doing this? Why isn't Saul stopping her? "Hand me a pot holder will you?" If he does, he is implicated.

"Here." Saul stands beside her. "Seems to me you should, as you say, bury the thing and let the maggots clean it off."

"What if a dog gets there first?" Jenny has no time to wait for maggots any more. She is almost forty; can't Saul see how far behind she is?

"If that doesn't work, you can try another method. There will be other chickens." Saul has no idea how Jenny feels. He never has known. He is taking food out of the refrigerator as if this work of hers does not count. "There are always more chickens." He sets his part of tonight's bird, bean sprouts, a jar of roast peppers, on her counter. "Just as there are always meetings. The one tonight went well." He expects Jenny to care. "I think we'll probably pull it off." He slides a cutting board into place.

"You missed a good dinner." She was willing to feed him; he does not have to take it upon himself.

"I had a little something at Timothy's." Saul tests the knife blade against his thumb.

"By yourself?" The burner is working. Jenny's bones are starting to char.

"With my allies." Smiling at an angle, Saul amputates, from a loaf of Jewish rye, a single slice.

"What allies?" Her carcass is on fire.

"Stan, Walter Kirkendahl, and Iris Wilde." Another slanted smile as Saul slivers white meat.

Jenny's bones hiss under cold running water.

"Walter thinks we should make an issue of the college's dismal record. The trouble is, Trinity hasn't been guilty of overt discrimination against women, just neglect."

"Mmhm." Jennny's mottled black and gray carcass now has the soft, strange beauty she wants, assuming it is there and not imagined, and if it can be salvaged.

"Iris Wilde came up with a great strategy." The crooked smile twitches on every time Saul mentions that woman's name. He slices his sandwich in two.

"I'll take half." Jenny hooks her fingers around his food.

"Sure." Startled, Saul looks at her. The corner of his mouth jumps up. "Iris says all we have to do is convince the administration that a Women's Studies Major will attract enough new students to pay for itself, maybe even make money."

If ever Jenny has seen one, that is a caught-in-the-act grin. Saul knows he is guilty. Pleasure bubbles up inside her. She almost smiles back now that he has given her something definite to work with. Jenny frowns at him.

"Iris thinks she can actually get a sociologist friend of hers to come up with a study to that effect." Good. Saul is sounding defensive.

"Delicious." Jenny savors her first bite. " Oh and there's news here too. Esther called." Jenny drops the dishwasher lid. Damn. Inside there are clean dishes.

"What did she have to say?" Saul helps unload.

Jenny wishes he would let her do it. The last things she wants to feel toward him tonight is gratitude. "Esther isn't coming home for spring vacation unless we agree to let her latest boyfriend sleep with her." Silverware jumbles together as Jenny slams the drawer.

"What did you tell her?"

"I said I'd have to talk to you."

"Want something to drink?" Saul's pale, graceful fingers slip ivory chicken, tomato red peppers, celadon beansprouts onto a brown plate. The Professor has made the work of art; the Artist has made a mess. And her half of his sandwich is gone. He still has his.

"What are you having?"

"A martini." Saul takes from the cabinet one of the glasses she just put away.

"Nothing for me, and before you start boozing it up, let's decide what to tell Esther. She wanted us to get back to her before ten."

"Then I better call right now." Saul puts down his glass and slips his address book from the shirt pocket under his sweater.

What other numbers does he keep hidden in there?

He dials and slips the book back, next to his heart.

"What do you plan to say?" She crams plates into the dishwasher.

"It's up to Esther who sleeps in her bed." Saul hangs up.

"Just like that?" Jenny drops a fork on the floor. "You're going to let your daughter sleep with boys in this house?"

"Why not?" Saul eyes the level of gin he pours into his glass. The level is high. " She can sleep with anyone she wants to here. It's her home."

"And mine." Jenny could have chosen Antibes. Tahiti. No great artist ever lived in Hartford. "I don't want Esther coming here to have sex." That is what Jenny did, and found herself stuck in quicksand.

"She's coming to see us. Sex isn't the central issue." Saul pares a translucent lemon peel. Just the zest, no pith, no bitterness. "You've got to get over this Victorian attitude of yours."

"My attitude!" That bastard. The one with the mistress. "What about—"

"Hey, I need an early dismissal tomorrow." Luke's hiking boots grind black curls into linoleum that already looks like the floor of a barbershop.

"What for?" Jenny has work to do tomorrow. Tulips and this chicken carcass.

"I told Nick I'd go for a bike hike with him."

"Give me a pink card and I'll sign it," Saul says.

"Why should he get out of school to go bike riding?" And why should Saul make every decision as if Jenny does not exist?

"Because, as I've been telling you for weeks, I don't have afternoon classes on Thursday. Dad remembers, but you, Mother,

38

every week you forget." A good mother is home to greet children after school. "This whole term I haven't had afternoon classes on Thursdays. For some reason, you just don't want to admit that." Luke hooks a gob of peanut butter on his finger and licks it off.

"Please." Taking a spoon from the drawer and a plate from the cabinet, Saul offers them to his son. "Be a little more civilized."

"How many times must I tell you that's not safe?" What if Luke does that when Jenny is not around? "People have been known to choke on peanut butter. You should always put it on something, a cracker, or bread. Never eat it plain."

"Name one person who choked on peanut butter. You can't, can you?" Luke screws the jar lid on.

"Why don't you try study hall tomorrow?" Jenny asks. "Your grades could use it."

"I remember I could never study in study hall." Saul always got A's. He knows Jenny did not.

"What did you do with the pink cards, Mother?" Luke careens through the kitchen, banging cabinet doors. "I left them right next to the phone."

"Right there, in back of the honey."

"Talk about slobs!" A gold thread connects the sheaf of cards in Luke's hand to the shelf. He rips it.

Jenny would like, just once, to make something as beautiful as that thread.

Saul sponges off cards and shelf. He signs a pink card. He does not say he agrees that Jenny is a slob. He does not tell Luke he inherited his uncouth habits from his mother. He implies.

As soon as Luke leaves, Saul clears a place for himself at the table.

"Okay, Jenny, I'm all yours." What irony! "What do you want me to tell Esther?"

"It's okay with you if she goes to bed with a guy she hardly knows right under our noses?" Her daughter's sheets will smell of sex. Esther's mattress pad will be stained with semen. Jenny will be expected to do the laundry.

"Esther's the age you were when you got married." Saul drains his glass. His ice cubes chuckle. "I'm flattered that she told us. Not many children can be so open with their parents."

"Why is she?" Jenny has always been careful to spare her own parents' details that would make them uncomfortable.

"Over the years, we've been frank with Esther." Saul must have told her filthy secrets behind Jenny's back.

"Isn't it possible she's asking us to set limits?" Jenny can hardly sit in the same room with this man.

"It's time she figured out how to set her own limits. We won't always be around to do it for her."

"What if she needs help now?" At nineteen, Jenny needed someone to stop her from making the mistake that ruined her life. But no one was there.

"You make too much out of everything, but particularly you make far too much out of sex." Brushing crumbs off his hands, Saul gets up, goes to the phone. "If Esther is making a mistake, it won't kill her. That's how people learn." He is calling screwing a stranger making a mistake. What about Mr. Goodbar?

Saul dials direct. No more names called out in dormitory halls. No more housemothers. No more sign-out sheets. Esther has her own phone.

"Ess? Dad here. How are things?" Saul's voice softens.

Jenny turns the water on full.

"Your mother tells me you're bringing a friend home for spring break."

A friend. Saul knows how to be casual about these things.

"Sure I remember. The one whose father is the economist at Purdue." Saul does not mention the boy's mother.

"Does Rick ski? If there's still snow on the north face, we can run up to Mount Snow."

Maybe this Rick's mother is liberated. A career woman. Or a suburban swinger who enjoys having her family leave to go skiing. Maybe where Rick's mother lives there is somebody she can turn to beside the mailman.

"Jenny will come round," Saul is saying. "Deep down she knows this isn't the Dark Ages."

There never were Dark Ages except for Protestants. Jenny calls it the Middle Ages. And no matter what he says she is there, in the dead middle, poised between that wall of pictures—Luke without front teeth, Esther on a pony, Aaron in a hobo costume, Jenny and Saul as bride and groom—and the window in whose shiny black night Jenny sees only herself, holding a snarl of chicken bones.

"So what else is new?" Stretching the cord, Saul picks up the fork she dropped. "Did Collins like your Nietzche paper?"

Jenny drops her scorched carcass into the crumpled fabrics at the end of the table.

"Did you get to the semiotics seminar?" Saul asks.

Jenny's green tissue paper clumps and red satin scraps look like a tenement Christmas.

"Nobody understands Derida", but he's still worth hearing—

Yes, I know. That's what I mean." Saul laughs a confidential laugh. "Next week then—Love you too, Ess." He hangs up. "They'll be here a week from Thursday." To see him. Saul walked in and took Jenny's only daughter from her. The whole family has changed. Only Jenny, except maybe for aging, has stayed the same.

"Want me to give you a hand in here?" Saul has the nerve to ask.

"No, I do not." At least not with the dishes. Those Jenny can handle. "Just tell me, honestly, what do you think of this?" She pushes the red to one side and sets green puffs, propping the bones so they do not cave in.

"I don't really have an opinion." Saul averts his eyes. "At this point, I can't visualize."

"Just tell me if you think I should keep the background thick to support the carcass, or if I should have it on something flat and stiffen it so it'll stand out on its own."

"I don't know what it is you're trying to convey." Saul pours himself more gin. "So I can't tell you how I think you should go about it."

"Try. All you have to do is look. It's something about keeping the ends of things to point at what's next. Like a ship's prow, see?" Jenny moves the carcass around. Maybe if she added some blue, to represent water. "And I'm going to preserve it with poly-urethane." Or maybe wax.

"I'm not the person you should ask," Saul says.

"Who else do I have?"

"Find someone who knows something about art." Saul riffles the pages of *Runners World*.

"You enjoy museums." It is Saul's idea that Jenny should find someone else, not hers. "It's only my work you won't look at."

"I did look." Saul moves toward the door.

"Then tell me what you really think." Jenny wants to know right now, one way or the other.

"I honestly can't tell the difference between what you've got here and trash." Saul's shoulders sag as if he is the defeated one, not Jenny. "Maybe somebody who knows more than I do could see more in it." Saul, the big Feminist fighting for Women's Studies; they should know at Trinity how he treats his wife. "To me it just looks like trash."

That is it! Only a Saint could go on loving the man who said that. Jenny makes her move.

"You just can't imagine a woman being great, can you?" Grabbing his briefcase, she pitches it into the hall. Good. It opens.

Let the professor's papers fan all over the floor. "Talk about trash; I'll show you trash." But his trash has status.

"Please Jenny, don't." Crouched on the rug, Saul slides orderly papers back into file folders. "Let's not fight." His eyes, like two shining black grapes, plead up at her.

Oh Christ, how beautiful he is! Jenny would like to kneel with him, put her arms around him, tell him she is sorry. But what good would that do?

"I just want you to know how I feel." If she kneels on the floor with him, she may never get up.

"I know. You feel angry and I'm sorry about that." Saul's papers whisper behind her back. "But you've been angry for years now Jenny, and there doesn't seem to be much I can do about it." Click—his briefcase—clicks shut. "I'm going to bed. I have to be up at six." He stands up.

"What for?" Whirling on him, Jenny watches Saul drag himself to the bottom of the stairs. "You can sleep late tomorrow. You don't have morning classes. Talk to me." She has no briefcase. No place to lock up her confusion.

"I'm meeting Iris at six-thirty. We're jogging around the reservoir."

"Jesus, you must think I'm stupid." Jenny can hardly breathe.

"No. I don't think that." Saul's voice is soft, even, under control.

"Then why do you keep pretending I don't know what's going on?"

"Please turn down the volume," Luke cries out. "I'm trying to study for an important test." His door slams.

"Iris Wilde." Jenny's lips move but her teeth stay clamped.

"You have no reason to be jealous of her, or anyone else." Switching the downstairs light off, the upstairs light on, Saul is caught, on the other side of the darkened hallway, a corpse already in his coffin, staring at Jenny from a box of light. "In twenty years I've never once been unfaithful to you." His voice is compressed but distinct. "Not once. And nothing erotic has happened between Iris and me. But I don't think it makes any difference, Jenny." Saul's eyes are glass. "It's how we feel these days about each other that's the problem."

"Just answer this: Are you in love with Iris Wilde?"

"I'm not sure I know what love is any more."

"That's not exactly a denial." Jenny grabs the door-frame and presses into herself its hard edge.

"No it isn't. Iris and I do like each other. I honestly don't know if it's more than that. If you like I'll invite her over so you can judge for yourself what's going on between us."

"This is your house." Not Jenny's any more. After this she has no excuse to stay. "Invite anyone you please." She slams ice into a glass.

Saul's shoes slide up the stairs.

Jenny pours scotch and gulps it like medicine. She hates scotch. But tonight it tastes good. Tonight scotch is a victory drink. Let Saul invite his Radical Lesbian Feminist girlfriend over. After that, Jenny will have every right to leave him.

Gathering every scrap but the purple velvet, Jenny crams paper and cloth into her shopping bag, she crams the bag into the trash, she walks with the wastebasket toward the back door. In the glass panel, she spots a speculative, sturdy, competent looking woman, the kind she is usually drawn to at parties. Reassured, Jenny walks out.

The rain has stopped. Jenny tips and shakes the wastebasket, dumping the last stinking cat food can, mail order catalogue, matzoh box into the trash barrel. Then she pauses.

Now that she is actually in it, the dark is not all that scary but hushed, and personal. Quite nice really, and it will be even nicer once Jenny has someone to keep her company.

Shivering, Jenny scampers back into the house. She tears her carcass apart, drinks, feeds each bone into the disposal's maw, drinks. There is no salvation. There is now and never, the past is garbage. The disposal clatters at the last knuckle, the last rib, the last hope of her construction.

Chapter V

ROUND THREE
• *Memorial Day Weekend: Saturday* •

Another wife might be angry if her husband invited his girl-friend to the house and out to dinner. Not Jenny. This could be the opportunity she has been waiting for. For the last month, Jenny has been sketching every day: tulips, mixing bowls, the cat, clematis, tea cups. She drew pictures of her kitchen walls and bought herself a new portfolio. And someday, when she can concentrate on making art, these quick studies will be the basis for paintings, constructions, assemblages. But right now, lying in her bath-tub, Jenny readies herself to meet the Radical Lesbian Feminist whom Saul finds so attractive.

What if Jenny also finds Iris attractive? Then, though untrained, she might not have to worry about Saul, or the kids, or what will happen to her when they are gone. She can simply, like her husband, enjoy doing whatever Iris does. And the beautiful part is, if that should happen—if Jenny and Iris should fall in love—Saul would have only himself to blame. Maybe that is what he wants. Why else would he have asked his friend to come tonight?

Jenny's palm slides over her own plump, baby-soft breasts, quivering buoyant in the hot water. Her fingers gather her nipples into crinkled buff-colored party hats. She wonders what kind of breasts Iris Wilde has.

Snap. Outside, Saul is opening lawn chairs. Snap.

He has no right to be angry. Not when every time Iris's name is mentioned, that special grin plays about his lips. Jenny is the one who should be angry.

She checks her belly button. Her finger comes out smelling like secrets.

Sssh. He is turning on the hose, washing off the chairs. Saul no longer thinks Jenny's secrets are worth knowing.

Time for some new ones. Jenny flexes her thighs and ass. Soon she will see Iris Wilde in the flesh. Making loops with her hips, Jenny palms her sauerkraut hair, her fresh hotdog-roll sex. Not old, not old, she has not forgotten the moves.

Sssh—He is turning the water—psst—off.

Now Saul can hear what she is doing. Jenny soaps her face, splashes to rinse, snorts like a sea lion, and steps out of the tub.

Stir-rip. He is tearing rags to dry the chairs. Stir-rip. Working in a fury.

Anything but furious, Jenny wraps herself in a bath sheet, and, waddling to their bed, flops down on her back, unwraps, and lets dampness float off her body.

"Can I come in?" Luke rattles the doorknob.

"No." Jenny flips the towel over herself. "What do you want?"

"To put away the nail clippers."

"Slide them under the door."

"Can't. Rug's too fat."

The door inches toward Jenny.

"Stop. I said don't come in."

The door retreats. Luke drops the clippers in the hall.

"I'm leaving them out here. Tell Dad I wanted to put them away like he said, but you wouldn't let me." Luke's feet clump down the stairs, his fingers no doubt leaving their usual trail.

This time, Jenny may surprise him and everyone else and just follow that trail right on out the door.

In the yard, Luke tells Saul how Jenny thwarted him. Saul tells him to take it up with her.

Flinging off her towel, Jenny stands up and makes sure the bedroom door is shut tight.

Saul gives Luke money for Burger King and tells him to go from there directly to Scott's house. Tonight Saul too is anxious to be rid of his beloved youngest.

Jenny pulls the shower cap from her head. Curls light as dandelion fluff tickle her shoulders and back.

"Have a good time," Saul calls out.

Whatever Jenny does, it will be all right. Saul is doing it too. Jenny waggles her hips at her mirrored reflection.

Saul is down in the kitchen, emptying ice trays, sliding cubes into the bucket.

Jenny enters the steamy bathroom, squeezes her breasts into Hollywood cleavage, gives herself a hug. At last it is her time to have some fun. If Iris Wilde is not one of those women who shaves the back of her neck. Saul has never mentioned what she looks like. But that smirk of his would not twitch on if Iris had tattooed biceps.

Jenny rolls deodorant under her arms. Last year she decided to stop shaving. This year maybe she will stop being ashamed of the surprisingly dark, surprisingly uncurly tufts sprouting out of her pits. She slips on see-through, nylon underpants and slides her feet into leather sandals. Casual, but underneath sexy is the effect she is after.

"When do you have to leave, Aaron?" Saul asks.

"I told Kim I'd stop by about seven." Aaron is out in the yard too. "I've got time to finish one last chapter."

"You want the Volvo?"

"You don't need it?"

"You can have it but you'll have to leave now," Saul says. "It needs gas. Here—take my card."

"Okay. It's a deal." Maybe Aaron senses that tonight his mother and father are also on the make. Whatever he senses, he knows enough to get out. The screen door slams.

Jenny leans forward, cups her breasts in seamless tricot, stands, hooks the bra. In fifteen minutes, Iris will be here.

"Just one thing," Saul shouts, "Get rid of those sneakers before you go."

Jenny sits down at her dressing table.

Aaron gallops up the stairs. Whop—His sneakers—whop—land somewhere in the vicinity of his room—their odor flies everywhere—he is going back downstairs, leaving.

"Drive carefully. No drinking." Jenny yells after him, her contact lens swimming, like a mini-diaphragm, in her palm. "Nothing crazy. You're too young too have sex."

"And too smart." The front door bangs shut.

Aaron is not that smart. Jenny is not that young. Anything can happen.

"Where'd you hide the vegetable peeler?" Saul calls up the stairs.

Jenny slips the lens into her eye as if, with it in place, she will see the vegetable peeler. Instead, she sees a blank, fishy eye. She puts in her other lens. "Try the dishwasher." Grimacing. she makes a mask of comedy and smoothes rose gel on its cheeks and across the nose. She drops the mask to daub blue-green on her eyelids, forest green in the crease under the bone. She pencils a line of silver right over her eyes, a line of brown underneath. She brushes her lashes into dark spikes, like her mother's, and combs them out to look like an Act of God.

Jenny takes a magnifying mirror to the window and examines the shadow of the girl painted on the face of the woman. Spitting on a finger, she rubs to blend the line between rose gel and her own skin.

Saul is banging kitchen drawers.

"Try the water pistol hook," Jenny calls down. Once it is warm, the boys cannot resist her water pistol and she cannot resist hanging things on the empty hook.

"Why didn't you tell me it was there in the first place?" Saul yells.

"I didn't remember." She highlights the bridge of her nose with pearl luster for a wide-eyed effect and smears her lips with gloss. Iris may be an art historian, but Jenny is a true artist, the woman in her mirror enchanting.

The doorbell rings.

Jenny stares at her reflection.

Saul answers the door. A woman says something soft. He chuckles. The mirrored face remains calm.

"Iris is here," Saul calls up.

"Be down in a minute." Jenny slides her arms into her favorite rust-colored cotton blouse. Soft over her shoulders and back, it hugs her like an old friend. She buttons three buttons, leaving the top open, as if by mistake. Stepping into her brand-new African print skirt, she takes a deep breath and hooks the waistband. Perfect with this blouse. She feels of a certain age, ripe.

The screen door creaks. She glides to the window. They are on the back porch, walking languidly down the back stairs.

Iris Wilde is short and bulgy, her backside in white overalls, one of the biggest Jenny has ever seen. No sharp edges here. This woman of Saul's has the sweet rounded outline of a long-expected bus. And the long blonde braids of a school-girl. Jenny's new skirt caresses her thighs as, slipping away from the window, she goes back to her dressing table. The other woman is very attractive indeed.

Jenny combs her hair. Silver glints from the coral tendrils dangling over her brow. She pouts in the mirror and thinks Fragonard. The woman in the mirror is adorable. Not unlike that woman outside.

"All we've got is ale," Saul is saying. "Aaron must have finished off the beer."

Iris says she hardly knows the difference. Saul says he is a connoisseur of alcohol. They laugh together. Jenny's heart is a bird trapped in her chest.

She sprays a veil of perfume over her head, neck, and chest, fastens a cluster of silver bells to her earlobe, and goes down stairs, tilting her head to put on her other earring as she walks out the door, thus including Iris in the intimacy of getting dressed. Charming. A perfect entrance.

"Ah Jenny." Saul beams like a proud Papa. "This is Iris Wilde."

He said she was thirty; with those petunia-yellow braids and the avid stare, Iris looks more like fifteen. Peering out of gold granny glasses, her eyes take in Jenny's hair, her mouth, her eyes. No one has paid Jenny this much attention in years.

"Hi." Grinning, Jenny offers her hand.

"Hi." Iris's hand is soft and cuddly. "I've been yearning to meet you." Her voice is rich, and furry as a peach skin. "I'm so glad to be doing it."

"What did you expect me to be like?" Jenny opens her eyes into the other woman's. This is the first time she ever let a lesbian see inside her and she is instantly, overwhelmingly reassured. Iris's eyes are as clear and purposeful as frog eggs, inside them a pulsing shadow like the start of a tadpole. Nothing perverted in those eyes.

"I knew that any woman married to Saul was bound to be outstanding." Iris flashes a dimpled smile.

"I like to think I'd be outstanding even if I wasn't married to Saul." Jenny flashes feminist credentials.

"I can see that." Iris laughs now with Jenny, not Saul.

Arching her back slightly, Jenny makes the most of her breasts.

"Either of you want a carrot?" Saul thrusts the plate between them.

"Not right now," Jenny says.

Taking one for himself, he reduces it to nothing with his teeth. Jenny chooses the middle chair.

"If you want a drink, you'll have to hurry." Saul swigs his gin. "Our reservation is for seven fifteen."

"Why?" Crossing her legs, Jenny clasps her hands in her lap. A model of self-possession.

"Because it's almost seven and it'll take us fifteen minutes to get there."

"I mean why so early?" Jenny leans back, exposing a sliver of breast white as a girl's slip.

Iris, sitting on the chaise next to hers, notices.

"I thought that's when you'd want to eat." Saul stands behind Jenny, nervously tapping her chair. "This garden's great." Kicking off platform-soled sandals, Iris folds her legs Indian style and looks eagerly around. "If I lived here, I'd never want to go anywhere." She understands exactly how Jenny feels.

"It's okay with me if we take our time." Saul makes no move to sit. "But Jenny usually doesn't like to eat too late."

"In the winter. Summer's different." Jenny moves slowly in summer. Seasons make no difference to Saul. "I'll have beer, or wine." Something to hold in her hand; the florid air is enough to drink.

"Which would you prefer?" He pretends it matters.

"Whichever."

Saul tears inside as if the phone is ringing.

Somewhere down the street a mower buzzes. No one is home nearby; the neighbors on one side are opening their house at the beach, the other side neighbors are spending the holiday weekend with his parents in Philadelphia, and white pines block the view in back.

Jenny looks at Iris.

Iris's white overalls strain against her chubby legs and crease in rays that point unabashedly at her private part. Her belly swells over her lap. She wears no bra, her breasts globes that spill out the sides of her bib, pulling her yellow shirt taut. Iris Wilde's mouth is a pink curlicue. Her cheeks are rosy. And, behind her gold granny glasses, her eyes watch Saul's wife, avidly, as if Jenny is the most fascinating woman in the world.

"Well, well, well," Iris says. "So you're the famous wife." Iris opens her mouth and laughs, the sound like bubbling juice.

"And you're the famous Iris Wilde." Between them a brightness flares that warms Jenny's face, swells her breasts, makes her remember the see-through nylon underpants, slippery between her thighs. All her life she has wanted to know what love at first sight feels like. Now that she has looked at a woman, she knows. It is like adoring Clark Gable. No rape, v.d., pregnancy—with a woman there is no potential for trouble. There could even be a chance for happy ever after.

"I forget whether you wanted ice." Saul dashes down the stairs clutching ice cubes over a glass of cold wine.

"Not really."

"Here then." Hurling the ice aside, he hands Jenny her wine. "I called Davey Jones and said we'd be late." Saul sits down. Jumps up to get his gin and tonic. Sits down. "So we're in no particular hurry." He taps his heel, bouncing his knee up and down.

Jenny stares as if his agitation is a stranger's.

"Good." She props her feet on the edge of Iris's chaise and breathes the deep smell of beginnings.

"I don't know why people wait for a holiday weekend to mow the damn grass," Saul says. "Maybe we should go inside."

"It's not that bad," Jenny says.

"I think it's a fine evening out here," Iris agrees.

"All right then." Saul sits back down.

"I love doing nothing, listening to other people work." Iris holds her beer in both hands as if it, like everything she sees here, is dear to her. "That's what is so great about the Women's Studies Committee." What is great about Iris is her enthusiasm. "No one expects me to do anything I don't want to do." Bubbles rise up and giggle out of her.

"Most of them don't want anything to be done." Saul's bubbles are all in his glass. "The know-nothings are terrified of change." According to him, most people are know-nothings. "The chapel is filled with their prayers. 'Please, O Lord, maintain the status quo." He expects Jenny to put up with his negativity forever.

"What's that?" She sniffs a new smell, pouring thick as smoke into the yard.

"Viburnum, I think." Saul knows what Jenny means. No one in the world knows her as well as he does.

The cat jumps in her lap.

"Jenny could also be smelling my afternoon bubble bath." Iris sets down her beer. "Honeysuckle." Lifting her arm, she bridges the space between her and Jenny.

"I love it." Jenny would like to nuzzle Iris's hand. "Delicious."

"But I'm quite sure it's viburnum you're smelling." Saul jumps up, tears a cluster of white flowers off a shrub, thrusts it under her nose.

"It smells better at a distance," Jenny says.

Saul tosses the viburnum aside.

"I'm fixing myself another drink. Either of you ready?"

"I'm fine," Iris says.

"Me too." Jenny moves her hand very slowly down the cat's flanks.

Saul races into the house.

Tree shadows lie, like downed bars on the grass.

The cat purrs voluptuous.

"What's her name?" Iris asks.

"His name is Siggy, short for Sigmund Freud." Jenny strokes his head, back, tail, over and over, in long, silky strokes.

"Let me see him." Bending toward Jenny, Iris looks at the cat. "Great. That dark patch under his mouth really does look like Freud's beard." Iris's fingers draw whiskers from her own chin, her hand in motion, the gentle hand Jenny has been waiting for, for years.

"Siggy understands my innermost thoughts." Jenny continues her slow petting.

"I doubt if the original had a clue about any woman's thinking process, but the name's marvelously emblematic."

"That cat's more of a Leon Trotsky." The back door bangs behind Saul. "Many times I've thought of whacking him with an axe."

No telling what the maniac will do. Jenny must get away from him.

"It's true, a male pussy is in some ways *ab initio* a contradiction in terms." Giggling, Iris retrieves her drink.

"Only if you accept acculturated stereotyping," Saul says.

How they sparkle together! If Jenny could talk to Saul like that, he might not need another woman. Jenny releases the cat. Jumping off her lap, he gambols on the lawn, chasing the white tip of his tail around the yard.

"Look. Freud's showing off his misplaced penile envy." Already, with Iris's help, Jenny is learning the lingo.

"I never heard anyone call it penal envy before." Iris's breasts jiggle when she laughs. "Given the strictures the patriarchy imposes on males, the term's great."

Jenny wonders what other people call it. Tail-chasing she supposes. Saul would know all about that. Maybe she better leave the brilliant dialogue to him and Iris.

"Let's drink up and get going," he says. "I told them quarter to eight."

"Okay." But Jenny would rather stay here. Now that it is getting dark, specks of light flash in the bushes. Fireflies, her first this year.

"I love fireflies." Iris knows what Jenny is thinking.

"Me too." How much Jenny has in common with this woman!

"I'll just go lock up." Saul heads for the kitchen.

"Want these glasses inside?" Scrambling out of her chaise, Iris wobbles her feet into the chunky platform sandals that make her look, not taller but rather pleasingly vain, reassuringly feminine.

"Thanks." Saul leads the way.

Passing Iris her glass, Jenny snuggles down in her chaise.

Inside, the two of them make comforting, gold-lit house sounds, getting ready to go out as if Iris and Saul are the married ones, and Jenny their child who could stay this way forever, watching fireflies.

Davey Jones Locker is meat locker cold. Most of its eerie blue light comes from fish tanks set in the wall. Pumps gurgle, plates chink, voices murmur, all very subdued. The hostess, her black acrylic hair tied back with an aqua chiffon scarf, leads them around a glass lobster vat to a booth. Dealing out menus that thud on the table, she goes away.

Iris slides deep into the booth and peers at the fishtank in the wall at the end. Jenny slides in opposite her, but only to the middle of the plastic seat. Tonight she will be observer, Jenny will be judge. Shrugging, Saul slips in next to Iris. Her yellow shirt and white overalls, his ivory linen, jacket, glow in the fishtank light. Jenny wishes she had worn long sleeves. Here, the lobsters heap themselves in the tank corners to keep warm.

"How'd you happen to pick this place?" Jenny has never heard of it. Maybe its clientele is limited to people having clandestine affairs. Maybe that is why it is so dark, mysterious, absurd.

"I thought we could try someplace new," Saul says. "I thought you love fish."

Across the room, a white haired couple is drinking coffee. They have already eaten. Nothing sneaky about those two, they look sewn together. But one never knows. Jenny always thought she and Saul were sewn together too.

"I love seafood." Iris turns from the tank in the wall. "Isn't it great the way fish swim?" Her little hand quivers through the air like a silvery fish.

"I just wish this place was warmer than the ocean." Jenny crosses her arms over her breasts.

"When the waitress comes, I'll get her to turn down the air conditioner." Saul snatches up a package of oysterettes, tears it with his teeth, flips crackers one after another into his mouth.

"Are you all right?" Reaching across, Jenny presses his arm. "You seem awfully tense."

"I'm fine." Crumpling cellophane, Saul jams it into the ashtray.

Jenny shivers, her arm, lying across the table, pimpled blue as a supermarket drumstick. Maybe he intends this dinner to be their last together, the meal of her choice.

"Here—take my jacket." Slipping it off himself, he gets up and drapes it over her.

"Thanks." The jacket resting on Jenny's shoulders is warm with Saul's smell, heavy with his wallet, pen, notebook, change, and guilt. As long as she has this on her back, Jenny knows her husband is not going anywhere, at least not without her.

"That's ideal with your blouse," Iris says, "which almost exactly matches your hair."

"Yes. That color is good on Jenny." Saul never said that before. It took Iris to make him notice.

"This is turning out to be a most excellent day." Iris flings back her yellow braids. "This morning I heard my grant came through."

"The Chicago one?" Saul asks.

"Yes. Cause for Celebration." She chortles, her lips parting to show tiny teeth.

"That's a real coup," Saul says.

"Congratulations." Panic swirls inside Jenny. "But isn't Chicago miserably hot in the summer? Do you really have to go there?" She wants Iris to stay here, in Hartford. Saul and Iris simply have to let Jenny into their brilliant circle. Jenny has nowhere else to go. "Exactly when do you have to be there?"

"I'm to go to California in two weeks and stay for July and August. I'm a replacement for some woman who had to drop out. I started piling up the books I'll need this afternoon." Iris can leave whenever she wants. She can teach Jenny to do the same. All Jenny would need to pack would be her new portfolio.

"I thought you said Chicago," Jenny says.

"Judy Chicago, but she's in California."

"The grant cover your way out?" Just like Jenny's father, Saul thinks of money first. Jenny left Simon, and lived through it.

"First class." Iris's dimples plunge deep into her pink cheeks. "I budgeted it in my proposal." Iris can show Jenny how to get money.

"Can you take a leave of absence?" Saul asks.

"They have to give it to me. My boss knows I could sue the museum." Iris grins. "There's absolutely no reason that loser should earn twice as much as I do. It's obvious sexism."

"Could you prove it?" Jenny asks.

"I don't have to. All I'd have to do is raise the issue. The museum's about to start a major fund drive."

"Crafty." Saul admires people who know how to use blackmail to get power.

"I'll have to remember that technique when my time comes," Jenny says.

"You folks care for a cocktail?" The waitress looks like a nurse, embroidered with anchors.

"I'll have a Brandy Alexander." Tucking a foot up under herself, Iris leans toward Jenny. "I just love anything to do with milk in any form. Don't you?"

Saul orders a martini on the rocks and asks to have the air conditioning turned down.

Jenny is no longer cold. She thinks about milk. She drank her last glass of the stuff when she was pregnant. Now it seems as if that was when she joined Saul in being old.

"I'd rather have a p.b. and j. with milk than most so-called gourmet food," Iris says.

"I'll go for these two and come back for your order later." The waitress whisks off with Iris's eyes fixed on her backside.

Her backside slithers inside her uniform. Blushing, Jenny shifts in her seat. She had not expected to change her orientation so quickly but there is no doubt. The waitress's ass is sexy.

"What's your favorite thing to eat?" Iris asks.

Jenny has not played 'What's your favorite?' in years. She had forgotten how much she loved the game until she saw Iris, her tadpole eyes gleaming, eager to play.

"Raspberries in cream." Jenny tastes the words as they come from her mouth.

"I love them too, but my absolute all the time favorite has got to be maraschino cherries," Iris says. "I once had a lover whose father imported them; we ate nothing else for a whole month. What a trip that was!"

"Weren't you worried about Red Dye Number Two?" Jenny envies a woman who can boast of having had a lover, one among many lovers. She wonders if it was a man or a woman. Iris, Saul told her, was married once.

"I get off on taking risks," Iris says.

The waitress brings drinks for Saul and Iris.

"You decided yet?" she asks Jenny.

"I guess I'll have a glass of white wine." Lifting her face, Jenny shows off her neck. Not a wrinkle on it.

Not like his.

"How about a bottle of Orvieto?" Last year, Saul took Jenny to Orvieto, to a former monastery. He got her drunk on wine. They made love.

54

"Not necessary." Jenny will not let him ply her with memories. "The house wine will be fine."

"Orvieto's like sunshine in a glass," Saul tells Iris. "I'll order a bottle and we'll all have some."

The menu Jenny opens in front of her face is heavy in her hands. "For the Hearty Adventurer," it says. She puts the menu down.

"How about your favorite color?" Iris asks.

Jenny stares into the fishtank where betas, like radium dial watches, hold the light. She once read that if you go to bed wearing such a watch you can gradually go blind. Flicked away from the fish, Jenny's eyes catch Iris's yellow shirt, her yellow hair. "Yellow, I guess."

"Greens are mine." Iris's hands draw leaves over her head. "Yellow and blue, I like the way they whisper together."

"Me too." Jenny has never admitted to anyone that she hears colors. "But better still, I like the way yellow bellows when it's alone."

When Iris laughs, her breasts jiggle.

"What's your favorite color, Saul?" She invites him to play too.

"I'm a puce man myself." Saul stares at a fish darting after two others. "What kind's that, Jen?"

"A kissing gourami," she says.

"Do you know what those other two are?" Iris asks.

"Betas."

"How do you happen to have this information?" Iris beams at Jenny as though she has discovered gold.

"Aaron used to have fish." Jenny is a motherlode of pet facts Iris can mine. If only she will want to.

"You folks ready to order?" The anchored nurse is back.

Saul starts forward as if to tackle her. "How are your steamers? Are they the big ones or the little ones?"

"Have you ever noticed size is a patriarchal preoccupation?" Iris leans toward Jenny. Iris wants. She wants everything she sees.

"That's true." Jenny had not thought of it before but Saul and the boys are always talking about what is bigger than what.

"Everybody up for steamers?" Saul asks.

"Sure." For once, Jenny does not care what or whether she eats.

"Fine with me, too," Iris says.

"Done." Saul clamps his menu and hands it over.

The waitress collects the other two.

"Where's your women's room?" Iris asks.

"Past the bar on your left."

"Excuse me." Iris bumps Saul off the seat, slides herself over, walks away, the pillows of her backside bobbing together like two giant marshmallows.

Jenny loves marshmallows.

"Well." Saul slips back into place. "What do you think?" His fingers drum the table.

"She's terrific." Setting her hand on top of his, Jenny muffles the beat. "Really."

"That's great." No more sly grin, this smile covers Saul's whole face. "You like her." He sits back as if now that he has made his point, he can relax.

"Anyone would have to." Jenny's skin glows as if she has plunged into deliciously cold water. She has no intention of jumping right out. "Iris is marvelous."

"You can see how it is between us," Saul insists. "In the old days, if a man had a woman friend, there was always an underlying sexual tension but now the women's movement has made platonic friendships between the sexes possible and Iris and I can be good friends." His eyes meet Jenny's head on.

"That's fine with me." Jenny has had this conversation before. 'Platonic relationship.' 'Just good friends.' When Jenny or Mimi, her best friend in high school, used words like that to describe a boy-friend, that meant it was okay for the other one to take her turn with him. "No problem." Jenny and Mimi used to love talking about each swapped beau. "In fact terrific." With the children leaving, Jenny must have something to talk about with Saul.

Iris comes back and slides in beside him.

"Where in California will you be, and do you need a place to live?" Saul asks. "I have a former colleague out there if that's any help."

"The grant includes an apartment in Santa Monica for visiting consultants. That's my official title." Iris pushes back her shoulders and her nipples show like medals under the thin yellow cloth. Licking her lips, Jenny tastes pennies. "Judy called to tell me about the deal. She says the place has everything and is a block from the ocean."

Judy Chicago who wrote *Through the Flower*, the Bible of Feminist Art, called Iris from California. Judy Chicago knows Iris Wilde. And now Iris Wilde knows Jennifer Reuben Weiss.

"You better bring earplugs for traffic, and your own sheets," Saul says. "Every place we've ever had that came with everything always had lots of noise and no bed clothes."

"They're giving me twelve hundred dollars in addition to my travel expenses. If I have to, I'll buy sheets."

"That's not really a whole hell of a lot of money for two months." Saul is getting more than twice that to teach summer school.

Jenny makes less than half of twelve hundred in a year.

"I'll still be on full salary from the museum," Iris says.

"If Judy Chicago asked me, I'd have worked for nothing." Jenny has so much to learn.

"Me too." Iris giggles. "But listen, you should get paid. Your collages at the bank were excellent."

"I didn't know you'd seen them." Jenny hopes Iris will not judge her work by those collages; she hopes Iris will mention her collages to Judy Chicago.

"I took Iris over there to see them." Saul has evidently decided it is now safe to tell Jenny about his outings with Iris. He thinks Jenny will give him points for being proud enough of her work to show it to his girlfriend.

Jenny smiles by clamping her teeth at him. From now on, she is keeping her points for herself.

"Could you ask Chicago if she needs more help?" Jenny sways in her seat as if she is already riding on her way. "Esther and Aaron have jobs on the Cape this summer. Luke'll be away at camp in Vermont." She delivers this as if it were a taped message; people are always asking Jenny what her children are doing. But now she adds a postscript. "I could easily go west."

"You're available any time in July or August?" Iris asks.

"Yes." Jenny can hardly believe her first move was so easy. Saul is not saying a word.

The kissing gourami presses its lips like suction cups to the glass.

Their waitress serves the steamers.

"Get you folks anything else?"

"A bottle of Orvieto," Saul says, as if a year later, in Hartford, he can have Jenny and Italy all over again.

"Someone's going to have to show me what to do with these." Iris holds her hands above the steaming pile like a priestess invoking spirits.

"You pull the clam from its shell. Like this." Saul flips the empties toward Jenny. "And peel off the skin." He hands the clam to Iris.

"Then what?" Iris holds the clam in her palm.

"Take the neck, dip the clam in broth, rinse off as much sand as you can, then dip it in butter, and enjoy." Saul shows her with one of his steamers. "Superb." His chin shines with butter.

"Don't let him kid you." Jenny dangles a clam. "Neck's a euphemism." She knows what they are flaying, rinsing, greasing, and sinking their teeth into. Nothing could be more phallic.

"Great for displacing aggression against the patriarchy." Iris understands too.

"I just like the way they taste." Saul is on a different wave length.

"Actually I've always wanted to go to California. Saul's been there, but I've never been further west than Buffalo." Jenny has never left him overnight, never been in an airplane or stayed in a hotel by herself. "Even if there's no work for me, let me know if you hear of a place where I could maybe arrange a visit." Jenny rinses off a clam as if it is the only thing on her mind. Nothing repels more than desperation; she takes care to keep hers from showing.

"You'd be welcome to stay at my place." Iris looks from one to the other of them.

"Saul's teaching this summer." Jenny unsticks her thighs from the vinyl seat. "I'd have to come out by myself."

"It would cost a fortune." Saul has emptied his shells and now clams lie, like worms, in his broth.

"I'll pay for it myself." Jenny does not have to give him every cent.

"Is that really what you want to use your money for?" Saul's shoulders sag. He may be cold without his jacket. "Is California worth a thousand dollars to you?"

Jenny tries, for Saul's sake, not to let him see that getting away from him is worth anything.

"Yes," she says, "I'm pretty sure."

"What about Luke, Jenny?" Saul asks. "We're supposed to go up to camp on Parents' Day. And your birthday; I thought we could go to the Cape and celebrate with Esther and Aaron." Saul mentions nothing about how he would feel if Jenny leaves for a while probably because he will feel nothing. She must not let herself pity him.

"Esther and Aaron have their own friends." Jenny's broth is salty and delicious, like tears.

"What about you, Saul?" Iris pants on her glasses and wipes them with her napkin. "Think you can get along without a wife?" Holding the glasses toward the fishtank light, she checks to see if they are clear.

"That's not the point. If Jenny wants to go, of course I can manage." Saul is not even looking at Jenny. He pushes Iris. "Let's get out of here, go somewhere else for dessert." He smacks his napkin on the table.

Saul has no excuse to be nasty. It is not Jenny's fault if she is a lesbian. It is not Iris's fault.

"That's all right with me." Iris clambers out of the booth.

"Don't you think you should maybe pay, Saul?" Jenny asks.

"Let's just go. I'll pay on the way out." Saul stands up.

Lobsters wave tiredly from their vat. Jenny understands. For years, with nothing else to do, she also stared out of glass walls. Now she has her way out, over the top. Jenny scuttles from the booth, joining Iris as easily as she would climb aboard a bus. Saul's jacket slips from her shoulders, knocking silverware and clam shells to the floor. "Oh God. Oh Saul, I'm sorry." Clam broth dribbles from the sleeve of his linen jacket. Jenny cannot help giggling. "I forgot I had it on."

"Give it here." Saul grabs. "My wallet. What did you do with my wallet?"

"It's probably on the floor." Jenny squats under the table.

"I'll help you find it." Iris's platformed sandals hold her great backside inches above the carpet.

"Never mind," Saul says, "I've got it."

Change rattles like hail on the roof above them. This is no time to leave shelter. Waiting for the storm to pass, Iris collects clam shells, clicking them together in a growing stack. Jenny gathers forks, knives, and spoons. Saul's legs flap away.

"Maybe I should put these shells in my yard and pretend they were washed up by the sea," Iris says. "I've always wanted a house by the sea."

"There's one." Jenny lets her hand drop to the other woman's knee. Iris does not pull away, her knee as familiar under Jenny's palm as a seat cushion. "Here." Letting go, Jenny picks up a shell and stands, her mouth flexed in the triumphant and guilty smile that belonged once, only to Saul.

Chapter VI

SEEING STARS
• *Four Weeks Later* •

So this is what it is like to be in love. A light, turned on inside Jenny, shines on everything she sees. This light heightens the beautiful and joyous. This light fades obstacles until they are all but invisible. Saul's wistful voice sings to Jenny as she floats on glittering currents down-river.

He said she was obviously determined to go. Jenny explained that her going was pre-determined. She brought about nothing. Introducing her to Iris, Jenny reminded Saul, was his idea. He fell in love first. He could not, he said, help it. Neither could Jenny. From the moment she met Saul's girlfriend, in fact even before she met Iris, Jenny could think of nothing and nobody else. Their love was preordained. Over and over she explained all that to Saul. And anyway, she is only doing what he expects. If Saul really meant for Jenny not to go, he would have stopped her.

Jenny was, for a moment, surprised by the vehemence with which he hugged her goodbye.

"I am coming back," she said.

"I wish I could believe that." Close to her ear, his voice was clouded with tears.

"Then do." Jenny is as determined to return as she is to leave. She stepped resolutely away from the steadfast body that comforted her all her adult life. "I'll be home in two weeks."

Leaving was as simple as walking onto the plane. Now Jenny smiles out the window at a brilliant sunlit sky she would never have seen from the murky ground below. Being in love—a single twist of the kaleidoscope—has changed the pattern of her life. It has raised Jenny into the light.

She licks dry-roasted peanut salt from her fingertips and flips down the last of her champagne. Engrossed in a paperback, her seatmate reminds her of Saul; same age, and reading when she wants him to talk to her. Jenny takes out Iris's letter.

My apartment is a basement with its own patio where every night there is an incredible sunset to watch. Inside I have a huge kitchen, living, bedroom with a phenomenal fireplace that burns at the flick of a switch.

Jenny always thought she disliked mechanical fires but now the thought of flames that need no coaxing, flames that just burst into being, dazzles her. It is the blaze that counts, not its source.

My only problem is that I'm lonely and your visit should solve that, at least for a while.

Jenny returns the letter to her purse. She is not leaving Saul; she is going to Iris. This trip will ultimately connect the three of them in a new marriage, the old subsumed in a triangle Jenny is already loving. Saul will love it too once they work out the kinks.

The man beside her tears his paperback apart, stuffing the pages he has read into his seat pouch, pocketing the rest. Jenny stares. Saul would kill himself rather than dismember a book.

"I believe in traveling light." Small and round, this man in his white leisure suit is airborne like a whiffle ball. "The older I get, the more I boil down to essentials."

"I know what you mean." Jenny ripped herself away from Saul with his absurd Hebraic reverence for the printed word, didn't she? The portfolio propped against her knees, a shopping bag stuffed with art supplies wedged under the seat, her sweater in the overhead locker, and one big suitcase in the baggage hold are irrelevant. Only Iris is essential. Iris warms the blood lining Jenny's body.

"I'm B.J." He offers his hand, his palm tough as the underside of a dog's paw.

"I'm Jenny." She loves dogs. Light glistens in the silver curls that bubble from her seatmate's open collar. Light glistens in the hair around his ears. Light shines, clean and bright, off the hairless top of his head. On her way to Iris, why fear entanglement? Jenny is taken. She lets herself like this twinkly tearer of books.

"Where you from?" B.J. asks.

"New York originally, but I've lived in Hartford, Connecticut for twenty years."

"We started out neighbors. I grew up in Jersey." He leans toward her, a gold horn swinging from the open neck of his black, saddle-stitched shirt. "But California is where it's at these days, know what I mean?"

Jenny knows very well what he means but she is through with phalluses, symbolic or otherwise. B.J. can stuff his horn back in his shirt. "My husband's the one who knows California." Jenny slides the word 'husband' like a bullet-proof shield between them. "I've never been west of Buffalo myself." Or on an airplane alone. Or away from Saul overnight. He is the one who has, up to now, done the leaving. "Are you married?"

"Was, but I split." B.J. pats the half-book in his pocket. "Like I said before, I travel light."

"Not me." Jenny would never leave her children; her portfolio hems her in.

"How long you staying in L.A.?"

"Actually I'm going to Santa Monica. A friend invited me to move in with her for two weeks." Grinning, Jenny lets the light shine through her face, lets B.J. see she is in love with a woman. She watches closely for his reaction.

"My place is a stone's throw from Santa Monica." He is like her father, more interested in real estate than in what Jenny may be doing. "We'll be neighbors again."

"Great." She blankets him with a smile. Simon's daughter is in love with a woman. All the real estate in the world will not change that. Jenny is ready to do cunnilingus. Pretending to scratch her nose, she sniffs at her fingers. No trace of her own juices, tasted in preparation. "Where exactly do you live?"

"In Venice. Lots of action there. But I miss most of it. I had to make three trips East in June. Now July's starting out the same."

"What do you do?" Jenny has never seen such a white, white suit, not even on a pharmacist.

"I'm a peddler." Wrinkles fan out from his eyes. "I sell heavy construction machines."

"Bulldozers? Things like that?"

"You got it." B.J.'s emphatic nod is a tribute to Jenny's intelligence.

"If I wanted to buy a bulldozer, how much would it cost me?" She has never met anyone with a bull-dozer to sell.

"Depends how big."

"The cheapest one that would really work."

"Look, if we're going to talk about a bulldozer, let's make it a big bulldozer."

"I'm for that." No one can think too big for Jenny.

"I could get you a heavy-duty machine somewhere in the seventy, seventy-five range."

"That's seventy or seventy-five *thousand*?"

"You got it. But exactly what do you want your particular machine to do for you? That has an effect on price."

"I want it for power."

B.J. laughs. "That's a new one on me."

"I'd love to be able to move earth." Driving a bulldozer she could crash through the door of the Wadsworth Atheneum and leave a great yellow super-tractor with her name on it as a permanent exhibit of her work.

"A powerhouse like you don't need a machine to get results," B.J. says.

"What makes you think that?" Jenny's heart quickens.

"I got a sixth sense." B.J.'s eyes enter hers. Jenny blushes. "So tell me," he says, "what you got in here?" The hand he rests on her portfolio is right above her knee.

"My friend is an art historian." Crossing her legs, Jenny squeezes them away from him. "These are some sketches I want her to look over." She needs support, contacts in the art world, and the sexual satisfaction that spawns great work, and Iris may just give Jenny what she needs. "I have art supplies with me." She points at the shopping bag bulging under seat. "But I probably won't have time to work." Jenny flashes B.J. the in-love smile she stole from Saul. "This is more of a pleasure trip for me."

"Sounds exciting." B.J. cocks his head. "First time in California and all. I could show you around."

"Ladies and Gentlemen, we are now starting our final descent. Please fasten your seatbelts and extinguish all smoking materials."

"I think my friend's going to keep me pretty busy." Jenny brushes crumbs off her lap.

"You'll probably have some free time." B.J. fumbles, for his seatbelt, in the crevice between them.

"I doubt it." Snapping her tray up, Jenny looks out the window. At bronze mountains. Swiveling around, she accuses B.J. "I thought, being next to the sea, Los Angeles would be flat." Jenny may have been wrong about other things too. The plane is flying close to the mountains. Wrapping her fingers around the ends of plastic arm-rests, she treasures the firm, smooth knobs so like bones. How Jenny loves certainty! But the plane does not crash. She is not yet to know how this will end.

"Those are the famous Hollywood Hills," B.J. is saying. "Nice place for a drive."

"I can't wait." Digging her heels into the floor, Jenny presses back into her seat. When she gets home, she will have so much to tell Saul. If he is still there. The wheels touch down. Letting out her breath, she opens her seatbelt.

"Please keep your seatbelts buckled and remain seated until the pilot turns off the sign."

B.J. is standing. Jenny admires his defiance. Saul never moves until he gets permission.

"Anything up here need to come down?" B.J. asks.

"A yellow sweater."

"Here you go. And take this too." His card. BENJAMIN J. LA MOTTA. SUNSHINE MACHINERY. "If you run into any problems, Jenny, just give me a call." His number is in the corner.

"Thanks. I will." She slips the card into her purse. The Iris of Santa Monica may turn out not to be, after all, the shining Iris Jenny is in love with. And unlike Saul, Jenny has no colleagues to turn to. She crams herself into the aisle in back of B.J.

He is short and wide like Simon. Jenny is done with father figures. B.J.'s brash white plastic loafers remind her of her mother's flashy clothes. She did not come all the way to California to be with her mother.

"Thank you for flying United."

"You got luggage?" B.J. asks.

"Yes." Jenny must get rid of this man.

"Downstairs." Carrying her shopping bag, he looks like Santa Claus. Such men are dangerous. "Come, I'll show you."

She follows him. All her life she has let some one lead her where she is going. She was planning, this time, to get around by herself. But B.J. knows the way and Jenny scurries behind him.

Her suitcase is one of the first to appear on the conveyer belt as if, because this trip was meant to be, every detail is perfect.

"Here," B.J. says, "let me take it."

"That's not necessary." Jenny lets him take it.

"My pleasure." B.J. hauls her bag toward the exit. Jenny trails him. His arm stretches, his body slants as he bears her weight. She, a traitor to feminism, blesses his dated chivalry. She blesses the anonymity that allows her to enjoy it. He, a traitor to his principle of traveling light, struggles to the door.

"How about—" Wheezing, "—if I give you—" B.J. drops the bag—"a ride?"—to the floor.

"No thanks." Damn it all, Jenny likes the man.

"You sure?" B.J. dabs sweat from his face. "Take me only—" He wants her to go to bed with him. "—a few minutes—" But if she did what excuse could Jenny give Saul? "—to get my car."

"Very sure." Jenny clings to her biological compulsion. She is leaving Saul because she is a lesbian. "But I really enjoyed talking with you." Even if he is a man. Bending with a quick impulse that pleases them both, she brushes her lips across his. "Ciao, B.J. La Motta."

She grapples with her portfolio, her shopping bag, her purse, her suitcase which gains pounds as Jenny staggers, like a wounded mule, toward the exit. Ahead of her, doors slide open. She stumbles out where pavement, windshields, and air glare in sharp patches of gilt. Through her tears, Jenny sees only light.

"Taxi?" The kid leans against his cab. His dungarees jut out, corrugated around the fly. His mirror glasses flash, in each lens, a woman with wild red hair and mammoth, kelly green breasts.

"Can you take me to Santa Monica?" Eyeing her reflection, Jenny is delighted. She chose just the right shirt.

"Cost you thirty." His is the only cab in sight.

"Done." Jenny knees her suitcase at him, hands over her art supplies. She clambers into his taxi, leans her portfolio against the seat, disentangles herself from her purse, slides a finger into the creases between her breasts, and, hooking the worm of perspiration before it can crawl another inch, lets herself go soft as the cushion underneath her. In this glowing heat, there is nothing more to do. Jenny can simply be.

The cabby slides in front and drives her out of the parking lot onto an elevated highway that reminds Jenny of the Cross-Bronx-Expressway but instead of brick tenements, high-rise projects, empty lots wadded with trash, she finds blond stucco bungalows, office buildings that gleam golden as beer, and, in the distance, tawny, tufted, lionesque hills.

"This is my first time in California." She seems to be the only green thing out here. "What are we seeing?" The landscape is as gilded as her dreams.

"Not much before the S-M." His arm is banded with leather, studded with metal teeth. Maybe Jenny has, after all, gone too far.

She grips a door handle. Driver number 47883. 47883. Dickran Tartulian. Definitely resembles the photo on the license. Feeling a kinship with survivors of genocides, Jenny has always liked Armenians. "So what's the S-M?" she asks.

"Santa-Monica Freeway. Right now we're on the S-D, San Diego." He looks into his rear view mirror and catches Jenny in his mirrored lenses, staring at her own image, her face multiplied in a dazzling tunnel of silver.

"You want to check out other forms of S-M while you're here?" He grins.

"No thank you, Dickran. That's not my particular perversion."

"What is?" His dimples remind Jenny of Aaron.

"I go for incest." Sitting back, she keeps hold of the door handle. "I adore my family." Three thousand miles away from her sons and their insistent sexuality, it is okay for her to confess.

"I could fix you up with stand-ins."

"Not to worry." Jenny lets the handle go. "It's all taken care of." She does not need another son, she has Iris.

"That's the story of my life. The chicks I can see right off they're dynamite, someone else always gets to them first."

"I'm too old for you anyway." Jenny is supposed to mind being called a chick, but the term makes her want to waggle her tail and strut.

"What too old, thirty? Thirty-five?" Dickran's glasses pick up Jenny's face. She cannot make out details, no wrinkles or puffiness, only mirror light.

"I'm almost forty. Old enough to be your mother."

"You said you were into incest. And I get off on older women." He turns off onto another highway. "S-M, here we go."

Many times Anna warned Jenny: A woman on her own is just asking for trouble. Her mother never mentioned that being out alone in the world can be fun. Jenny's sister has never once gone off alone. Jenny sits back, her T-shirt tight across her breasts. Calvin Klein. Not on sale. Her mother would be horrified by its price. Jenny smiles. This shirt is worth every cent she paid for it.

"Was that a thrill or what?" Dickran veers off the highway onto a street. "And now for Lincoln Boulevard." He stops at a red light.

A blue van with orange and yellow flames painted on the side flashes by. A little boy munching glow-in-the dark cotton candy crosses the street wearing a twinkling rhinestone bracelet. Why not? Palm trees, like ratty feather dusters, stretch over the roof of Bob's Big Boy. This is a funky tropics with no sexual stereotyping. Paradise. They speed by Paul Bunyan who stands astride a discount house roof offering a rolled up Rug-O-Rama carpet to the reddening sky.

"Look, Dickran." Jenny crams her head out the window. "Look at that." She loves the giant muscled legs, chest, arms. She brings her head back inside. "I wonder where he comes from? I'd love to bring one of those home." Jenny likes fake men; only real ones make trouble.

"That dummy's got to be at least twenty, thirty feet tall." Dickran's typical male preoccupation with size reminds Jenny where she is headed. Iris Wilde would hate Paul Bunyan.

"He'd look spectacular in my garden." Maybe Jenny could find a female version. She imagines a photo of herself in her backyard, looking up between the giant's legs, *Hartford Courant* page one.

"How would you get him there?"

"I don't know." She is not even sure she can get through the next two weeks. "Somehow I guess." What if she cannot amuse Iris? What, exactly, will Jenny have to do?

"Like I always say, different strokes." Dickran pulls a cigarette from the pack rolled in his sleeve. "That type of thing looks pretty scuzzy to me." The arbiter of taste has a dragon tattoo on his bicep.

"You a native Californian?" Happy to re-focus on Dickran rather than Iris, Jenny assumes his contempt for indigenous folk art is a case of profound self-contempt.

"Nope." A flame spurts from his fist. "Fall River Mass. Been out here three years come next month."

"You glad you moved?" The closer he takes Jenny to Iris, the more she feels as if she has on a tight girdle. Painfully tight.

"Glad? This'll blow your mind." Dickran emits coils of smoke. "I split Fall River with a B.S.A. 500, rode out here, and traded in less than two years for a Harley Panhead."

"What's that?"

"Best damn high performance bike in the world at the present time, that's all."

"I mean Gravity's Foe." Must be a kite store. "Go back there for a minute." Kites on the beach she used to fly them with the kids, now Jenny can fly kites with Iris. "I want to buy a few kites." She imagines a dragonfly darting, high in a flat blue sky, between a caterpillar and a box kite.

"Gravity's Foe is a head shop." Dickran twists around. "Still want me to turn back?"

"No, never mind." She avoids the mirror eyes. "Keep going." This is no time to learn about head shops. Later, maybe Iris will take her. Shivering, Jenny cranks up her window.

Dickran turns into a side street.

"This here is Lomas Drive." He flicks his cigarette stub out the window. "What did you say that number was?"

"Nineteen seventy-six, same as the year." In Hartford that sameness seemed a good omen. Now Jenny passes a dry tongue over her dry lips.

Climbing a steep hillside, the cab clears its throat. Jenny coughs. She forgot about smog. Dickran shifts gears. Jenny glimpses the sea swallowing the sun, the Pacific not a beautiful blue, or Atlantic gray, but brown, sullen brown.

"This what you want?" Dickran yanks the emergency brake. The cable tightens. Numbers next to a tarred driveway glitter like steel nails. "Nineteen seventy-six."

She should have called from the airport. Iris may not even be home. Iris may be waiting for her. Jenny does not know what to say. This whole trip could be a disaster; she hardly knows Saul's girl-friend.

Dickran has the trunk lid up. No sidewalk, Jenny's bags dumped on a crabgrass strip. Already he knows Jenny is no dynamite chick. How long will it take Iris to realize?

"That's thirty like I said." Dickran waits for Jenny to get it out.

"Just a minute." As if this is a bad watercolor scene, Jenny's topaz afternoon has turned brown. Tropical shrubs point blades at a darkening street where there is no child's bike, no Good Humor man, no sign of life, not even a doorway. On Lomas Drive everything is sealed off.

Dickran leans against his cab watching Jenny with eyes. No mirrors.

Jenny turns away.

A red hibiscus thrusts its tongue at her. She shoots her tongue right back out at it. Behind that bush there are cars in a carport, one of them probably the Volvo that came with Iris's apartment. Iris must be here. Every basement is down. Just beyond the mailbox, next to a waist-high jade tree hedge, there are stairs. In Hartford, those plants would cost thousands, though at this moment Jenny cannot think why. Still such riches must mean she has arrived in heaven.

"You take that." Jenny points a toe at her suit-case. "I'll get the rest."

"Come off it, lady." Behind her, Dickran bumps the heavy bag down each railroad-tie step. "This wasn't part of the deal."

"Just a little way now." Jenny leads him to a brick patio, glass doors, soft gold light.

Iris bends over a sink. Naked, the globes of her cream-white ass glow like twin rice-paper lamps. Iris is washing her hair.

"Just leave that." Pulling out her wallet, Jenny grabs bills, drops bills, stamps on bills, snatches up bills.

"Take your time." Dickran stares at Iris. "No sweat."

"Here." Thirty-five is too much or too little. Jenny thrusts it at him; he takes it.

"Sure you can't use me for anything else?" His teeth and eyes glisten with Iris Wilde's light.

"Very sure." Jenny plants herself between him and the glass doors.

"Catch you later then." Waving, Dickran climbs the stairs. Jenny waits to hear the slammed taxi door, the engine.

She turns back to the gold light.

Iris is wrapping her head in a yellow towel. Her breasts shift, soft as fresh-baked rolls shaped and re-shaped by her arms' languorous movements. Every part of Iris is smooth. Her belly, curved and shiny as a lima bean, rests on a honey triangle. She ties on a shimmering, white, silken kimono and her pale nipples emboss glistening rosy discs in the cloth as if her magic radiance gleams through matter.

Through Jenny. The heat from Iris's light pools in Jenny's chest, her breasts. She raps on the window, smearing away her own steamy breath.

Iris plucks her granny glasses from the kitchen counter, puts them on, peers outside. She grins.

"Perfect timing." She slides back the glass. "I was just thinking about you, O Empress of the Night."

"You look wonderful." Jenny moves inside.

"So do you."

They hug, their bodies fitting like yin and yang. If Jenny is Empress of the Night, in her yellow turban, Iris is Empress of the Day.

"My God it's good to be here." No more scaly history for Jenny. The walls of this apartment are as blank and glossy as the skin of an orange.

"I was just getting ready to go out to supper, unless you're too exhausted."

"I'm fine." Past Exhaustion, Jenny is into Euphoria.

"Good. I'm starving. Haven't eaten since yesterday." Iris grabs a comb from the bureau. "We can go to Mother Nature's." She has everything planned.

"I love the name." Jenny wants only to be told what to do.

"There's gin under the sink. Pick a lime from the tree on the patio." Iris goes into the bathroom. "I'll be ready in a few minutes." The door swings shut behind her.

Jenny leans her portfolio in the corner nearest the glass doors. She drags her suitcase into the same corner. Normally, she unpacks immediately, turning every place into a replica of home as fast as she can. But this home is Iris Wilde's. Too high and hollow for gin, Jenny prowls.

A double bed, a single studio couch, maybe Iris expects Jenny to sleep by herself. Jenny perches on the arm of a leatherette lounger. If she knew where the switch was, she would turn on the famous fire. Tomorrow, when her mind comes down from space, she will figure it out; right now she will just be cold. Jenny has no right to be disappointed. All basements have mildew in the air. From the bathroom, Iris's hair blower whines. A dog whimpers upstairs. Jenny gets up and walks outside.

Below a great bowl of gray lambswool—the California sky—she hears the Pacific. She presses her hand against a tree trunk. It is real. Jenny is here. She lies down on a chaise.

"You all set?" Iris leaves her apartment without turning off lights or locking the door.

"Yes." Jenny's portfolio is in there. Also her Italian slippers and her silver rain cape. But she must stop worrying, in this bourgeois capitalist way, about being robbed.

She follows Iris up the stairs, through the musky evening and below that ample ass in white painter pants, Jenny's tongue remembers the soft powdery sweetness of marshmallows. The Volvo's padded bucket seat supports her limp body.

"How nice to see you again!" Iris's hand on the gear stick shifts along Jenny's thigh.

"It turned out to be a very easy trip." Jenny waits to see what Iris will do next. "I can't believe it took me twenty years to get out."

"It is unbelievable. Last night I dreamed I went to the train to meet you." Under sodium vapor street lamps, Iris is phantom yellow. But this is no fantasy. If she has Jenny in her unconscious mind, their love must be profound. "Saul was standing at the gate so I pretended you weren't coming." Iris has him in there too, the three of them linked forever. "After I woke up, I went on the assumption the dream was accurate in case you didn't show."

"I said I'd be here."

"I'm not used to such good fortune." Iris told Saul she grew up in an orphanage.

"I always keep my promises." Jenny is determined to make up for the love Iris missed, to restore to her beloved a sense of security.

"How noble of you!" Iris reaches over and clasps Jenny's knee. Jenny keeps her legs relaxed. Whatever Iris wants, she can have. Withdrawing her hand, Iris steers the car into Mother Nature's parking lot.

After dinner, coming back to the apartment is like coming home. Jenny knows the way down. Sliding back the glass door, she steps over the threshold into incandescent light.

"You can have the bottom two dresser drawers." Iris takes a plastic bag of marijuana out of the freezing compartment. "Hang things in the right side of the closet." She rolls a joint on the kitchen counter.

Jenny stuffs her flowered chintz cosmetic kit in a drawer swiftly, hoping Iris thinks her pink cheeks are natural.

"Want a hit?" Iris squints through smoke.

Jenny is ready. A week ago, she and Saul sprawled on the floor like their own children and he showed her how to smoke pot which made her see the den carpet as deep crimson with a sheen, like raw beef. Lit by the honey of a Brahms Sextet, the air that night shone gold as if Iris had already touched everything Jenny would ever see with her magic wand. Now Jenny inhales.

Iris smiles. Jenny must have done it right. She lets out her breath.

"Far out." Iris picks up Jenny's mylar raincape and holds it around her neck. "You even brought me your Moon Goddess costume."

"Why not?" Jenny's Fairy Godmother turns ordinary clothing into enchanted rainment.

Iris twirls before a mirror, the silver cape fluttering and billowing behind her. She crouches to clack a cassette into her tape recorder.

"BRING MUSIC" her postcard said. In Jenny's day, tapes held gauze pads in place. Now, leaving in her suitcase the records and sheet music that prove she is overdue for an update, Jenny takes a deep puff of the joint.

"Here comes the sun," the Beatles sing.

The sun is Iris, lighting candles in bottles, candles in star holders, candles in saucers, her flames turning this room into a golden grotto. Oh yes, Iris will inspire Jenny and Jenny will amaze the world with fantastic cave animals; creatures like no one has ever made, ever seen. Iris blows out her taper, turns off the lamps.

71

In the magic candlelight she dances, whirls, loops around. Iris crouches and leaps, her silver wings spread wide, folding. Even Jenny's sister Barbara cannot dance like this. Iris's fingers, like butterflies, light in Jenny's hair.

"I've never known anyone with such curls," she murmurs, the silver cape dropping to the floor.

"I used to wish my hair was straight." Now Jenny is afraid that compared to all the others Iris has known, she will be found wanting. Getting up, she pinches her contact lenses, drops them into her case, squirts in saline solution, tightens the lids, sets up her sterilizer, presses the button as if she is not expecting going to bed to be extraordinary.

Iris pulls rubberbands off her braids. "I used to give myself perms so I'd have curls." Now she unfurls, around her face, spaghetti waves, their satiny sheen like the nightgown Jenny pulls from the drawer.

At home she goes to bed naked.

"Where do you want me to sleep?" Without her lenses, Jenny sees Iris the way a moth must see a flame, as a brilliant blur. "On the couch?"

Laughing, Iris slides her straps over her shoulders, pushes her overalls down.

"Only if, for some occult reason of your own, you prefer the couch to my bed." Iris lifts her shirt over her head, her face reappearing like a clouded moon.

Jenny drops her nightgown. She unties her skirt, pulls off her shirt, unhooks her bra. Her breasts quiver and tighten, nipples puckering as if already sucked by imaginary lips.

Smiling, Iris steps out of her underpants.

Jenny slides hers off.

Iris puts her glasses on a night table.

Jenny unbuckles her watch.

Each woman, on her side of the bed, slips under the covers.

The moment of contact is cool, startling, fluid. Iris's body is sleek as water. Nothing abrades. Her fingers flutter over Jenny's breasts, belly, thighs. Jenny's own fingers, touching Iris the same way, know exactly how every touch feels.

("You're supposed to move, not just lie there like a corpse," Saul said after the first time. "How should I move?" Jenny wanted to know. "Up when I go in, down when I go out," Saul said.)

Now she moves the way she wants to. The way Iris moves. Iris does not go up and down. She slides around loose and free. Jenny gyres and gimbles with the wabe. She sloshes. Saul's cock floats into her head like a sodden log. She thrusts it away. Grasping Iris's cushiony shoulders, Jenny rides the surf. Her skin dissolves. She is the surf. Feelings of love, held in for years, slip out of her into Iris.

"Ohh." Iris's voice comes from outside the dark mass that is both of them. A jolting current connects clits, flashes, switches off. "So good."

Adrift, Jenny for the first time understands why shock treatments work. She is a different person now. A lesbian. Her problems solved by sex, blissful sex. She curls around Iris in sleep.

Jenny dreams of an ice-cold bowl of potato salad and wakes up hungry.

Where is she? Lost. No, in Santa Monica, California. She is in the fetal position, naked in bed, with Iris Wilde in a white silk kimono standing over her.

"Want a gin and tonic?" Crystalline bubbles cluster around a lime disc in Iris's goblet.

"Looks beautiful, but isn't it awfully early to start drinking?" Never never before breakfast, Jenny has assumed all her life. A bed lamp shines on her watch. Seven-thirty. Hartford or California time? Morning or night? The light outside is the gray that comes right before or after dark.

"You're on a holiday." Iris hands her the glass. "Time doesn't count." With silky hair flopping, she looks like a pekingese puppy.

"If you say so." The drink slides into Jenny like a cold snake.

"What an amazing collection you have!" Iris picks up Jenny's deck of credit cards. "Mind if I look?" She pulls the rubber band off the pack.

"They're just the usual." Jenny minds. Here she does not want to be Mrs. Credit Card.

"Saks, Macy's, Lord and Taylor."

"Saul always calls it *Gott und Schneider*."

"Why?"

"That's Yiddish for Lord and Taylor." Jenny and Saul both have a little Yiddish. No matter what happened last night, Jenny and Iris have only the fact that they are women in common. Maybe that will be enough.

"Bloomingdale's, Bergdorf Goodman." Iris tosses the cards back on the bureau. "I once ripped off a suede shirt from Bergdorf's."

"Everyone steals at least once in their life." But what if Iris never stopped stealing? Jenny knows nothing about her lover's character except that Saul seems to think it okay. "Excuse me." Saul would say his back teeth are floating. "My back teeth are floating."

Snatching up her T-shirt, Jenny clutches it in front of her, tears into the bathroom, shuts the door, sits down, and lets go.

("If the Department of Environmental Protection ever finds out about your farts, they'll give you a life sentence," Luke claims.)

What if Iris heard that? Until she gets home, Jenny will have to hold farts in. She turns the faucet on loud.

("Did you wash your hands? Thoroughly?," her mother used to ask. In those days, Jenny never had.)

Now she washes thoroughly, ignoring the hair blower with a mouth like a sea monster on the back of the toilet.

("You sure you want to go through with this?" Saul asked on the way to the airport. Then, Jenny was sure.)

Now she pulls her T-shirt down and sidles into the bedroom. She must look like an ass. She is an ass. Jenny scoots under the covers.

"All the lonely people; where do they all come from?" the Beatles ask.

Iris is busy. She sits crosslegged on the bed with a small wooden tray tilted in her lap, her kimono gaping around the exotic iridescence of her vulva. Iris sifts grass, rocks her tray, chops with her cardboard matchbook. Jenny used to watch her grandmother chop chicken livers, cabbage, onions, fish. Grandma rocked her big wooden bowl, her blade chopping and scooping, knocking out the same clip-clop Iris makes now.

"My grandmother left Odessa with a trunk full of oranges she sold one by one on the ship." Jenny wants Iris to know everything about her Saul knows. "By the time she got to Ellis Island, she had enough cash to set my grandfather up in business as a tailor." Beginning at the beginning, she repeats, word for word, her father's favorite story. "All my grandfather brought with him was a violin and a pair of scissors."

"Highly emblematic." Seeds and stems skitter down Iris's tray. "The woman as nurturer of the body." She scoops shreds into a creased paper. "The man controlling the tools of art and trade." She rolls and licks a joint, sliding it in and out of her mouth. "A classic." Iris lights up, inhales, passes to Jenny.

With Iris's spit between her lips, Jenny feels like she is french kissing grandma. Shame heats her face. Iris chuckles.

"Tell me, beautiful lady, what is it like being rich?"

"Mostly I feel guilty."

"Why?" Iris scowls.

"There are people who don't have anything." People like Iris. "I

74

feel responsible for them. I envy people who earn what they have."

"How do you make your money?"

"From my father's investments."

"You earned that. Every daughter pays for whatever her father gives her. Mine killed himself when I was thirteen." Iris sucks the joint.

"That's awful."

"Now that is where you are wrong." Holding smoke, Iris presses her lips. "I'm better off without the creep." Her voice sneaks out pinched.

"You don't really mean that." Jenny must help Iris to release the love she is pressing back.

"Sister, have you got a lot to learn!" Iris passes the joint. "Lesson One." She gathers up a handful of Jenny's hair. "You have as much right to your father's money as you have to your curly hair." Iris tugs. Jenny's hair is rooted. Like her white skin, her Jewishness, her brain, her artistic bent, and the legs that could never run better than a fifteen minute mile, the money her father gave her is Jenny's. She must make the best of it. Jenny is great at making the best of things.

"I never thought of it that way before." She feels a power surge in herself that could turn on a million lights, light up a million canvases. How grateful Jenny is to Saul for introducing her to Iris!

"Let's see what other goodies you're hiding." Iris's thighs and belly gleam smooth and white as sacks of sand. Gently, she draws the sheet away from Jenny.

Jenny strips off her shirt. She remembers the jade plants. Some people like succulents.

"You have a fine body." Iris stares at Jenny's stretch marks. The Beatles click off. Something hisses. It is the room. Or maybe the tree looming outside in the spongy dusk or dawn, its leaves rustling like dried minnows.

Iris tickles Jenny's nipples with the ends of her kimono sash. The Russians used to tickle people until they laughed themselves to death. This is not funny. Her room smells like being buried alive but there is some kind of spice she uses to cover it up.

"What's that smell?" Jenny crosses her arms over her breasts.

"Eucalyptus from the tree right out there."

Jenny's mother used to keep eucalyptus leaves on the table by the elevator. Maybe Jenny did come all this way just to be with her mother.

"Is that the Pacific I'm hearing?" Whispering secrets. Secrets. Jenny listens. Anna too had secrets.

"No. This is California." Iris gets up. The sliding door rumbles. She locks it. "It's traffic." She closes the curtains. "They've got highways between the people and the sea here." Her body blocks Jenny's way out. "They've fucked up the whole state." Iris's voice has hypodermic needles in it.

Jenny clutches the mattress. She must not close her eyes no matter how much she wants to. The room is tilting. She holds tight to keep from falling off into those huge pillows, that smothering comforter, Iris filling up this room, her head almost to the ceiling. Jenny should never have left Saul.

She pulls the sheet over her head, curls up, and shivers. "I feel sick." As if the outside of her is collapsing into her own hollowness.

"Here." Iris tucks the blanket around Jenny. "I'll warm you up." She rubs Jenny's hips, her backside. She massages Jenny's thighs and calves like Jenny's mother used to do to keep her from getting infantile paralysis. Turning off the light, Iris slides in beside Jenny. This Anna never did though Jenny wished her mother would. Now Jenny closes her eyes.

Their tongues touch. Inside Jenny, lights flick at blackness that belongs to them both so she is not sure where she is or which of them is which. Pulling away, Jenny sees Iris with her hands, sees the cushiony shoulders, the smooth bones of her spine. She squeezes the yielding generosity of Iris's ass and licks the gully between her breasts, damp and smelling like honeydew. Jenny licks Iris's midriff, her belly that is hard and soft as a balloon. She licks the tiny threads around Iris's belly button, licks a line down to taste forbidden fruit. Fibrous and sweet, not after all a raspberry or an apple, but a plum, a marvelously ripe, juicy, Santa Clara plum pulses between her lips.

"How nice, my seething trollop, that you get off on country pie!" Iris pets Jenny's head. "Not everyone does."

Jenny presses her ear to Iris's belly, listens to the gurgling, is content with what it means to be a lesbian.

BLAST. CRASH. PIP-POP-PIP. Bombs. Jenny yanks herself away from Iris. The war has started. Here. To punish her for what she just did. She will die three thousand miles away from Saul and her children.

Grabbing her glasses, Iris springs out of bed. "Look." She flings back the curtains. "It must be fireworks for the Bicentennial."

Glitter explodes behind the eucalyptus tree. "Let's go where we can see better." She scrambles into her overalls, her sandals. "Hurry. Get dressed." Iris pulls on a shirt.

At the kitchen sink, Jenny swipes water at her mouth and chin. "Never mind that." Iris slides the door open.

No time to put in lenses. Jenny jabs her legs into her underpants. Her shirt barely restrains her breasts. Her denim skirt flips around her thighs, like hands.

"It'll be all over before we get there if you don't hurry." Iris pushes Jenny just as Saul does. Jenny tags after her, out across the patio, through prickly bushes, down hidden steps to a sidewalk into a dim, dank, pissy tunnel.

"Wait." A stitch pierces Jenny's belly.

"See you there—" Iris—"there—" disappears—"there—" around a curve, "—there," echoes all of her that is left.

Leaning against a wall, Jenny takes deep breaths. She cannot stay here. The stone beats with the footsteps of her own heart, her own feet, running.

GEORGE JACKSON LIVES in swollen underground graffiti. But George Jackson is dead, only an un known artist makes him live. Unknown, like Jenny up to now. She races out of the tunnel.

BLAM. Pink strings hang in the sky. Jenny stumbles into strangers.

"Watch it." A woman clasps her elbow. "Place is mined." She points down at a brown blob.

Dog turd.

"Thanks." Jenny zigzags toward the water, her eyes to the ground. And up. Around her, tilted faces mirror every shock of light.

CRASH. SISS. A mammoth yellow palm tree spurts into the sky.

Hartford has nothing like this. As soon as Jenny gets home, she will describe this magnificent spectacle to Saul.

SSH. SSH. Frenzied green worms writhe.

"Imagine, if they could see all this, what our founding foremothers would say." Coming up behind Jenny, Iris winds her arms around Jenny's waist. Jenny tenses. "What's the matter?" Iris shoves her away. "Afraid people will know you're a dyke?"

"No." Jenny is afraid because love has not fused her to this woman. "Just startled, that's all."

BAM. BAM. Bursting dandelions go to seed in a vast black field. BAM. BAM. Generation after generation of dandelions. CRASH. Sparks shoot at the sea, the beach, the hills. Globes explode, blasting spasms of light that drip tentatively, down the sky, toward the world.

"We better start back." Iris moves with the crowd.

Jenny pauses. People jostle and nudge her, She stares up into the night at tiny fists of smoke that open, widen vanish. In Jenny's hands the shape of Iris's shoulders, ass, waist, breasts, her taste in Jenny's mouth. Jenny shuts her eyes.

Inside her lids, spheres bright as grandma's oranges, swim. At last, Jenny has fireworks of her own to add to her father's vision. Opening her eyes, she smiles. A young woman smiles back. Maybe she knows Jenny is a lesbian.

"WHOOHEEH!" The woman's boyfriend throws a beer can high into the air and it flipflops, in a spangled arch, back onto the shit bedecked sand.

Chapter VII

NURSING WOUNDS
• *Eight Days Later* •

In California a little over a week, Jenny is tired of doing nothing. Her shopping bag, stashed in the corner right where she left it the first night, is as fat, sloppy, and useless as Jenny is, propped up, on pillows, in bed. She has not unpacked so much as a paintbrush. More important, Jenny has not kept Iris from falling into a whirlpool of anger.

"Look what Judy's getting away with." Iris smashes eggs, one at a time, smash, smash, smash, against the side of a steel mixing bowl. "In the name of sisterhood." She thumps a giant chunk of butter into a cast iron pan. "Her project is one big scam."

"Are you cooking eggs for me too?" All that fat will make Jenny fatter, it will clog her arteries, she will die which is what she deserves after what she has done. Three thousand miles away from Saul, Jenny remembers his body with pleasure. It is Iris whose skin is becoming routine. If Saul sometimes felt like a needle sewing Jenny to the mattress, last night, Iris felt like an eggbeater, the sensation not so much different as the same. Jenny may have left her husband for nothing.

"Obviously." Iris's knife rasps as she scrapes more butter onto toast. When she was young, her mother deserted her. Her father killed himself. Of course she assumes Jenny will also hurt her.

Jenny must prove her wrong. Getting up, she scoops her raincape off the floor and buttons it around her neck, mylar cool as wind on her skin. She must stay cool. She begins by restoring order, pulling back curtains. Jenny may never make it as an artist but she will always know how to be a mother. At this hour, the patio is sunless, bricked in, the jade tree hedge like barbed wire around a prison yard. Jenny turns away.

"You look beautiful this morning, Iris Wilde." She will smother the child's turbulence with compliments. Jenny will heal past hurts.

"You're the only one who thinks that." Iris tears a carton of juice open with her teeth. "And even if it's true, why waste beauty on creeps? I think I'll call in sick."

"I wouldn't if I were you." Jenny has not worked in more than a month. "Naturally you hate going back after time off." California images are ready to explode inside Jenny. "Go. You'll be happy you did." Jenny is not just being selfish. The longer a child stays home from school, the harder the return. "Accomplishing even a little something will make you feel better." Sitting down on a dinette chair, Jenny twists her legs around chrome tubes that remind her of her own sturdy shins, her own need to accomplish something.

"If you really loved me, you'd want me to stay home with you." As always, Iris demands proof of love.

"I do love you." Jenny's work now is Iris, not art. She lets her raincape slip open, switching, once again, the impulse to work, over to sex. "I want you to do whatever's best for you."

"If I knew what was good for me, would I take a lover who's married to somebody else?" Iris slams plates on the table. "Would I accept a job in a chaotic studio?" She plops down opposite Jenny, her backside overflowing her chair. "Chicago's on the most incredible ego trip." Iris spreads her arms on the table. "She's actually invited her men to work on our project." Leaning forward, she squints as if she is about to thread Jenny's eyes. "What do you think about that?"

Jenny thinks she is under attack.

"You talk as if it's my fault." Wrapping her cape wings across her lap, Jenny decides that, longterm, sex as a palliative is a flop.

"You think everything is your fault." Iris shoves back. "Well right now I happen to be talking about a feminist principle, but you wouldn't understand."

"Then take it up with Judy." Jenny has let Iris's tantrum go on too long.

"There's no point discussing anything with Judy either." Iris stares out the window. "Most of the other dykes have already quit."

"Dykes. Kikes." The words slap Jenny's ears. "I can't stand those labels." Whether she deserves them or not.

"Stop being paranoid. The word dyke has entirely different connotations than the word kike."

"Both are negative."

"False." Iris smacks the table. "Becoming a dyke is the most positive thing I ever did in my life." For Iris being homosexual is definition enough. "But that's not the point." Stirring she clanks her spoon against china. "The issue is Judy. She's so out of it she has no idea who's there and who isn't." Thrusting her wet spoon into the sugar, Iris coagulates beige pellets, like kitty droppings, in the bowl.

"Do whatever you want." Jenny's images never embody her intentions. Maybe Iris is right. Jenny should forget Mother and Artist and declare herself simply Lesbian.

"The women Judy hasn't driven away couldn't mount a show of any scope within five years, let alone next year," Iris is saying. "Someone's got to do something about her fucking 'Dinner Party.'"

"Could I?" Jeans, a workshirt, contact lenses, and rouge, Jenny could be on her way in five minutes.

"The ceramics are a joke." Iris stabs eggs with her fork. "Any plate that doesn't disintegrate inside the kiln falls apart as soon as it comes out." She crams eggs into her mouth. "What do you know about making porcelain?"

"Not much." Nothing, in fact. Jenny's eggs taste like fleece. Her toast smells of ashes. "But I'm a quick study." Her presence here with Iris proves that.

"If I did the research I was hired to do," Iris says, "Judy probably wouldn't use it. All she wants is names so her project will qualify as a collective effort for funding."

"She's welcome to my name." Jenny has only her father's or Saul's to offer. Maybe those are not good enough. "I'm thinking of changing it." People would want to see art by a woman named Connecticut O'Fantastic. All Jenny has to do is make images worth looking at. She is back on square one.

"You're better off out of this debacle," Iris says.

"Isn't there something I could do to help?" Working on Judy's project would be so much easier for Jenny than having to make up a project of her own.

"Nothing short of assassinating the queen bee." Iris gets up from the table.

"Without a queen, the hive dies," Jenny says.

"As far as I'm concerned, that would be great." In front of the mirror, Iris twists a braid ponytail that ends up like a paintbrush. "The whole thing's gotten to be a drag." Jenny prefers the two-braided Iris, even the enraged Iris, to this pointed hair Valkyrie, looking forward to the destruction of her gods. "Don't look so sad. I'm not abandoning you. I thought you said you wanted to sketch."

"I did." Squatting in the corner, Jenny's shopping bag is all packed for the trip home. "But I may not bother." After almost a month, she cannot even think how to begin. And she has breakfast dishes to wash, a kitchen to clean. And, once Iris is gone, the bathroom will be all hers. And by the time she is through in there, the sun will be perfect, and Jenny can go out on the patio and work on her tan so she will have something to show for her vacation when she gets home. "Will you be here for lunch?" Jenny can plan something special; she will have no time to work.

"Probably." Iris jiggles her back-pack. "Have you seen my keys anywhere?"

"On the mantel."

"What about my sunglasses?"

"On top of the sink in the bathroom."

"Anything else you think I should have?"

"Your wallet. Top bureau drawer."

"That it?"

"No," Jenny says, "come here and I'll give you a kiss."

"Why not several?" Iris engulfs Jenny in the smell of sunshine.

"If you want." Jenny is beginning to feel as if her problem may not be marriage but coupling of any kind. It takes so much time.

"Maybe I should call in sick," Iris says.

"Out." Jumping up, Jenny pushes Iris through the door.

"If you really loved me—"

"We'll discuss that when you get back."

Nothing forgotten. Iris is really gone. Wind, cars, ocean whoosh solo minutes around Jenny. The place is hers.

She washes dishes first. Then she makes the bed. She sits on the toilet, reading an ancient *Art News*, exploding super farts and unrepentant stinks.

Jenny shampoos her hair. She creams her elbows. She still has an hour and a half until Iris comes back, plenty of time to go to the beach. Jenny cannot enjoy the beach until she first at least tries to work.

Lifting her shopping bag out of the corner onto the kitchen counter, she cuts the cord around it, takes out her paintbox, opens the lid. Scarlet. Mars and cadmium yellow like the hummingbirds, appearing helter-skelter outside, blurry pinwheels buzzing the lime tree. Jenny rubs a blank canvas board that feels, against her palm, like the inside of a tangerine rind, cream white tinged with gold, the same California colors that swirl in her, this place still happening. She has no idea what to make of it.

Besides, getting Iris off to the studio was work enough for one day. Jenny has earned the right to lie in the sun. Unhooking her bathing suit bra, she stretches out on a chaise.

Soon her warmed white breasts feel like floats that will carry her up to the sun. This is what Jenny wants to paint. Light. And love. Now that she knows what it is, she wants to show passion seething hot and gorgeous as molten steel. Wriggling her bottom, Jenny swipes away a sweat mustache.

She is melting out here. Her arm dangles off the chaise like a Dali watch. Her fingers curl around a stick, no, a paintbrush. Sable. Like Luke's eyelashes. Or the coat her father gave Anna on their fortieth anniversary. If Jenny mentions sable, Saul knows she means paintbrushes, Luke's eyelashes, her mother's coat. Jenny may lose Saul, this fear in her an ice cube swallowed whole.

Jenny cannot lose him. Her marriage is a triangle now, fragile and silver with that little opening where two sides do not quite meet. Maybe that is what she should paint: the tiny space where music crosses over, sparks fly, shapes swell or shrink or are forged into permanence. All it takes to make a triangle is steel and heat. Light. That's it. Jenny will paint fireworks.

Jumping up, she paces across the patio, back, across. Her colors must come out looking like brilliant streaks of speed. She has Verplex for a transparent background. Jenny loves transparency. She needs glitter. There must be something in this land of light she can use. Jade leaves look oily, she wants sparkle. Maybe broken glass, or even more brilliant, a shattered mirror. But broken mirrors are unlucky and she does not want such a literal reflection. Jenny wants glitter.

Under the sink in the kitchen, she finds a roll of aluminum foil and a hole-punch. Obviously this work was meant to be. Why else would there be a hole-punch but for Jenny to make sequins? She has gold in the paper around a box of sugar wafers. She guzzles Tab out of a can with a matte aluminum shine that will give her an illusion of depth, and squeezes scouring powder out of its metallic green tube. Jenny punches silver discs, cuts green shreds and gold triangles, punches out tin sequins, heaps her colors on *Art News*.

Carrying this palette out to the patio, she sets it down on the bricks. Jenny sits, holding flat on her lap, the limitless possibilities of an untouched canvas. Images flop around inside her. This time, she will pin down at least one of them.

Jenny begins by spreading polymer gel across the center of the canvas. Her swath immediately turns tacky. She sprinkles it with an arc of Tab discs to represent shooting star trails. Adding islands of gel, she dabbles them with green shreds for bursting worms. The shreds look only like shreds. The gel is clouding up. Jenny hurls silver sequins at both arc and islands.

She overdid. The silver is too dense. It makes nothing light up. Yet, slamming foil sequins at the canvas, Jenny feels her work explode, and, circling and throwing, she is whirling bits and pieces of dizzy ideas out of herself into the world.

"I rushed home because I thought you wanted me here for lunch." Iris's shadow falls on Jenny's canvas, her hand on Jenny's sun-warmed shoulder, a fresh fish.

Jenny did not hear the car, the door, Iris's footsteps; she has no idea what time it is.

"I just have to finish this one thing." Her gel is hardening.

"Hurry. I'm starving."

"You're blocking my sun." Saul, the kids, Iris, they all expect Jenny to drop what she is doing the minute they appear. "Move."

"Don't speak to me in that tone of voice."

"I can't work with you there." Jenny's children know better than to interrupt her when she is working.

"Fuck you." Iris frisbees a letter into the hedge and flounces into the apartment.

By now, Jenny's children know they cannot always have her full attention. She is damned tired of training children, damned tired of being a mother. A letter from Saul mocks her from the jade tree hedge. She left him for Iris; she must take the consequences.

"You want to smoke?" Iris stands in the doorway. "It might help if you got stoned."

"In a minute. This is about to dry." Jenny slams a fist full of gold triangles at her canvas.

Iris saunters outside, a joint bobbing between her lips. After squinting at Jenny's work, she turns away, lowers herself onto a chaise, puts up her feet, and closes her eyes.

Now Jenny sees what Iris saw. Aluminum circles spattered like grease, shirred foil, green shreds bunched like grass clippings on a wet lawn, gold pointing like loose arrowheads.

"What do you think?" California is an incoherent excess; Jenny has caught that.

"I should have stayed at the studio." Iris puffs at her joint. "I could've had pizza."

Jenny lifts her picture, sets it on the hedge, tucks jade leaves over the corners. Her materials shimmer in the sunlight as if she really did capture daytime fireworks. Of course that would make Iris jealous. Iris spends hours avoiding work, hers as well as Jenny's. Jenny plucks Saul's letter out of the hedge.

"He didn't mention you in the letter he wrote me." Iris does not say what Saul did mention.

"He's into denial." Or else, once they get back to Connecticut, it will be Saul and Iris with Jenny on her own. Jenny takes a deep drag of the joint.

"Saul's letting you do whatever you want." Iris's knees sway, her thighs smear.

"I suppose so." Shivering, Jenny pulls a T-shirt on over her bathing suit.

"I thought you came out here to have fun." Iris's lips form a straight line.

"Only partly." Jenny twists the top of the gel tube. Good and tight.

Iris waves her joint at the house.

"What's the disaster in the kitchen sink?"

"Scouring powder."

"Get rid of it. The odor's foul." Iris shifts around to face the sun, her zitsy back a wall.

Jenny goes inside. She turns on the kitchen faucet so the sullen aqua heap blossoms into spit-white bubbles. She needs time off, a vacation from her vacation, Jenny needs to go back to living. She tears open her letter.

Dear Jen,
    The house is quiet without you. I've been working my way slowly through the freezer. Tuesday I ate blintzes from the paleolithic era. Last night was sweet and sour cabbage soup.
    If you get a chance, please send me your flank steak recipe. I've invited a friend over for dinner.
    In the meantime, I miss and love you. Give Iris my best.
                                                                              S.

Saul is entertaining while she is not there. Jenny shuts off the water. Who? He is eating cabbage soup on a July night in Hartford. This morning, Jenny downed Iris's woolen eggs. What are they doing to themselves?

Jenny swats a cabinet door with her hip. Probably peanut butter sandwiches for lunch with milk. She is sick of this return to childhood. There is no wine. Or tonic. No point. The patio door rumbles in its tracks.

"I'm sorry I threw your letter." Iris's feet slither across the linoleum. "But you weren't exactly welcoming when I arrived."

"It's okay. No problem. You want help with lunch?"

"What a fucking drag! All morning I put up with Judy's hostility and now I have to deal with your passive aggression." Iris plunks a jar on the counter.

"I'm sorry. It's just that you surprised me when you—"

"Let's just drop it, okay?" Iris plasters peanut butter on Wonder Bread.

"You going back to the studio this afternoon?"

"Looks that way." Shoving Jenny aside, Iris swings open a cabinet door and takes out apple jelly, not even grape, but apple.

"If I drop you off at the studio, can I take the car?"

"What for?"

"I have some errands to do." Jenny feels like a kid, having to plead for a car. Iris must understand. She is no kid. Jenny has to call her husband. She has to buy glitter. Jenny has to stock this place with food that is neither pure fat nor pure sugar. "I'll pick you up whenever you say."

"Don't bother." Iris slaps two boxed Table Talk pies on the lunch tray. "Sarah can drive me home."

"Fine." Jenny has heard quite a lot about Sarah, the ex-nun turned dyke. Maybe Sarah can give Iris the love she needs, compensate her for the deprivations of her youth. A nun's dedication is more than Jenny can offer. Jenny will just go back home to Saul. "Are we eating outside or in?"

Jenny grasps the Volvo stickshift and pulls it toward her. Jammed between cars on the freeway, the car jerks forward like a dragon segment in a Chinese New Year Parade. She is celebrating. Iris has gone back to work; Jenny is on her own.

"A-A-Afternoon Delight," the radio sings.

In the next lane a man with bright blond hair glistening on his arm swigs a can of beer.

"Way to go." He toasts Jenny.

"You wouldn't have another of those would you?" Taking a dollar from her purse, she waves it at him.

"That ain't all I can give you, girl." Without reaching for her dollar, he flips a beer into Jenny's car.

"This is fine." Jenny stares at the dewy aluminum on the seat beside her. She had not realized it would be Coors. Iris boycotts Coors because they do not hire gay people. But Coors fuels its burners with recycled garbage. Jenny clamps her mouth over cold foam and gulps the tainted brew. Ah yes! No matter what Iris says, Jenny now remembers, there are advantages to being impure. "That was a lifesaver," she calls out to the next car.

"One be enough for you, little lady?" The blond leers at her. The driver, a Latino, bends down and waves.

"Plenty thanks." Letting a Jeep cross into her lane, Jenny drops back to let her beer suppliers pull ahead. She has time. At home it is only six. Saul may be out for dinner. She is more likely to catch him later.

He is home when she calls.

"I'm fine." His voice is as narrow as the glass booth around her, but much cooler. "How are you?"

"Okay." Jenny is sweating like a knock in kraut. "Except it's hot here, and I miss you a lot." She unfolds the door. VROOM. "What?" A motorcycle caravan snatches Saul's voice out of her ear. VROOM. "What?" She closes the door on Hell's Angels.

"How is Iris?" Saul is asking.

"Okay. Fine. I just dropped her off at work." Jenny does not tell him how much fun she is having. "What's going on in Hartford?"

"Not much. We had a letter from Luke. He's got poison ivy. I mailed him his cortisone spray." Saul sounds impatient, maybe because Luke always gets poison ivy, and should have taken the spray with him in the first place.

"How does it feel having the whole house to yourself?" Jenny wishes she could see him. It is probably broiling there. He is either downstairs in the kitchen, or shut up in the air-conditioned bedroom wishing she was in bed with him. Maybe Saul is naked.

"Fine," he is saying. "Haven't we already been through that? I thought I wrote you."

The phone coughs in Jenny's ear.

"Deposit two thirty-five for the next three minutes please."

One. Slide ring. Two, slide ring. Three, slide ring. Four. Five. Will Saul wait? Six. Jenny is not ready to let him go. Seven, eight, nine, finally the dime.

"You still there?"

"Yes. But I don't see much point in wasting this money." Saul does not want to talk to her. "You'll be home in five days."

"I got your letter this morning." Jenny must tell him to eat cold lobster and drink champagne not cabbage soup.

"I've been getting yours also." Ice cubes clink. He is drinking. Jenny must speak to him about that too. "Sounds like you and Iris are having a swell time."

"To cook a flank steak," Jenny says, "mash half a clove of garlic in each side with mustard—the good kind—and Worcestershire sauce. Then broil for five minutes on a side. Who's it for?"

"Angela. Angela Corvino. She's here with me now as a matter of fact." FUCK, scratched into the booth, has a swastika for the K. "She's teaching me to fry Italian sausage with peppers."

"Sorry I interrupted." Jenny can see the department secretary in her kitchen. Teaching him to fry. That bastard.

"The smoke alarm went off a while ago but now I've got it under control."

"You always get everything under control, Saul." Jenny's belly churns. The receiver smells from strange, slimy mouths.

"Under the circumstances, I don't see how you—"

"I'll explain when I get back. Bye." Jenny hangs up, unfolds the door, stands outside. What he is doing is not the same as her being here. Jenny is a being lesbian, shivering as air chills her wet back, not like him an adulterer.

She should have realized it was a set-up. Asking her for the recipe. "I invited a friend over—" Saul threw out the damned bait and she grabbed it. Now, a hook in her gullet, Jenny thrashes which is what he meant for her to do.

Sun flashes off windshield after windshield in an agony of light, neutralized by the sting of tears. Mica chips twinkle in the pavement. This is California, the Sunshine State.

Jenny is walking by stores, a pocketful of change meant for the phone, thudding against her thigh. She cannot remember what it was she came out here to do but instead of solving her problem, now Jenny has Iris and Angela and maybe Sarah the nun to deal with.

In an optician's window, frames arranged on glass shelves— each frame a delicate arrangement of specially colored bars of light, pure, elegant, and rational as Euclidean geometry—attract her. Back when she first met Saul, Jenny wore glasses instead of contact lenses. She saw everything through a shield.

She pushes a glass door, entering a shop where mirrored walls reflect a middle-aged Orphan Annie, Jenny, and an earnest young saleswoman, her glasses suspended by threads of gold. Limpid chunks of gold and silver shadow cling to this vision's hair and skin. She embodies California as Jenny's work does not.

"What's your sign?" The optician has the clear blue eyes and pert nose of yet another fairy godmother.

"Leo," Jenny says.

"No wonder you're up. Your sign's in ascendance." Practical plastic pads on the nose piece of the magic glasses make this fairy godmother look, up close, like a Sunday School teacher. But, as Iris says, in California everyone is too engrossed in constellations, cusps, gibbous moons, fire, water, and celestial movements to study the Annunciation, Crucifixion, Holocaust.

"I don't feel very up," Jenny says.

"Temporary setbacks are not uncommon." The optician waves them away with a glossy little hand. "This is the perfect time to choose glasses that will express the really real Leo."

Knowing this is a sales pitch, Jenny is still reassured.

"The thing is," she confesses, "I don't have a clear image in mind."

"How about something like this?" The optician is holding green butterfly wings. "The color should go great with your hair."

The frames make Jenny look like Bat Girl.

"These better?"

"Not really." In wraparound plastic, she is an over-age motorcycle moll.

"How about these?"

Now she is Benjamin Franklin.

"Still not right." Jenny has to look beautiful and wise. She has to impress Saul and Iris. Angela and Sarah. Frames pile up like tangled driftwood. In the magnifying mirror on the table, Jenny's face is a contour map of exhaustion. Maybe she should go with granny glasses. Maybe she should have run away with the studs in the beer car. With red hearts around her eyes, she is a freak, the kind of freak that hangs out in packs. But Jenny is on her own.

"Try these." The optician's touch is deft and soothing as she lifts Jenny's hair and angles tortoise shell over her ears.

"Are you married?" Jenny can guess the answer. This competent young woman fits the middle American mold. "A, my name is Alice, and my husband's name is Arthur; we live in Altoona, where he sells Apples—"

"Not any more." The optician wrinkles her nose. "But me and my present old man have been together almost eleven months now. How about you?"

"Twenty years in September." It is a perfect fit. The bottom of the tortoise shell frames rests lightly against Jenny's cheeks.

"Oh wow." The optician flops back and stares. "Far out. Nobody I know ever got past five years, and not too many made it that long."

"At this point, I'm not sure staying with one person your whole life is a good idea." Jenny has no back-up except Iris. She looks in the mirror. These frames make her look smart, like Saul. She loves them.

"My old man and me talk about packing it in just about every day, but we're hanging in there for now. I don't know, though. Three years is the longest relationship I ever had. I was only married seven months."

"I've been married more than half my life." Turning her head, Jenny inspects her profile. She first got tortoise shells as a teenager. These frames take her back to the beginning.

"Those look real good on you."

"How much are they?"

"Forty-five. Plus your prescription. That Annie Hall look is real big this year."

"What else have you got?" Jenny does not want to be in style. She wants to look unique.

"These are only thirty-two."

But not that unique. The fat black frames make Jenny a raccoon.

"I can just hear my husband." She pulls off the mask.

"Yeah, they can get real nasty." The optician laughs. "My ex turned into a creep the minute we left the church."

"My husband waited. For years in fact." Jenny is startled, but not displeased, to hear herself confiding. "I just called him back home in Connecticut." Who else can she turn to for sympathy? "And the whole time I was talking to him, he had a girlfriend right there in my kitchen."

"My present old man tried that on me once. But I told him. No way. A little something on the side's one thing, my home's something else."

"In my case it was partly my fault." Jenny needs more than glasses to solve her problem. "I came out here to be with my husband's old girlfriend."

"What's so bad about that?"

"We're lovers." After this confession, Jenny curls her fingers around her chair and ducks into herself.

"Hey that's cool. If you and your girlfriend are ever up for a threesome while you're out here, give me a call." The optician slips a business card across the table. It has the store name in the middle and says "Pansy Frazier" in the corner. "Nothing I like better, every once in a while, just to break up the monotony of balling the same guy all the time." These words are coming out of the most quintessentially normal-looking mouth Jenny has ever seen. "Try the Annie Halls again. They're you."

"But Annie Hall was such a loser." Jenny has been making too much of sex, too much of lesbianism. Women who enjoy sleeping with women are not perverts. People in California have sex the way people in New England have conversations.

"Really." Pansy's tone expresses complete understanding. "But if you stop to think about it, Diane Keaton is no loser, and she's the one looking real good in the glasses, see what I mean?"

"Yeah." Jenny is alive and curious like Diane Keaton. "I'll take them." Old and determined like Louise Nevelson. "When will they be ready?" And with contact lenses to fall back on, cagey like Bette Davis.

"Day after tomorrow." Pansy is writing up the order. "You want plastic lenses don't you?"

"Yes. That's my birthday, day after tomorrow. I'll be forty." Jenny's life is due to begin.

"Oh wow." Again, Pansy flops back in her chair. "I had no idea you were near that old."

Jenny wonders how much older she could look at her age. She wonders how Pansy would react if she saw her naked, not that Jenny plans to call her. Pansy stamps a sales slip with her credit card. Signing, Jenny is careful not to notice the total. A great artist needs magnified eyes.

"It's been real nice talking with you." Pansy puts frames, prescription, charge slip in an envelope and neatly licks the flap. "Forty, and still having a blast. Gives me hope."

"You wouldn't happen to know where I could buy some glitter nearby?" Jenny remembers what else she needs.

"I think Pounds of Paper has it." Pansy takes her to the window and points. "And check out Cupid's Garden, just a little further down. Lots of goodies in there." Pansy's Sunday School eyes twinkle with sin. "My old man manages this branch. Let me tell you, he carries some excellent turn-ons. What am I saying?" She smacks her forehead. "Listen, it's your birthday in two days." She writes something on the back of a prescription blank. "Take this over and give it to Ray. He's got something I want you to have for a present." Pansy tears off the prescription and puts it in Jenny's hand.

"You don't have to do this. Really." Jenny has never been in a sex shop.

"I know. But I want to. I'm pretty sure it will give you and your friend some laughs." She nudges Jenny's arm. "And don't forget. Give me a call if you're in the mood, and while you're over in Cupid's Garden, kind of check Ray out too. He's not one to say no to a little orgy action." Pansy guffaws.

Outside, the prescription crackles in Jenny's hand. Of course she should throw it away. She knows that. But a sex shop. And a surprise porno present. When in California. Jenny buys her glitter and walks on to Cupid's Garden.

The windows are covered by curtains the color of raw liver. No one outside could see if Jenny was attacked in there. Or kidnapped by white-slavers. Now she is getting crazy. White slavers do not want forty-year-olds, and there is nothing to stop Jenny from holding the door open while she cases the place. She can always run out.

"You must be the lady Pansy called about. I'm Ray." Dead white, facing her from behind a glass case in back of the velvet-lined store, he glows like a slug. "I have your present right here, all wrapped up." He holds out a package. In order to reach it, Jenny must let go of the door and walk across the rug.

"Thank you. Tell Pansy I said thank you. It's very nice of her. I appreciate it." Why does the veil of words covering her excitement have to be transparent? "And I really did enjoy my conversation with her." Jenny's hand rests on a glass case where dydee doll rubber penises with the same apoplectic veins, the same heart-shaped rims, the folds, even the same slotted dome Saul has, are displayed. Amazing. What Jenny always took to be an unmentionable deformity is evidently what penises look like, except Saul's is raspberry red.

And dipping in and out of Angela.

Shoving the thought out of her head, Jenny covers the dildoes with her present.

"Tell Pansy I said thank you." The package is soft and puffy, like a little pillow. "I'm sure I'll love it, whatever it is." What if Ray wants her to open it here? Jenny knocks over a plastic torso wearing a bulging black leather jock strap patterned in nailheads. Her father's favorite chair is black leather, its bulges held by hammered nailheads. "Even years ago, Greenberg charged a fortune for work like that." Jenny hears her father here, in this sex shop. Never can she escape her family.

"Don't worry." Ray comes out from behind the counter. He smells damp. "I'll take care of that." He reaches for the torso. "Me and Pansy'll catch you later then?" He grins.

92

"I'll let you know." The door opens easily. Outside the sun is still shining. Jenny waits until she is in the locked car to open her gift. Cherry-flavored, edible underpants. Bikinis. Outrageous.

Iris will love them. She will love hearing about Jenny's adventures. If Sarah comes home with her, Jenny will amuse them both.

Leaning on a shopping cart, Jenny rolls through a supermarket past cans, bottles, boxes, and bags, lines of food stacked up, each variety of fruit and vegetable in its separate bin. The orderliness comforts and inspires her. Surely she can establish a similar glossy regularity in her own life.

Jenny buys a large bag of shrimp. Celery. Mayonnaise. A gallon of wine. Chocolate cake; Iris loves chocolate. As long as Iris is pleased with her, Jenny does not have to worry about being fat. She does not have to think about Saul and Angela. One thing this trip has made clear, Jenny has no need, any more, for a husband. She can manage perfectly well by herself. Jenny squeezes back tears.

She feels better once she gets back to the apartment, puts groceries away, tries on her new undies. They stick, especially in the crotch. Imagining Iris nibbling them off, Jenny pretends they are not itchy and that she is not rubbing her thighs to scratch, but rather out of arousal. Iris should be home soon.

Going to the door, Jenny holds up a new tube of glitter to catch the light of a reddening sky, dark in her hand as evil. The dying sun picks up something in the hedge too, her fireworks, still out there.

Jenny's canvas bristles with eucalyptus leaves. Brushing them off, she cannot get rid of dark specks, embedded in the surface. Instead of catching light, Jenny has hardened what looks like the contents of a dustpan. She slides her canvas board behind her materials in the corner. Still, the background did dry clear. She might get it to hold sparkles, keep them forever light.

Pulling the glitter tube cork out with her teeth, Jenny spills shiny gold grit into her palm, and trickles it back. Next time she can try a black background which will be about burnt rubber as well as sky, Hell's Angels a part of California glitz. The good part is that Jenny has gone back to work.

Sighing, she busies herself with dinner. How Jenny has missed cooking! On its platter, her shrimp salad is tropical junk piled on a magic barge—coral tires, celery blocks, a mayonnaise tarp. Plenty there for Sarah too, if Iris brings her home for dinner.

Iris should be here any minute.

Jenny goes into the bathroom, peels away her underpants, rubs the last sticky tufts off with wet toilet paper. By now she should know: fantasies are best just that. Fantasies. Jenny dries herself off and smoothes some of Iris's baby powder around her stomach and between her legs. She puts on cotton knit underpants, her old jeans, and the baggy mohair sweater she bought when she went to college. Forty really is time to start over.

Rolling herself a joint, Jenny lights up. She carries a platter of cheese and crackers outside. She strikes three matches before she can get a candle in a glass sleeve to light. This may be a sign. Three. Jenny examines the shriveled black match sticks. All have smooth heads. All are bent, as if in pain. But one of those matches stayed lit long enough to transfer its flame to a candle. She lies down.

The sky above her is black, strewn lavishly yet precisely with stars. Some day, Jenny will make her own starry universe, her vision impeded just now by eucalyptus leaves that twitch and blow out of reach like the bits and pieces of her California trip. A shadow on the patio turns out to be a toad, hiccupping from brick to brick.

Watching the fat, liver-spotted body heave itself out of dirt on one side of the patio, into dirt on the other, Jenny weeps for the poor creature. She weeps gusty sobs for herself because all she wants to do is save Iris, do her own work, be a great mother, and now that rotten husband of hers is making Jenny go back to straighten him out. Jenny sobs, savoring the delicious flavor of mucous and tears. In five more days she will be home.

Chapter VIII

THE RE-MATCH
• *Five Days Later* •

Jenny's garden looks the same. Planting annuals before she left Hartford, she expected to come home to a riotous thicket of marigolds, but each plant still stands prissy, alone. Withered. Faded leaves, on the mock orange bush next to the back door, hang wilted, in thick July heat, like Jenny herself. Nothing at home has changed; things have only gotten worse.

Iris is here with her now, having quit the project. Saul picked them both up at the airport. Now, unlocking the door, he leads Jenny and Iris into the house, into moist, gray air. The same old family photos curl from the kitchen wall, refrigerator, cabinet doors. *Hartford Courant*s rise from the table, each newspaper folded around the names of people who died while Jenny was away. On top of a mail heap, a Wayside Garden catalogue tells her to "Order Bulbs Now in Time for Fall Planting."

Iris drops into a chair. Jenny follows Saul on into the front hall, clumsily, as if already the house has hardened, like a body cast around her.

"Why isn't the attic fan on?" Stuffing her art supplies inside the closet, Jenny squeezes the door shut. It may be weeks before she can work again.

"When the temperature outside is higher than the temperature inside, turning on the fan is self-defeating." Dark hammocks sag under Saul's eyes. His shirt sticks to his torso in banana-rot blotches. "The house is better kept sealed during the day." No more the fastidious husband, now he wants her to feel sorry for him.

Jenny cannot stand the sight of the man. She cannot stand listening to that voice saying the same old things. In winter, Saul cites data to prove a fire in the living room makes the rest of the house colder. In summer, he explains that the attic fan brings in hot air. No matter what he says, Jenny sees for herself.

Her two weeks of fun over, she is home with the usual heavy inevitabilities: air that must be stirred, windows that must be opened. The house smells like old people. Jenny must get rid of dust and cobwebs. She must bring in fresh flowers. Saul, a near corpse in this tomb, needs her to bring him back to life.

Gratefully, she sinks into a chair next to Iris. As long as Iris is here, Jenny cannot succumb to her old routine no matter what Saul needs. Iris's lips are slick as cherries. Jenny's own mouth waters. Her breasts blush. Jenny grins up at Saul. Their lives simply cannot go back to where they were as if falling in love had never happened to her. And to him. They are committed now to Iris.

"You'll have to excuse me." Saul darts into the bathroom.

Standing up, Iris goes to the refrigerator and looks at photos curling off the door.

"Who are all these people?" she asks.

Jenny identifies Esther, Aaron, Luke, her sister Barbara, her niece Emily. She tells about her mother's wart medicine to explain the picture of the rabbi's finger. She wishes Iris would go home so Jenny could have it out with Saul.

How dare he fuck the Department Secretary here in Jenny's house! How dare Iris stand there as if she owns the place! How dare Jenny, after all Iris has done for her, wish her lover away!

"There's room for you right here." Jenny quickly points to a space between graduation portraits of Esther and Aaron.

"Stop pushing," Iris says. "I'm not in your family yet."

"As far as I'm concerned you are." Slung over Jenny's shoulders, like a silver-blue mink stole, another albatross.

"So." Iris sits down again. "How does it feel being back home?"

"Hot." Jenny pulls her hair up off her sweating neck. Her breasts lift toward Iris. Iris's eyes massage her skin. Saul comes out of the bathroom. Jenny hastily drops her arms into her lap.

"I'll turn on the fan if you want," he says, "but the sad fact is, it isn't going to make a hell of a lot of difference. You'll still be hot." He hurries off to do whatever Jenny wants.

Damn Saul. He has no right to kill Jenny with kindness. It is not as if she ran away with a man.

Jumping up, Jenny throws the back door open. Heat presses at her through the screen.

"I'd forgotten how awful Hartford is in July." Jenny juts out her lower lip and shoots breath up into her face.

"I told you we should've stayed in California," Iris says. "I can't see why we came back here, except to suffer. If we spent a few weeks in San Francisco, Saul would've survived without you."

"No doubt." Jenny's husband would have survived with Angela.

"He might've preferred being left alone," Iris says.

"Yes." All the more reason for Jenny to come home.

"Don't forget, Saul has a brand new girlfriend now." Iris persists.

"Yes." Jenny will not be goaded into hated Iris no matter what the bitch says. The poor thing is sick. Afraid of intimacy.

"Is that why you had to come running home?" Iris stares, through her glasses, into Jenny. "Because you couldn't wait to break up Saul and Angela?"

"No." Jenny's eyes shift to the floor. Filthy. She longs to be on her hands and knees, scrubbing, making it up to Saul for what she did to him. But how could she help it? Jenny must be a lesbian if she enjoyed sex with Iris. "On the contrary." Jenny is glad about Angela. If Saul feels guilty enough about her, maybe, just maybe, he will forgive Jenny for leaving him and they can go back to loving each other, especially if Jenny includes Iris in the deal.

"You and I could've had a perfect honeymoon." Tilting her chair back, Iris piles her legs on top of the table. "But when I quit work and we finally had our opportunity to achieve all-encompassing, day-and-night lovemaking, you had to run home."

And none too soon. Those full days with Iris were like being caged with a lion; Jenny never knew when her lover would decide to turn on her.

"It was better than nothing," Jenny says. "Certainly an improvement over my first honeymoon." If Saul hears this, maybe he will throw her out, force Jenny to be on her own at last. Or give her back to Iris.

"Speak up!" Iris slams her feet down on the floor. "You're muttering."

"I just said our honeymoon was wonderful as it was the best vacation I ever had."

"We should've had more time together." Iris insists on this lie. "I never even got to do lizard licks down your back."

Hot as she is, Jenny shivers.

"Another time." For now, Jenny holds onto the adventure of leaving, and carnival L.A., and the good times in bed with Iris, and the hours Jenny had to herself in California, with her sketch pad closed as she gazed at the Pacific, its water yawning to show polished almost clarity, over and over the not quite clarity rising smooth, curling over itself and inside her. Iris brought Jenny to this ocean. "I do love you, you know." Jenny will love Iris forever. She owes her that. Saul's feet are hammering down, down, he is stamping down the stairs.

"How about a drink?" He offers his standard solution to their problems except this time, the glass Saul holds out to Jenny, trembles slightly.

"Sure." She will drink with him but she will not go to him, hold him, beg his forgiveness. She will not give in, once again, to being a wife. Lifting the piled newspapers off the table, Jenny shifts closer to Iris.

"I have dinner all ready." Usually Saul moves with graceful restraint, but tonight he could be playing basketball. His arms thrust out. Ice cubes shoot from his fingers and rebound to the floor. "When do you want to eat? Seven? Seven-thirty? Eight?"

"Whenever you say." Airplane food bubbles inside Jenny, about to erupt.

"I'll go wash up." Iris is leaving them alone.

"It feels funny being home." Jenny will not put her arms around Saul, she will not join the rivers of their feelings. "I'd forgotten what it's like." How easy, but demoralizing, it would be to go on being what she has been. No. She is not going to show her love for the gaunt man on the other side of the room. "You should've seen Venice." She has never seen this husband before. "It was just amazing." The pictures on the wall behind him come out of some other life Jenny wants, no longer, to be hers. "And crazy." The Weiss family, middle Americans, lined up at Aaron's graduation, only two months ago. "People skate-boarding all over the place. They have this purple cotton candy out there, and little kids wear make-up. I kept thinking of *Miss Lonelyhearts*. Oh Saul, I missed you." Giving up, Jenny goes to him.

"No one forced you to leave." Turning away, Saul opens the refrigerator. "And West's Hollywood book was *Day of the Locusts*." The platter of raw vegetables he sets on the table is as bright, pleasing, stylized as a Hallmark card.

Jenny is safe. If this is Saul's welcome, there is no slipping back into her old life.

"No matter." She feels miserable. She touches him. Jenny forgot

Saul's strength, his arm ropy as a Tarzan vine. Always she could depend on Saul. Letting go, she sits back down. "I missed you terribly."

"So you say." Saul slaps leftover flank steak onto a carving board, grabs a knife, rubs the blade across the cushion of his thumb.

Jenny recognizes that meat, the remnants of his orgy with Angela.

"So how was your dinner with the Department Secretary?" Jenny scoops the cat onto her lap. She still has him.

"Basically—" Saul makes slices thin as kelp. "—it was boring." The raveled strips look used.

"Really." Jenny expected something else. This sounds true. Boring. "In what way?"

Saul faces her, his mouth loose, no guilty smile twitching at his lips. "Just boring." His heavy eyes dare Jenny to make too much of what he did.

If she cannot use Angela, she will have to find something else. Jenny will not have Saul pinning the guilty party label on her. What she did was a question of biology.

"What else went on around here while I was away?" Jenny glances at a letter from Mimi Deutsch suggesting a Saratoga weekend for the four of them. A few weeks ago, Jenny would have accepted. The Weisses were a couple then, on the couple circuit. What a relief, even if she does love the ballet at Saratoga, to be done with all that! If Jenny wants to, she can still go. With Iris. And Saul. If Iris likes ballet. If Saul is finished with Angela. If. If. If. Sitting here, in the old familiar kitchen, Jenny is bombarded by hypotheses.

"Place was very quiet with you gone." Saul stares at the cat in her lap. "Sigmund had no idea what to do with himself."

"He's acting like I was never away." Purring when Jenny rubs the bridge of his nose.

"I envy him his resilience." Saul holds himself tipped back slightly, like someone who thinks he is about to be hit.

"I do love you. A lot." Jenny feels, at this moment, as if she left Saul just to hurt him.

"I'm glad to hear that." He slams his eyes into her face.

"Guido claims he never got my letter." Iris comes in. "He assumed I wouldn't be home for another month. I told him to get out tonight. You think he will? After the divorce, it took me six weeks to get rid of him."

"You are back early," Saul says. "Wasn't your grant until Labor Day?"

"No way could I survive another six weeks as a Judy Chicago underling." Iris plops into a chair. "The intrigues, machinations, and power ploys in that studio make the Athenaeum look great."

"I thought you told me you love intrigue," Saul says.

"Inside an institutional setting, but without a solid infrastructure to fall back on, rivalry between women is self-destructive. And what a bummer that can be!" Iris throws back her head and whoops like a sea-lion begging for fish.

"You admit then that male hierarchical values have intrinsic stabilizing worth as a safety net." Saul hoots too.

"Notice where we always seem to end up?" Laughing with them, Jenny thinks that now that Iris is in the family, being home may be okay.

" 'The Dinner Party' is a disaster." Iris kicks off a shoe, puts her foot on the chair, props her head on her knee. "It will never make it to a museum."

"You surprise me." Saul is smirking.

"Is it okay if I eat now?" Maybe Jenny can stop him from gloating. "I'm starving." Maybe Jenny can make Saul and Iris see how much she would like one of the jobs they complain so endlessly about.

"No problem. I've got everything ready." Saul sets out tomato salad, cucumber salad, mushroom and onion salad, macaroni salad. "I'm getting to be an expert in the kitchen."

"This is like a wedding." Jenny is really thinking of a funeral. Soon, he will be doing the cooking; she will be useless.

"Try some of this wine." Pouring for her, Saul stands by like a sommelier, or a man who cares. If this were for real, Jenny would scrap all her schemes, give up her work, love Saul full time. But it is an act he is putting on in front of Iris. Jenny tells herself she would have to be a fool not to see that. "What do you think?" he asks.

"It's turned." She shirrs her lips. "How long has it been open?"

"Five days." That was when he cooked for Angela. "Try the steak." Saul watches Jenny cut, he watches the meat enter her mouth. "How is it?"

Chewing thoroughly, Jenny swallows, nods. They understand one another very well.

"Boring." She looks him in the eye. "Overdone, Saul, with or without the wine." He need not make so much of a victory that is only temporary; yes, Jenny went pretty far, but now she is back, ready to take him on again.

First this dinner must be got through. Iris lights up a joint and passes it. Jenny sucks in, again and again. Let Saul keep his liquor; she has found something better. Saul and Iris shoot words at each other across the table. And Jenny feeds herself, bit by bit, like a kid having dinner with mommy and daddy.

"A paradigm of unsisterly attitudes," Iris says.

A tomato chills Jenny's teeth.

"The rest of us are confronted by a chairman whose deviousness is unmatched in the memory of man," Saul says.

His mushrooms are as slippery as frogs.

Saul is taking out a hash pipe.

"Where did that come from?" Jenny asks.

"Angela gave it to me." He cuts a chunk of hash the size, color and shape of a peppercorn. "For a house present." Dropping it into the pipe, he pokes at the lump with a lit match, draws at it to to make it flare, passes to his wife.

There is something about smoking Saul's girlfriend's dope out of Saul's girlfriend's pipe that fits Jenny's need to do penance. Sliding Angela's wet stem into her mouth, Jenny sucks at it, and smiles, stroking with every breath, heat at her fingertips.

Not until gold glitters in Iris's hair, Iris's glasses, Iris's skin, does Jenny pass the pipe on. Esther's glossy self-portrait reflects candles Saul lights in the darkening room. Macaroni gleams in Jenny's plate, like a creamy worm orgy. She was crazy to think nothing here changed. In only two weeks, Saul has taken over her kitchen. He is better at it than she is. The room spins, lights smearing around the photo of the rabbi's finger until that finger is steady and flat as a compass needle pointing constantly at sin, at Jenny, not just at her, at the three of them.

"Something is making me sick." Jenny pushes her dish away. "I think it's the meat."

"We all ate it. It's fine." Saul stands up over her, huge and shadowy, but with glittering patches of tooth and eye.

"Give her some sugar," Iris says.

"What'll that do?" Saul plunks the sugar bowl on the table.

"It'll bring her down," Iris says.

"I'm not high," Jenny says. "I'm sick."

"You'll be all right," Iris says. "People under tension sometimes have bad trips is all."

"Jenny and I have gone through a hell of a lot together, most of it before either one of us ever laid eyes on you, Iris." Saul stands at the end of the able, clutching the back of a chair. "There's no particular reason for her to feel tense about coming home unless there's some secret you two are keeping from me."

"No secret," Iris says. "But let's face it, Saul, a bourgeois, well-established home is, like a prison, conducive to tension."

"It didn't used to be." Saul releases his chair. "For twenty years, Jenny and I led a rather uncomplicated and pleasing existence, at least I always thought that's what we had." His eyes plead with Jenny not to contradict. "How do you feel?"

"Much better." Jenny goes soft as a baby, and warm. Saul really does love her. Later tonight they will make love; she will show him all the great new moves she learned from Iris. Her mother always said Jenny would regret it if she had premarital sex; Anna never mentioned that Jenny might regret her lack of sexual expertise, might have wanted to know, as she now—thanks to Iris—does, how to help her husband pleasure her. "Luscious, Saul." Jenny tongues grains of sugar from the creases in her palm.

"But your relationship was predicated on oppression, your wife was your slave, Saul." Iris grins. "No wonder you adored her."

They both laugh.

"I can still adore her." Saul sits down beside Iris. "Relationships can change. We can make a new kind of marriage work."

How uncertain he sounds! How close to Iris now! Curling her fingers around her chair seat, Jenny presses her feet into the floor. This is her house. She is not going anywhere. Any change in their relationship can happen right here, right now.

"What sort of new marriage are you proposing?" Light clings to Iris as if she were a mirror ball. No wonder Saul, and Jenny, are both in love with this woman.

"That's something we'll all need to discuss," Saul says. "It's wonderfully cool out now." He stands up. "Why don't we go in the yard and talk?"

"Is anybody else tired?" Jenny is tired of letting Saul build his word boxes around her. She wants to act. Get this three-way new marriage settled once and for all.

"These issues aren't going to disappear. They have got to be addressed," he says.

"Not tonight," Jenny says. "As you say, they're not going to disappear."

"Remember how we watched fireflies out here?" Iris asks.

"Firefly season is over." Saul's shorts scratch, twill against twill, as they walk to the garden. "But the yard is still lovely." He slides into a chair, stretches his elegant legs in front of him, crosses his slender ankles. Mosquitoes never bite Saul. He is king here, a woman on either side of him, a man with all the grace Jenny remembers, the grace she treasures. "All our theoretical talk tends to becloud an important point." His hair holds moonlight.

"Full moon tonight." Jenny loves Saul's silver sheen.

"No wonder we're all insane." Lying on a chaise, Iris raises her face to the sky as if she is sun-bathing.

"I've concluded it would be foolish for me to give Jenny up unless that's what she wants," Saul says.

"No one's asking you to give Jenny up." Iris keeps her eyes closed.

"I thought you wanted to get rid of me." How else could Jenny have left this beautiful creature? And what can keep her now from going back to being, once again, Saul's house slave?

"There aren't many women around like you and me." Eyes still shut, Iris giggles. "Saul's too smart to dump us." Us. Iris thinks they both belong to him.

"Understand, Iris." Saul leans forward, his back and shoulders curving like a shield. "I'm a fierce competitor."

"Amazing." Sitting up, Iris opens her eyes "Sounds like you're challenging me to a duel."

The idea of Saul and Iris fighting a duel over her leaps inside Jenny, but she does not move. This has to be their decision.

"I love you both," she murmurs, noticing that spotlighted by hidden sun, the moon above her is stained from within like bad plaster. Jenny loves Iris now.

"This isn't something we can settle tonight." Saul leans back, his hand on her armrest, his fingers not quite touching her thigh.

Jenny takes quick breaths.

"Triangles never work." If Iris thought they did, she might lose interest. Iris is not looking for dailyness.

"Why not?" Saul asks.

Jenny could tell him. Day by day, love grows, insidious and controlling as a fibroid tumor inside a woman.

"All I know is that no three-way relationship I was ever in lasted long," Iris says.

"Lenin did it," Saul says. "He had a *ménage à trois* for years."

"If we all three went up to bed, do you think we could just go to sleep together?" If Jenny goes up there with Saul alone, she will be right back where she started. "I mean literally to sleep, nothing else." Like a stripper, she twirls this possibility under his nose.

"I don't see why not." Saul stands up, lust glowing from his eyes.

"At least we can try." Iris stands up too.

"I'm exhausted." And scared. Jenny is finally going to bed with her father and mother. After this night, nothing between them will ever be the same. Jenny's earring, caught in chaise webbing, yanks at her earlobe. "I'm stuck." A reprieve.

"Let me look." Saul bends over her, his shirt billowing with body breath. Jenny stares up—cloth grazing her cheek—at his chest, the hair in the hollow, the swelling muscles. She turns away.

"Just hold still till I get you unhooked." He is on top of her, his sweat-smooth shoulders a horse ready to be ridden.

"Never mind. You'll hurt me." Jenny pulls, tearing the earring from her ear. "Shit, where'd it go?" Down on the ground. Scrambling to her feet, she waits for the yard to stop rocking.

"A disappearing gold ring, the perfect touch. I don't see how she does it." Iris laughs. "Jenny your whole life is a work of art."

"A tragedy." Jenny loves these earrings. Saul gave them to her in Italy. Now the unmatched single will remind her forever of what she has lost.

"Not at all. A gold ring is only one link of a chain." Squatting beside her, Iris rakes her fingers through the grass.

"Please." Jenny grabs Iris's arm. "I'll find it in the morning." If they wait any longer, she will lose her nerve. "Right now." Jenny stands up. "Let's go to bed." She heads for the house.

"Whatever you say." Saul follows.

"Does she ever bother with subterfuge?" Laughing, Iris hurries to catch up.

"Let's just say it's not Jenny's characteristic mode of expression." Saul chortles.

Jenny grabs the banister to steady herself.

"Definitely a full moon." Iris giggles.

Jenny climbs the stairs, leads them into the house, through the hall, up the stairs, pretending, like a concierge showing a honeymoon couple to their room, that these accommodations are for sleep. Saul and Iris play their part too.

"I think we better keep some clothes on, just to be safe." Jenny peels off her jeans and slides under the sheet.

Getting in, Iris takes off her white canvas pants and drops them over the side.

Saul stands at the foot of the bed, smiling down at them.

"I really mean it." Jenny's heart is pounding, pounding. "We are here to sleep and to sleep only." Drawing the sheet up under her chin, she clamps her legs together.

"Right." He takes off his shorts. Nothing pokes at his underwear.

Jenny relaxes her legs.

Saul climbs into bed.

Lying in the middle of the bed, flat on her back, Saul on one side, Iris on the other, Jenny folds her hands over her belly.

Saul faces the window. He is first to fall asleep. He is always first to fall asleep, his back and ass smooth, cool, infuriating.

Iris slides her underpants off.

Jenny pretends not to notice.

Iris falls asleep.

Jenny lies between the two of them. How can anything happen? She is a bundling board. The attic fan whirs above her but nothing in this house spins. Three meals a day, seven days a week, twelve months a year, in this house Jenny counts thirty, breathing in and breathing out. She thinks gray. How can she fall asleep when she wants so badly to make love? With Saul. With Iris. Penis and vaginas sliding, creamy as macaroni salad, in, out, around each other.

Turning over, Saul wakes her. It is morning. He presses his cock, hot and hard, against her hip. He gropes for her nipple. Pulling away from him, Jenny fits her body behind Iris. Saul reaches over and caresses Iris's breast, his cock rubbing Jenny's ass. Iris circles moist, naked skin around Jenny's thighs, her belly. Jenny cannot breathe in the wet, dark whirlpool of sex. No!

Hurling back the sheet, Jenny leaps out of bed, runs to the door, flings it open.

"I can't take this." She slams the door, and stands in the hall, shivering. Nothing on but shirt and underpants. They have her jeans.

Jenny rushes downstairs, races from room to room, snapping up shades. Saul is an animal. She knew she could not trust him in bed. And Iris. Some sisterhood. Iris must hear these shades flapping at the rollers, but she is not coming down to Jenny, she is too wrapped up in Saul. It was always like that. Jenny is the extra.

Jenny meant to throw herself into *La Vie de Bohéme*. But this vile eruption of traditional values proves she is nothing, nothing but a hopelessly straight Hartford housewife. A real artist would be up there in bed, getting it on with her husband, her lover, anyone remotely attractive.

Jenny's suitcase is in the front hall. Wrenching it open, she grabs her wraparound skirt and sweater, puts them on, tears out into the yard. Her earring does not glint in the grass. Wet blades crisscross her bare feet. Her hair. She will get it cut.

Stubbing her toe on the stairs, Jenny accepts the stinging throb as her due and hobbles into the kitchen. She opens the phone book to the yellow pages. Beauty parlors. The names mean nothing. Jenny will call Angela and ask where to go now that, playing her own game, Jenny has lost.

Saul sidles into the kitchen, his eyes sweeping the floor.

Chest heaving, Jenny shuts the phone book.

"Iris and I only fooled around," he says. "Really. I swear it, Jen."

"Why should I believe you?" Why, oh why, should it still matter? Jenny's knees wobble. She grasps the counter, its steel rim cold and tough as she too must be. So what if Saul is like her, both of them with their Victorian hold-overs. "Anyway, it doesn't matter." Which is not exactly a lie. Whatever Jenny did with Iris, Saul did more, Angela and Iris, the double negative a positive. Saul has given Jenny every justification for leaving him no matter what else he is or does, no matter how she still feels about him.

"I'll make breakfast," he says. "What would you like?"

"Suit yourself." This time, she means it. Jenny is finished with Saul. Finished with Hartford all together.

Iris bounces into the kitchen.

"You look so funny, standing up there by the door, like a little girl," she says.

"I didn't feel very funny." Jenny wheels past Iris into the front hall. Squeezing her suitcase, she lugs it upstairs and throws it open on top of the rumpled bed. This is Jenny's space. Whether Saul and Iris like that fact or not. Whether she herself likes it.

Her children will be home soon. In the bathroom, Jenny turns on hot water. The children will expect to find their mother and father exactly as before, exactly as they have found Jenny and Saul every other year. Jenny goes back into the bedroom.

She shoves underwear in her underwear drawer, shirts in her shirt drawer. She restores her clothes as if she was never away. Jenny was away. For two weeks. And she must make the children accept the fact that she will leave again. Jenny is on her way out. Crouching in scalding water, she winces.

Chapter IX

UPDATING THE RULES
• *Two Months Later* •

Saul may never see Jenny as his good old wife again, but the children expect certain things of their mother and, caught in their web of assumptions, Jenny is still, the day after Luke's Bar Mitzvah, doing what they expect. She is obeying the rules of Nature.

House plants must be brought inside for the winter. A spider's web, like cheesecloth stretched over a berry bush, nets her gloxinia. Last year Jenny hosed the glox, shooting off leaves soft as earlobes. She shot off fat pearly buds. She spent the winter nursing a brown stub back to life. This year Jenny snatches at the damn web, tearing off a bud that drops, like a milky eyeball, next to her foot. Spider hairs cling to her fingertips.

"I don't see why you've chosen this particular day to bring in plants." Saul comes outside with the Sunday *New York Times* and coffee. Nature makes no difference to him. His time is his own.

Only Jenny is in thrall.

"There's supposed to be frost tonight." She has to act fast.

"In outlying areas." Saul lies down in a chaise in the sun. "Not here."

"Ess wants to know when's lunch." Luke kicks through the back door. "Her ride's coming at two."

"It's only eleven-thirty." Last night after the Bar Mitzvah, Jenny cooked and served dinner for thirty-five. "Tell her it'll be at least another hour before lunch." Spading up a clump of impatiens, Jenny jams it into a pot.

"How many blankets can I take?" Aaron sticks his head out of the window in Jenny's room.

"As many as you want," Saul says.

Aaron slides the window down and goes about the business of stripping his mother of her belongings, stripping Jenny of her time. Tomorrow, she will have to go out and buy blankets.

"Did you call Dr. Teisch yet?" Luke is back.

"Not yet," Jenny says. "Remind me tomorrow."

"If I don't get a medical card signed by Friday, I can't go to school."

The door slams.

Iris is on a bike hike over Avon Mountain today, on this perfect day for a bike hike.

One by one, Jenny lugs plants over to the patio.

"Where do you expect to put them all?" Saul asks. "The sunroom's full of paper flowers."

Not even Jenny's cousin Myra took home the tissue paper poppies Luke and Jenny made for Bar Mitzvah decorations. According to the world, Jenny's work is worthless.

Yet she keeps doing it.

"Never mind." Plucking a slug off her avocado, Jenny flings it to the ground, stamps on it, smears mother-of-pearl flesh on a flagstone, wipes off the work boot Saul hates—gone his dainty wife—on the grass next to him. "I'll find room for every single plant."

"You want me to give you a hand?"

"No, thank you." The fingerleaf philodendron Jenny drags over to the back stoop sprouted two new babies over the summer. She does not need him. Setting the plant down, she takes a clippers from her pocket. "I have my own system." Jenny cuts back a spindly bromeliad so it will either branch out, or be permanently misshapen.

"Vendler's got a fascinating review in here," Saul says.

"What of?" Jenny asks.

"Adrienne Rich's new book about motherhood."

"Why should that interest you?" Jenny can keep nothing for herself. Mealy bugs stick, like tiny gobs of spit, in the ruffles of her Boston fern.

"Everything Vendler writes interests me. Listen to this: Rich says, 'Poetry was where I lived as no-one's mother, where I existed as myself,' and Vendler, pointing out that Rich isn't concerned about herself as a poet being someone's daughter or wife asks, 'Is it simply that one can separate herself from other adults but not from children?'" Saul turns toward Jenny without seeing her, without seeing that she might have some feeling about this point. "Now that's exactly the kind of provocative question, based on a close and thoughtful reading of a text, that I'd expect from Helen Vendler."

He expects nothing of Jenny. Saul likes brilliant women. Turning the hose on full, Jenny blasts mealy bugs into eternity.

"I suggested to Iris that she go to Boston for Vendler's Stevens course this fall," Saul says. "It's only two nights a week."

Jenny can guess which two. She plans to be with Iris on Tuesday and Thursday nights, when Saul's class meets. She grabs a spindly angel-wing begonia in one hand, a glaucous rubber tree in the other, neither worth house room. Jenny would be better off leaving them both out here to die.

"I'm absolutely convinced there's a correlation," Saul is saying, "between the visual art of the period and Stevens' images. With her background in art history, plus the work we've done together, Iris is uniquely qualified to explore that connection." His plots are always complex.

Jenny prefers the simple approach.

"Listen, I love Iris." She warns him: if he throws his professorial weight on the scale, Jenny will fly off with or without his uniquely qualified scholar. "Shipping her out of town on your Trinity nights is not going to change that." The cat flicks its paw at a baby, dangling from Jenny's favorite spider plant; Jenny flicks a foot at the cat.

'Songs in the Key of Life' pour from the house.

"When's lunch?" Esther is louder than Stevie Wonder.

"Soon." Jenny spots a Norfolk pine behind the forsythia. "I just want to finish up here."

"Hurry." The window slides down, and up. "Okay if I pack the shampoo from your bathroom?"

"Take whatever you want." Pine needles chafe Jenny's arms. She sets the pot down on the bottom step. Enough is enough. If Jenny lets this go on soon there will be nothing of hers, nothing of her.

"Saul, could you please come inside with me?" She stamps dirt off her boot soles. "There's something I want to discuss before Esther and Aaron take off."

Saul rises, sinuous and elegant in his Irish sweater and silver corduroys. "Sounds ominous," he says.

"Take those—" Jenny points at the rubber tree and the bromeliad, now a ringed stick. "—two in with you, please."

Saul holds the plants well out in front of him. Jenny follows to the sunroom, hugging her spider plant and the avocado she raised from seed, getting dirt on the overalls she will have to wash, working like a field hand. For what?

Their children, they are pulling out as if they were not parts of their mother, parts like her arms, her head. And Saul does nothing, he will do nothing, to stop them. "Esther!" Pain and fury spurt in Jenny. "Aaron!" Her voice is as high, sharp, demanding— "Luke!"—as her tea kettle's. "Come down, please." They cannot leave her. "Right now." Not before she leaves them. "I want to talk with you." Jenny will tell them who their mother really is. "All of you." Then they will stop taking her for granted. "Before you go." She shoves aside paper poppies to make room for live, and quasi-live plants.

"How long is this going to take?" Her head sprouting tiny braids, her body swaddled in a robe, spiky fluff slippers on her feet, Esther scuffs in looking totally adorable.

"I can't stand it!" Jenny screams "Aaron! Luke! Get down here! Right now! Your sister is in a hurry!"

"I'm going to boil water," Saul says, as if someone here is giving birth. "Anyone else want coffee?"

"Tea for me, please. Red Zinger." Esther plops down on the loveseat. "Where's Sidney Omar? Maybe he says something about me taking a trip today." Maybe he will convince her not to go.

"I'll have coffee." Jenny subsides next to her daughter. She should not have pruned that bromeliad. It looks ready to die back instead of branching out. Every year she brings in plants wrong. She tries to hold onto summer instead of welcoming winter's starkness and the gorgeous simplicity of death.

"Only assholes read horoscopes." Luke comes in slurping cream of tomato soup out of a pot. "What's mine say?"

"Be sure you wash that pot when you're done," Jenny says.

"There's crud in the bottom. Someone else may want to eat it." Pretending he is saving leftovers, Luke often stashes dirty pots in the refrigerator.

"Throw the crud out and wash that pot or I'll stop buying soup," Jenny says.

"The playoffs have started." With a television addict's soft stupefaction, Aaron clouds into the room. "How about fast-forwarding the goodbye sequence?" He yawns and stretches. "Like go for a finish during the station break."

"What a space cadet!" Leaning back in a Salvation Army rocking chair, Luke clunks his feet onto the table, his hiking boots standing like useless bookends. Yesterday, in his navy blue Bar Mitzvah suit, he was gawky and serious as a giraffe. Today, white cotton knit bulges from a hole in his green corduroy crotch and he is as obscene and improbable as a baboon.

"Sidney says, 'Consider proposal from someone of opposite sex favorably.' Think that means I should get married?" Esther asks.

The kettle howls.

"Like somebody's really about to ask you to marry him, too." Aaron throws himself into a chair.

Maybe they will none of them ever marry. Only Jenny, younger than Esther is now, was stupid enough to marry. Her children have settled themselves into this house. They will never leave their mother. Never.

"Here." The coffee Saul hands her is battleship gray because here, like Jenny pretending to be what she is not, skim milk masquerades as cream.

"Get those feet off the table," Saul barks.

Luke stomps his boots down, the rickety rocker Jenny loves, creaking as he shoves it back, away from the rest of them.

Jenny's coffee is a dancing fish on the ceiling, never touching Saul's fish, or Esther's fish, each fish dancing with a life of its own, separately.

"This one of your power trips, Jennifer, or what?" Aaron's bare legs stick out; Jenny wonders if he has anything on under his robe. "Watch the eyes, Jocasta." Aaron clamps his knees together.

"I've got something important I want to talk to you about." Jenny has to get away or go crazy. "It's about me and your father." About Jenny and her children.

Esther tears rubber bands off her braids, snapping rubber bands, snap, snap. Her tea is red. Her mother is a dyke, or an ordinary housewife, nothing in this house what it is supposed to be.

Eighteen carat sun, gauzy when spread outside, glares through the window.

"It also concerns Iris Wilde." Jenny blinks tears.

"What about her?" Esther tosses a hairy rubberband on the table. Jenny used to straighten her hair, her daughter is making kinks. Nothing makes sense to Jenny any more. "She seems kind of weird but interesting."

"I've been trying to figure it." Aaron gnaws the skin around a fingernail. "Like the minute I left for college you guys got to be best buddies or something. "

"It's a little more complicated than that." Only Iris keeps Jenny from backsliding to that earlier status that now seems so demeaning, Jenny everyone's household convenience. Once they know Jenny is a lesbian, everything will be different.

Esther tosses her last hairy rubber band on the table.

"Will you get rid of that mess?" Saul waves his arm at the glass top which now looks like a three-dimensional biology slide.

Esther sweeps her rubber bands into her lap.

"That too." Saul points at her tea bag, lying in an ash tray like a dead mole. "Take everything into the kitchen."

"Later," Esther says.

"Later you'll forget." Saul jumps up. "Do it now. This minute."

"Welcome to Tension City, Ess," Luke says. "Dad doesn't mellow out these days until after at least two gins."

"Hey twit." Aaron nudges Luke. "You leave me any chili?"

"Be serious." Luke rubs his belly, strains, farts. "I ingested the last bean hours ago."

"Not very considerate, Greta Grabbo." Aaron jabs. Luke jabs back. ("Entering manhood entails serious responsibilities," he announced yesterday from the pulpit. Another phony in this family.) Luke maneuvers the screeching rocker around his brother.

"Stop fighting, you two." Saul's ice water voice freezes the action.

"So, mutha, tell us arready, what's goin' on around here?" Coming back from the kitchen as if she is walking on stage, Esther chews imaginary gum.

"I don't know how to begin." Jenny breathes deeply. The song she is about to sing is very long.

"Try words." Fingers curled, Aaron examines his nails. ("That's one of the tests," Jenny's high school friends said. "If they look at their nails like this—" Someone would hold up a flat hand. "—that means they're queer." Jenny sometimes looks at her nails one way, sometimes the other; for this her friends had no test.)

"Last July, I did something I've wanted to do for a long time," she starts.

"Big deal. You went to California." Aaron is again gnawing. "We all know that."

"Maybe they know as much as they need to," Saul says.

"I want to tell them everything." Jenny is half-way there. "I went to California—" She clings to her couch cushion. "—to spend time with Iris." Reaching down, Jenny strokes the cat winding around her ankles. His back slides under her hand, his tail, he is gone.

"I thought Iris was Dad's student." Esther's hair stands out, a globe of question marks.

"Iris is a friend of your mother's and she is also a friend, and former student, of mine." Saul emphasizes each word as if this, really, is all that needs to be said.

Behind him, the cat jumps onto the shelf.

Plants and paper poppies stand, a crowd waiting for a train in some other direction.

Jenny is alone.

"Friend is a euphemism," she goes on. "Iris and I are lovers."

The cat tips Jenny's favorite spider plant off the shelf in a terra cotta crash that dumps soil and pot shards onto the floor.

Saul rushes from the room.

"You shouldn't even try being funny, Mother." Luke's chair groans in rhythm with his rocking. "You're pathetic as hell at it."

"I'm sorry, Luke," Jenny says. "It's not a joke." Yet she does not want anyone to take it too seriously.

"Oh shit." He rocks faster.

"Cut that out!" Saul comes back with the dust-pan and brush. "You'll break the chair."

So much broken here now, what difference does a chair make?

"Wow. This is heav-vy." Esther falls back, widening the space between her and Jenny.

"I know this seems like something sudden. In a way it is; in a way it isn't." All around the room, giant red tissue paper poppies stand like open sores. Last week, Jenny and Luke sat, every afternoon at the kitchen table, making those flowers. Four years ago, Jenny did the same with Aaron. Now there will be no more of those times. "I told your father years ago that I wondered if I was a lesbian. Then this summer, I fell in love with Iris and found out I am gay, or maybe bisexual." Jenny and Saul have gone back to making love every day, her life a confusion that belongs, as it never used to, to someone else. "I know this is hard to understand." They just have to accept that Jenny is not again to be plain housewife and mother. "At the same time, it feels wonderful, having what I am out in the open." Simple.

"I'm glad you trusted us enough to tell us." Esther's arm, flung around Jenny's shoulder, is a lifeline.

Once Jenny was on guard whenever her own daughter touched her, in case the lesbian in her took over. Now she lets herself feel pleasure. "I don't want any of you to do what I did." Jenny used to think the merest touch could turn her into a lustful beast; she still thinks that could be true with men.

"Not to worry," Aaron says. "One queer bait in the family is enough."

"I mean explore all your options." If Jenny had done that, they would not be here. "Adolescence is the time to experiment." She would not know the people she loves best in the world. She would not be entangled.

"That's what I've been telling you," Esther says.

"Well now, I know you're right. It is okay to be a sexual person. More than okay, in fact, absolutely terrific." A five-thousand-watt grin inflames Jenny's face. Across the table, Saul is dead white. Jenny's smile floats in front of her hot face.

"Great. My mother wants me to butt-fuck. Oh my God, what'll I do? Where will I live?" Luke keens.

Jenny's spider plant baby lies under the coffee table, its leaves like feathers, torn from a bird to decorate some vicious woman's hat. What made her think her life as a housewife and mother was all that bad?

"I figured it had to be something like this," Aaron says. "Part of Mom's new artist image; artists swing both ways. And then there's that women's lib crap she's into. They're all dykes. Everyone knows that."

"I get home from school. There's nobody home. Half the time there's no food." Luke's rocker beats against the tile floor. "Nobody tells me where they are any more. I don't know who to call in an emergency." He twists away from Saul's out- stretched hand. "Every night my father drinks a quart of gin. And she's always at that fucking Iris's house."

His pain, catching Jenny in the gut, empties her of breath. She did that to Luke.

"The important thing to remember is, your mother and I love you and we always will," Saul says.

"This is starting to sound like you guys are working on a divorce," Aaron says.

"Couldn't wait till I got out of here to break up, could you?" Luke's chest heaves. "Bitch!"

The word 'bitch,' hitting Jenny like spit on stone, restores her.

"No one's talking about divorce." Leaving Saul is unthinkable. Without Iris, Jenny would be stuck here forever.

Esther's arm, tight around her shoulders, feels like a trap.

"If we do try a separation, you might like it." Saul keeps bringing up the subject of a separation as if he will leave Jenny no matter what she decides. Jenny has figured out what furniture to take and how she will decorate her own apartment. "It's no fun being in the middle of a conflict."

"I'm not going with her. Ever," Luke says. "You can either send me to boarding school, or I'll stay at Scott's."

"Really, you guys. You're too much." Aaron shakes his head. "This is such a classic over-reaction."

"I know it's only your way of defending yourself, Aaron," Esther says, "but your Mr. Cool act is the pits." She drops her arm off Jenny's shoulder.

"So what if Mom has a little fun? And Dad, too. About time if you ask me." Leaning back, Aaron stretches his arms over his head and yawns. "Open marriages are in now even in the bush league." He brings his arms down. "Only thing I don't understand is why you two picked Iris to mess with. You could have done a lot better than that bonzoid."

"We love her." Whenever Jenny thinks she could have chosen someone better than Iris to fall in love with, she stamps the thought out before her brain catches fire. "And you will love her, too—" Jenny and Saul fell in love with Iris because, like a mountain, she was there. "—when you know her better."

"Don't bet anything vital on that," Aaron says.

"What's she like?" Esther asks. "I only talked to her for a few minutes yesterday. She seemed sort of weird, but nice."

"Iris is one of those thinks-she's-a-tough-shit intellectuals," Aaron says, "Trapped in an Earth Mother bod."

"Stop that." Jenny knows what he means.

"It's one forty-five. Suppose I make everyone an omelet for lunch?" Saul wants a normal family on a normal schedule.

And Jenny does too. She wants to go back to what Iris calls, 'living death.' Jenny longs again to be simply a housewife and mother. But she cannot now that she is a dyke.

"I don't think anyone's really hungry right now, Dad," Esther says.

"You guys don't know how lucky you are." Luke's voice flutters. "You don't have to live here any more." Pulling his T-shirt up to his nose, he wipes. "I won't even be able to have friends over any more."

"Sure you will." Saul passes him a handkerchief.

Luke takes it. Jenny is grateful to them both.

"How can I?" Luke asks. "You think I want any of my friends to know my mother's a gaybo?"

Saul stares at the floor.

"Your friends are probably a lot cooler than you think," Aaron says. "Look at you. Could you care less if Todd's mother does it with the hockey coach?"

"That's not the same," Luke says. "The hockey coach is a man."

"You guys going to be all right?" Getting up, Esther leans over the back of Saul's chair, nestles her face against his head, clasps her hands around his chest.

If Jenny leaves, Esther will stay with Saul.

"It's tough just this minute," Saul says, "but your mother and I are in better shape than we were when we acted as if everything between us was hunky dory." Eyes closed, he circles his head in his daughter's hands.

Love melts in Jenny and overflows onto Saul and Esther. But it took Iris to bring this love out. Jenny must remember, she owes Iris everything. Gratitude covers her with its full length cape of lead.

"Be honest, Luke," Aaron says. "Do you give a rat's ass whether Brian's mother smokes grass or not?"

Jenny thinks Brian's mother is a sicko.

"A slut or a druggy isn't half as bad as a dyke," Luke says.

"It's not like you can trade your mother in," Saul says.

"I'm not sure he'd swap me even if he could," Jenny says.

"Fuck you, bitch." The rocking chair gives a final yelp as Luke shoves it and stomps out.

"Come back here." Jenny would gladly wash his dirty dishes, wash them with her own tears, if that would make him love her. But enough has changed around here. She was never one to buy love. "Take this pot and wash it thoroughly."

Snatching up the pot, Luke holds it over her. Jenny looks up, meeting his eyes, meeting in him her own steel.

"Put that down," Saul shouts.

Luke springs out of the room.

"Fuck you. Both of you."

"Maybe I should call the dean and apply for a leave of absence. Family emergency," Esther says.

"No. We'll be all right." Diving down, Jenny scoops up the baby spider plant. She will root it, replant it. "It's only a month and a half before Thanksgiving." Jenny can do a lot in a month and a half with only one kid at home.

"Listen up, Ess. What we have here is your typical mid-life crisis." Aaron lifts himself out of his chair. "They have to handle it by themselves."

"Are you sure they can?" Esther asks.

"Does the Pope shit in the woods?" Aaron strolls out of the sunroom with his sister.

Saul stands. Jenny slumps, inert as a sandbag.

"Want some sherry?" He is already pouring.

"Absolutely." She wants the whole bottle.

The man who hands her a glassful is white and indistinct, an over-exposed photo of the real Saul.

"Maybe telling them was the right thing to do." He is pale as a negative, already almost a ghost, almost dead.

"I wanted them to know." Jenny sips sherry as if the scene she just played was from a British comedy of manners. Always she pretends to be someone she is not. A lesbian would not worry about her husband dying, she would not enjoy sleeping with a man. Maybe Jenny is no one at all.

"As you see fit." Saul pours more sherry and sits down next to her. "Oh God, Jenny." His voice breaks. Putting her arms around him, she eases him close against her body. Saul is quivering. Tears stream down Jenny's face. They have not cried together in years.

"Halloo!" Jenny's sister barges into the front hall. "Anybody home?" Barbara pounds into the kitchen. "Luke, darling, you were terrific yesterday, just tee-rific."

Other people are shuffling into the kitchen.

"And so handsome." Jenny's mother is one of them. "Simply stunning, like you Aaron, another Adonis."

"Will you excuse me please?" Esther asks. "I've got to get dressed."

"Don't run away," Jenny's father says. "Anna doesn't mean that you are not even more gorgeous than those two *paskoodnyak* brothers of yours."

Tooting his nose, Saul goes into the hall.

"You coming down with something?" Marvin asks.

"My ride's picking me up in fifteen minutes." Esther dashes upstairs.

"Scuse me folks. I also have to pack." Aaron gallops after her, leaving Luke to face the enemy alone.

Jenny hauls herself up from the loveseat.

"I thought maybe we could all go out for lunch," her father says. "Where's your mother and father?"

Jenny imagines Iris, coasting down Avon Mountain on her bike.

"Inside." The soup pot bangs against the sink. Luke must, after all, be washing up.

Jenny smears tears from her eyes, her nose.

"Where does she keep her tea bags?" Barbara slams cabinet doors.

Poor Iris has no family to flow in, like an ocean, inexorably to smooth rocks. Iris will have to make it back up the mountain alone. Maybe she is lucky.

"I've got some delicious Russian spice tea." Calling out to her sister, Jenny joins her people in the kitchen.

Chapter X

TACTICAL REVIEW
• *October* •

Some years ago, with classic Yankee ingenuity, women calling themselves the Farmington Fair Forty organized cheap, regular trips to New York. A few year later, Jewish women chartered their own bus, on the third Wednesday of each month, October through May. For five dollars a person, untitled, they left a West Hartford shopping center parking lot in the morning, rode to Rockefeller Center for a day in the city, and came home.

Jenny is today starting her fourth year on the Jewish bus. These days off, returns to the land of her birth, were always refreshing, but now, reentering the routine of previous years, Jenny feels as if she has caught hold of a rope that will stop her from being swept out to sea.

Her bus friends have not changed much since last year. Rosalie Feinstein is a treat, even this early in the morning. Rosalie's gold hair and earrings shine, her pearly nails, eyes, lips gleam, her ivory trench coat glows.

"You saving this seat for anyone?" Taking her coat off, Rosalie folds it around its shining white lining.

"It's all yours." Jenny has always liked Rosalie.

"Thank you." When Rosalie stretches overhead, her champagne knit sheath creeps up her perfectly controlled figure. Before sitting, she makes sure her skirt is pulled down, smoothed out. Neutral, neat, lustrous, Rosalie is Jenny's ideal opposite. "Have a good summer?" she asks, eyeing Jenny's effusive curls, her brown velvet, rust jersey, floppy leather. Rosalie smiles.

"Excellent." Jenny smiles back. Hers was a daring summer. Yet safe. Jenny has emerged from the maelstrom of the last four months to land on these predictable shores.

Sighing, the bus rolls off.

"How about your summer?" Jenny asks.

"Very relaxing." Unlike Jenny, Rosalie can lift a plastic lid off coffee without spilling. "Nothing special." Her eye twitches.

The bus jounces out of the parking lot. Rosalie keeps her coffee under control. How Jenny would love to be able to do that!

"Oscar and I have been going to Neptune Park for over thirty years now." Rosalie's twitching eye flashes a signal. "Oscar is crazy about the beach." But all is not perfect, the eye says.

"What about you?" Jenny will liberate this poor woman who spends he summers in a ticky-tacky bungalow on the Connecticut shore just to please her husband.

"I'm used to it. As you can imagine, by now we have quite a crowd down there." Rosalie curves her lips up, tight, superior. "Playing golf, swimming, going to parties, what could be better than that?"

The question exhausts Jenny. Such heavy work liberating a person of limited vision! Yet not so long ago, Jenny was also content to be her husband's slave. If she made it this far, Rosalie can too.

"Have you ever tried going some place else?" Jenny asks. Maybe if Rosalie once saw a beach with surf, a beach without wall-to-wall houses, a beach far from the nuclear submarines that feed, like a litter of giant sharks, off General Dynamics' Electric Boat Division dockyards, she would do what Jenny did. Declare her independence.

"Every year Oscar takes me for a trip," Rosalie says. "Aruba, Hawaii." She counts off on her fingers. "We've been to Israel twice. This year it was Ackapoko." She throws her hand. "I could not wait to get home. I mean, why should I leave when right in my own house I have the best? I never understand the girls who are crazy to fly this place and that place. East, West, if you ask me, home's best." Rosalie is vehement.

"Sometimes you appreciate home more if you go away for a while." After California, Jenny treasured the swiping up, sweeping, throwing out, and rearranging that, like successful art, reorders chaos.

"I get enough of that going to New York," Rosalie insists. "Tonight, when I walk in my front door, that's when I'll be happy." Eye twitching, Rosalie reminds Jenny of her mother.

120

Anna too is always reluctant to leave home and always afraid she is never going to get back. The last thing Jenny wants is to be reminded of that part of her heritage. Leaving home is hard enough as it is. Jenny squeezes close to the window, reaches into her shoulder bag, takes out an *Art News*.

"Excuse me." She turns pages.

The bus bumps over seams in Interstate Eighty-Four.

Jenny's eyes slide over glossy pictures in her lap but her mind follows the voices, crisscrossing the bus, thin and sharp as a jumble of pick-up sticks.

"Have a nice summer?"

"Terrific. And you?"

"Wonderful."

"Get in a lot of tennis?"

"Never enough."

"I just heard you were up at the Cape. How was it up there?"

"Just gorgeous. Unbelievable."

No one admits her summer was awful. Jenny is tempted to tell them about Iris. That would make them know for sure. She is not one of them, not a woman who does what everyone else does, year in and year out.

The bus ticks off seams in Interstate Six-Eighty-Four.

"Thelma gave me this fabulous recipe for sweet and sour meatballs. You cook them in a gravy made out of equal parts grape jelly and chili sauce."

"I'm not making anything with a sauce until Seymour takes off twenty pounds."

"We just got back from Israel ten days ago. What a magnificent experience that was!"

"You got pictures?"

"Here's Harry, standing by the Wailing Wall." Even the trips that should be extraordinary are standardized. "And this is me with our tour guide in front of the Knesseth."

The bus lurches through pot holes on the Major Deegan. Jenny slides her magazine back into her bag.

"So how's your family?" Rosalie asks.

"Fine." Jenny sighs. "My youngest was just Bar Mitzvahed."

"Tch." Rosalie shakes her head sympathetically. "Goes so fast. My Scott is graduating from Tufts this June."

"What's he planning to do?" Jenny is always looking for ideas.

"Oscar's starting him in our Manchester store." There are no ideas in Rosalie's life, no loose ends. "So, what do you think?" She takes a beige linen swatch from her pocket book. "Now that the

children are gone, I'm redoing my whole house in desert tones."
Same color as her dress, her coat. "Like it?"

"Sure." Jenny shrugs. Why not cover empty rooms with sand?
Why not, like her mother, buy wholesale, bleach your hair, spend
two days out of every seven in a beauty parlor? Turning from
Rosalie, Jenny stares out the window.

A few brown people cluster in front of steel meshed stores. Last
year one of them threw a rock at the bus but the bus was
impervious, shiny and bland, its corners rounded, its windows
blank, all the women inside as safe as they would be in their own
living rooms.

"I can't decide on my den colors," Rosalie is saying. "They're
showing a lot of charcoal and beige again, but I don't know."

"Your necklace is a beautiful color." Even if Jenny cannot free
this woman, she can at least give her confidence in her own taste.
"Why don't you use something like that?" Instead of whatever
'they' are showing.

"That's real jade." Rosalie deepens crescent moons around her
mouth. "Oscar gave it to me for our thirtieth anniversary." For her,
the rewards of marriage are more than enough.

They mean nothing to Jenny. If she lived in one of the sunny
apartments here, along one-hundred-sixteenth street, she would
grow potted trees on her fire escape, sprout potato vines and carrot
tops on her window sills, eat fried green tomatoes, and keep a
baseball bat handy. She could be poor and happy. Single and
happy. But Jenny cannot go back to living like her mother and be
happy.

The bus turns down Fifth Avenue. Not much farther to go.

"Excuse me." Jenny climbs over Rosalie's knees.

"Have a good day."

"You getting out here?"

"At the Metropolitan if he'll let me," Jenny says. This bus, thick
with coffee, cigarettes, and old lady perfume is hot as her grandmother's oven.

"Have a good time."

"Enjoy, darling. Enjoy."

The women call to Jenny as if she must have, for them, the fun
they cannot take for themselves.

Standing by the door, she reads street signs. Eighty-four.
Eighty-three.

"Here, please."

The driver releases her in front of the museum.

Because Anna would hate her doing it, Jenny dashes, against the light, across Fifth Avenue. The gingko trees remind Jenny of her mother's old friends—skinny, blotched, leather-tough women who never had to worry about what they would do when their children grew up. They would play mah-jongg and golf, volunteer at the hospital, entertain.

Crossing Madison, Jenny pats a yellow taxi as she might a steer's forehead.

"How you doin'?" The driver grins at her.

"Great." Jenny grins back, delighted to make eye contact that tells her the cape flapping around her is perfect for this apple juicy day. With it on, she knows who she is. A New Yorker. These buildings are her mountains, this bus and auto exhaust, her Alpine air.

Breathing deeply, Jenny bounces as if the sidewalk is a trampoline under her feet. So what if she is too old to be a child? No matter what either of them has been through since high school, Jenny has not outgrown her friend Mimi Deutsch. With Mimi, she can be a teenager again. "How are you today, Miss?" Mimi's doorman greets her as if she belongs in his building.

Jenny does belong here. Long before Saul there was Mimi. Jenny and Mimi were inseparable until Jenny made the impulsive decision that took her out of New York.

Now she is back, sitting, for the last half hour, legs up, arms limp, in Mimi's all-white kitchen. One tiny window, looking out at airshaft murk, reminds Jenny of being stuck last spring, in the elevator. Otherwise this room is pure paradise.

"Would you rather have pâté, or Smithfield ham, or brie, or a combination of any of the above?" Mimi asks.

"I want everything." High above Jenny, the ceiling is a sheet of light.

"That's what I love about you." Mimi pads back and forth, from refrigerator to counter to drawers to counter to table, satin slippers lapping at her heels. "Your capacity for gluttony."

"I love being cosseted," Jenny says.

"Good." Mimi twists a squeaking corkscrew, pulls a creaking cork, pops open a bottle, pours red wine with routine expertise.

"No doubt about it, you are class." Cupping ruby light in a crystal bubble, Jenny drinks. "First class."

Skinnier than ever, her skin stretched over her cheekbones and creasing at the edges of her face, Mimi gives the appearance of having changed, but she is the same. Instead of going to her own school, she sits on School Boards, attends Friday Philharmonic concerts, plays weekly bridge. On Wednesdays, their old early dismissal days, Mimi hangs out. Today she has not yet dressed but wears a marabou-collared peignoir that could have costumed Jean Harlow because, with Mimi, the good parts of the past go on happening.

A distant vacuum cleaner whines.

"Lunedi-Cambiar las Savanas y los Toallas. Lavar las Ropas," says the list on the refrigerator. The language changes but the facts remain the same. Mimi has always had a maid. Today, *Miercoles*, Malta the maid is *aspiraring el Salon* before *limpiaing el Piso*.

"Tell me about Luke's Bar Mitzvah," Mimi says. "I wish we could have been there. Did it go off all right?"

"More or less." Jenny sighs. Now that Luke's childhood is officially over, she too must grow up. Not like her mother. "My mother prescribed wart medicine for Saul's Department Chairman." Brie oozes like caterpillar blood from both ends of the french bread Jenny bites. Pulling off the swollen cheese, she stuffs it into her mouth. No need for manners, not with Mimi.

"What about your father?" she asks. "Did Simon do one of his crazies?"

"Actually he was fairly restrained. " Jenny moves on to the ham, saving pâté for last. "Outside of attacking my brother-in-law because he voted for Carter, and Aaron because his hair was too long, Simon wasn't all that bad."

"Some people say that about Hitler, too," Mimi says.

"That's true." For years, Jenny and Mimi have commiserated with each other about their parents, particularly about Jenny's father and Mimi's mother.

"Dolores pulled one of her numbers last week," Mimi is saying "She asked for a scarf for her birthday. I said, 'Go pick one out. Charge it to me,' but of course that missed the whole point. She wanted me to buy the scarf so when she took it back she could say she could not believe the money I wasted, fifty dollars for something she wouldn't be caught dead wearing."

"Typical." Jenny smiles, lulled by the variation on this familiar theme. "Oliver pretended none of it was happening?"

"Poor Daddy. He puts up with anything the woman does."

"Just like Anna," Jenny says. "As far as she's concerned, Simon is God."

"He must have been right at home in the Temple," Mimi says.

"My niece showed up with her boyfriend." Jenny introduces another relaxing topic, other people's dates.

"What's he like?" Mimi asks.

"Omar Sharif playing a Moroccan medical student. This pâté is amazing."

"It's got green peppercorns in it."

"My sister kept telling Esther she wants to fix her up with Omar's brother the rabbi. Can you see me with an Arab rabbi for a son-in-law?"

"Sounds just like your sister," Mimi says. "What did Esther say?"

"She told Barbara to have the rabbi submit pictures, preferably featuring frontal nudity."

"My god-daughter always was a practical person" Mimi says.

"Esther?" Jenny's daughter is a loving person, but practical?

"From day one, full of common sense." Mimi gets a bowl of raspberries and a pitcher of cream out of the refrigerator.

"My favorites," Jenny says.

"I know." Mimi takes out dishes, spoons, and her silver muffineer. Jenny would not know such things as muffineers existed if not for Mimi. "What do you want to do after lunch?"

"I thought we were going to the theater," Jenny says.

"What do you want to see that we can get tickets for?"

"What is there?" Jenny and Iris are going to 'For Colored Girls Who Think the Rainbow is Enough' in two weeks.

"Nothing I'm too interested in," Mimi says. "But it's almost one o'clock. I have to shower, get dressed, so you pick."

"Why bother?" On Broadway, the wind will be raw, grit will fly up in their eyes, Jenny will have to watch out for Times Square creeps.

"You only come in once a month," Mimi says. "We ought to do something."

Jenny has the guilty pleasure of secret trips. Her secrets used to include Mimi.

"Are there any good movies around here?" Jenny smoked her first cigarettes with Mimi in the Trans-Lux Theater around the corner.

"If you call 'Humanoid from the Deep' and 'Bruce Lee's Revenge' good."

"What about the museum?" Years ago, Jenny and Mimi wasted whole days hoping someone, anyone, even one of their mothers, would come up with a good idea for something to do. Too old to go on waiting, now Jenny must decide for herself. "Anything interesting going on there?"

"Not that I know of," Mimi says. "Why don't you check the

paper, in the den, so Malta can watch her soap operas in here?" The mistress of this house, so like a Fiji chrysanthemum in her marabou-collared peignoir, does not own her own kitchen.

Malta stands in the doorway with her vacuum, her eyes sad and accusing.

"Sorry." Jenny leaps up. If only she could explain that usually she works too, only she does art. Not that art, she admits, really counts for something useful. Not like a job that pays money. Adults get paid for doing the world's work.

Jenny follows Mimi, down a dark hallway, into a brown and leathery den that smells of money. Gold falls from the coffered ceiling like shafts of sunshine in a forest too deep for milky, outside-the-window light to penetrate a copse of russet, black, and crimson-bound law books.

Taking her raspberries and cream, Jenny sinks into a couch soft as piled leaves. She puts one fat, fuzzy berry in her mouth, inserts her tongue, flicks it back, and swallows. She eats the rest of her berries with cream, rationing so she has enough to coat the last fruit.

"I'm exhausted." Jenny puts her bowl on the desk and lies back, safe in this deep, still, magic forest, to pick pips from her teeth.

Mimi takes a silver tube out of a desk drawer and tosses it over. The tube contains toothpicks.

"Is there anything you can't provide?" Jenny takes two. She loves picking her teeth.

"I do my best." Mimi grins.

As Rosalie Feinstein said only this morning, why leave home when home is perfect? Looming over Jenny, Mimi's husband's law tomes cast shadows as heavy as institutions—courts, hospitals, bridge clubs, symphony orchestras—as eternal as stone walls. Jenny grabs a newspaper and turns to the entertainment page. She must find a movie, any movie, to get them out of this jail.

Cups chink like keys. Malta enters. Sliding a tray onto the desk, she picks up the dirty bowls and walks out, her behind, pillowy like Iris's, shifting from side to side in a rhythm, a rhythm that has a dignity Jenny envies, a dignity Malta has earned.

Plopping two cubes into a demitasse, Mimi hands it over.

"You really in the mood for a movie?" she asks.

"I gather you aren't." Jenny stirs her coffee.

"I don't think there's anything worth seeing." Mimi stirs her coffee.

"Then let's forget it." Jenny shoves the paper aside. Her bus leaves at five-thirty. It is not even two. There is nothing left to talk

126

about. A thick, hopeless stupor settles over Jenny. "Want to do up some dope?"

"I can't," Mimi says, "but you go ahead."

"You sure?" Jenny takes a joint from her pocketbook.

"Very." Leaning forward, Mimi snaps flame from a gold table lighter.

Jenny takes a hit, releasing the sweet naughty smell of grass into this sepia room that looks and feels so like a bank.

"Highly recommended," she says. "This is great stuff." The illicit is just what any bank needs.

Mimi shakes her head.

"Can't. Not good for the baby."

"What baby?" Holding the joint outstretched, Jenny neither moves nor breathes.

"I'm pregnant," Mimi says. "Due the end of April if the results of the amniocentesis are negative."

"That's terrific." Jenny remembers newborn baby skin against her face. And infant fingernails, like miracle shells. A baby in here will be like an elf in a deep dark forest. "I love the idea."

"Me too." Mimi can stay home and take care of her new child. "It's been a long time." She will not have to face the world.

"But are you sure you want to go through it again?" Now Jenny remembers babies screaming, their spastic grabbing, the scratches from those miracle nails, and the stools spreading like mashed squash out of diapers, out of rubber pants, horror movie bowels taking over the world. She drags, drags deep at her joint. "I don't think I could." No. A new baby, like her old ones, would only grow up. "I'm trying to get a job." Something Jenny can hang onto for the rest of her life.

"What kind of job?"

"Facilitator at a Feminist Art Gallery."

"You should be good at that," Mimi says.

"If they hire me, but that's a big if," Jenny says.

"If you have nothing better to do, have a baby. Mine could use a friend." Mimi is like a siren, luring Jenny onto rocks. No matter how awful they are, Jenny loves babies. She lashes herself to the mast. Saul.

"The way things are right now between me and Saul, the last thing we need is another kid."

"What's the matter?" Mimi's marabou shivers.

"Saul seems to prefer women a little younger than I am these days." Jenny is furious. Tears thicken her voice. She should be happy. She wanted to be rid of Saul, wanted to be free.

"I'm sorry." Reaching over, Mimi touches Jenny's hand.

"Don't be. Saul Weiss is not the only person in the world. I don't really know why I'm making so much of this." Jenny thrusts her head back to keep tears from seeping from her nose. "I always used to say I didn't care what he did as long as I never found out about it." She feels as if she said that years ago, not last spring. "But we've lived together too long. When he did it, I knew."

"It's the mid-life crisis." Mimi passes Jenny a box of Kleenex. "They all go through it. Most of them recover."

"I'm not sure I will." Now that Jenny is crying, there is so much to cry over. "When Esther left, I lost my only ally. I'm living in an enemy camp. Even the cat is male."

"Sounds divine." Mimi, who always liked Saul, is liable to start praising the bastard.

"It's hell," Jenny says. "I've gone through some changes."

"I would hope."

"I think I'm—I've fallen in love, too." After the dope, Jenny's wine tastes sour.

"Just when you get to the juicy part, I have to go to the john. Don't forget where you are." Mimi rushes from the room.

As if Jenny could forget. Telling Mimi now that she is a lesbian could cut Jenny off from her best friend forever. Outside, on the window ledge, pigeons gargle as they used to outside the apartment where Jenny grew up. Getting up, she takes a book from the shelf. *Admiralty Law*. Solid. Heavy. Like Bill Deutsch, and Saul, and every other man. An anchor that must be cast off. Jenny wedges the book back where it belongs.

"Now." Mimi flops into her chair. "With whom are you in love, and is it requited?"

Jenny found a way to tell her children. There are words for Mimi as well.

"Saul and I are both in love with the same woman." Jenny is conscious of the masculine way her legs are crossed. "I should probably never have married. I think I've always been a lesbian." The silver coffee service is Georgian or Queen Anne. Mimi could tell Jenny which. All four of them, Mimi and Bill, Jenny and Saul, have gone sailing together on the boat in the photo. No matter that Jenny hates sailing; she may never get to see the new baby. She makes herself look at Mimi's face. Mimi meets her eyes.

"I've known for years." Mimi knits her brows. "I thought you realized that."

"Was I that obvious?" Has Jenny spent years hiding behind cellophane?

128

"Obvious to someone who knows you as well as I do." Mimi smirks at her. "So what if you're not a bit of fluff?"

"Oh." Shame slides off Jenny, leaving her to flutter free, to fly unprotected.

"So who is this woman and what is she like?" Mimi asks.

"Her name is Iris Wilde." Jenny utters the sacred syllables. "She used to be Saul's student and jogging partner, and then he fell in love with her." Jenny feels a surge of pleasure. Iris will take care of her. "And when I met her, I fell in love with her too."

"That'll teach Saul." Mimi laughs. "I love it."

"Me too," Jenny says.

"What's this Iris do?"

"She's an art historian."

"Perfect. Sounds like you and Saul are having fun. Gives one hope," Mimi says. "I was beginning to think my days of having fun were over."

"If my parents ever find out, I'll have to kill myself," Jenny says.

"Aren't you a little ancient to be worrying about what Mummy and Daddy think?" Reaching into a magazine rack, Mimi pulls out a magnifying mirror. "Anyway, who's going to tell them?" Tweezers in hand, she inspects her face.

"I already told the children," Jenny confesses.

"Why?" Mimi's mirror flashes down into her lap.

"I wanted them to know." Talking about Iris establishes her reality even if talking to Iris does not. Then, Jenny feels as if she is a character in a story she and Iris make up for their own amusement, neither of them thinking, for a moment, that it is true. But if the children believe—

"How'd Esther take it?" Mimi asks.

"She went to a shrink." Jenny cannot understand it. Her daughter was so supportive when she told her, so calm. But now Esther is telling a stranger her mother is a dyke.

"Sounds very sensible of her." Mimi picks up her mirror and again gazes at her face. "I tell you, my goddaughter is an amazingly practical young woman."

"The shrink told her the situation is typical, a symptom of the age. It isn't important that I chose to act out with a woman instead of a man." Jenny cannot understand how anyone could possibly think her homosexuality, or maybe bisexuality, is a side issue.

"Sounds like he knows something. Where'd Esther find him?"

"Her. She's a social worker in the Wesleyan Health Department."

"What about the boys?" Mimi asks. "How did they react?"

"Aaron played it cool. Luke cried at first. Now, every time I speak to him, he just says, 'Shut up, gaybo.' Oh shit." Jenny is crying again. She should not have done dope after wine, wine after dope.

"Don't worry about your kids." Mimi lays her hand on Jenny's arm even though Jenny is a dyke. "They're good people."

"So are you, Mimi. If I didn't know that before today, I'd know it now." Tears come too fast now for Jenny to go on talking. She helps herself to one of Mimi's Kleenex. Even in such small matters, she depends on her friends. "I still can't bear the thought of not being glad to see Saul walk into a room I'm in." She may never stop crying. it would be just like Saul to press a clean white handkerchief into her hand, just like him to remind Jenny that she cannot function properly without him.

"The situation sounds pretty unbearable," Mimi says.

"Not really," Jenny says. "Iris is wonderful."

"I assume she must be if she hooked you two." Squinting at her mirror, Mimi plucks a stray hair.

"Woman, you are amazing." Hundreds of times, Jenny has watched Mimi tweeze her brows. "I tell you I'm gay, and you act as if it's nothing."

"What'd you expect me to do?" Mimi keeps tweezing.

"I thought you might throw me out." Jenny will never leave if Mimi goes on being so terrific.

"I like you." Mimi beckons for her to lean forward. "Besides, I'm not sure either of us will be here long enough to make new old friends." Pulling a hair from Jenny's eye-brow she shows her, it is white. "Best to make the most of the time we have." Mimi smiles extravagantly.

Jenny looks away. She adores Mimi. Of course she wants to be just like her. Jenny wants to be happy staying home. But she is not, damn it, she is not.

Lights speckle the building across the street.

"It's already getting dark," Jenny says.

"Standard time does that." Reaching behind her, Mimi pulls a cord. Silk curtains the color of dead leaves, sliding across the glass, block off outside lights. "It's not really all that late."

"It's time for me to get going." Jenny must tear herself, once and for all, out of the past. "I have to leave." Limbs mired, she cannot even get up off the couch. Jenny is woozy with dope and emotion. Pressing her hand on a cushion to push herself up, she sinks further down. "You may never get rid of me."

"Fine with me," Mimi says. "Bill will be home in a few minutes. He'd love to see you. Stay for dinner. Sleep over."

"Another time." Jenny cannot stay with her beloved Mimi no matter how she is tempted. Jenny has a husband waiting for her at home.

She forces herself to stand up, almost colliding with Malta who exchanges the tray on the desk for a new tray holding crystal glasses that shine, like sunlit trees after an ice storm, beside a silver lotus bowl filled with macadamia nuts.

"Your bus doesn't leave for an hour. Stay. Mix yourself a drink." Mimi points at the new goodies.

"I can't." If Jenny puts even one single smoothly delicious macadamia nut in her mouth, she could be like Persephone, stuck forever in this dark hell. "I have to go." Her eyes follow Malta's soft butt which bobbles from side to side as the maid turns to leave. Women's bodies interest Jenny. She is not normal like Mimi. Jenny trails Malta into the foyer. "Getting a cab at this hour is impossible."

"The doorman can radio one to be here in half an hour," Mimi says. "I'll call down."

"Don't." Jenny opens the guest closet door. "I don't want to get stuck in traffic." She pulls her velvet cape from ghost shoulders and buttons it around her neck. "I'm better off walking." Jenny swoops into the library and bends to kiss Mimi's smooth cheek. "It's been a wonderful day." She gulps back new tears. "Thank you."

"My pleasure." Mimi looks up at her. "You'll be in again next month?"

"I don't know. If I get the job, I'll be starting right away." Jenny will have to give up her seat on the bus. She cannot look to older women for help. "I'll let you know." And the friends her age who know what to do now are women with special training. Like Mimi, the rest are going on the way they always have. "One way or the other." Jenny must look to younger women if she is to find a new way to live. And when she does find it, she will come back for Mimi, and show her too. "I love you, you know."

"That's nice," Mimi says. "We love each other."

Pressing her arm, Jenny dashes away.

"*Adios*, Malta," she calls out. "And *gracias*." Jenny plunges from the apartment, into the elevator, down, out of the elevator, out of the building past a couple huddled in the doorway, past the doorman fruitlessly trying to hail a cab. Dazzled and exhilarated by a glittering stampede of cars, taxis, limousines, Jenny races along the sidewalk, into the sharp night.

Chapter XI

BACK TO BASICS
• *Fall to Winter* •

Jenny at last has a job. Before she goes to it, she surveys her kitchen. Her counters are clean, her sink scoured. Gleaming photos curl from the wall like whitecaps on a sea of memory. Her work here is done.

She switches off the lights. Nothing stops Jenny from getting out now. Except Saul.

"How about more coffee?" He shuffles in, an unshaved beggar holding out his mug.

"You'll have to make instant." Jenny thumps the jar on the counter between them. "I've packed the regular to take to the gallery." If only a bitch would leave a husband with the day off, Saul might as well know right now, Jenny is that bitch.

"Fine," Saul says. "Care for some cinnamon toast?"

"No thanks." And Jenny is not staying to clean up the mess he is making either. She grabs a pack of paper napkins and stuffs them into her electric coffee pot, then sweeps her eyes across the bare chest that would feel so delicious against her breasts. Damn the man. He will do anything to keep her here. Snatching up a half-sack of sugar from the counter, Jenny wedges it into her carton.

"Hey, I need that," Saul says.

"Take what you want and put the rest back. I'm leaving."

"I thought you hate being early."

"Not today."

"Why is that?" Saul asks.

"I'm not just trying to get away from you if that's what you're thinking."

"Until you mentioned it, it never occurred to me that that's what you're trying to do," Saul says.

"Then I should also mention that three thousand bucks is a lot more than you pay me to stay here." Clutching a wet sponge, Jenny ostentatiously swipes his crumbs off the counter. She is not the only one around here who should feel guilty. For years Saul was content for her to be his slave. The hell with him. Jenny wrings the sponge as if it is a turkey's neck and drops the limp corpse into the sink.

"Three thousand is a pittance." Saul crunches into his cinnamon toast.

"You sound money-hungry, just like my father." When she was a little girl, swallowing wishful spit—she swallows now—Jenny used to lie in bed next to Simon while he ate his breakfast and read his newspaper. She is not going on watching, waiting for a taste of this or that. "Maybe all men are interested in making tons of money, but this job means a lot more to me than that." Jenny pulls off her apron and hangs it up.

"You're the one who brought up money." Flapping his newspaper open, Saul examines it despite the gloom. "I thought you wanted to be an artist." Slap. He turns a page. They both know Jenny could do art at home.

"Right now, being a Gallery Director makes more sense," Jenny says. "It's a big opportunity for me."

"Yes. I assume Iris will be there," Saul says.

"She got me the job, if that's what you mean." Jenny is proud of making it, at her age, off a casting couch.

"Now you two can be together every day." Slap.

"Just as you and I are together every night." Twenty-four hour sex is closing, like a flesh-eating plant, over Jenny. For weeks she has not painted, sketched, attempted any art.

"Never mind. If you and Iris get it on at the gallery, I'd have no way of knowing." Goading Jenny to adultery, Saul would rather have a lesbian sex kitten than a working wife. And he is naked under that robe, his pink cock warm and ready to be ready.

Jenny is tempted to give in.

"What about Angela?" Invoking the Department Secretary's name strengthens Jenny's resolve to leave. "You could be getting it on with her at the college." Jenny swings her raincape over her shoulders, the fact of her leaving billowing between them. "Guess we'll just have to trust each other, Saul." Bending, Jenny slides her tongue between his lips. She tastes his coffee, his cinnamon, his warmth. "See you later." Jenny rises, spinning, unsteady.

"Yeah." Saul does not look up. He sits alone, in rainlight that glows like aluminum, plushy shadows pressing in at him from the walls. Slumped over his newspaper, Saul sits alone.

Jenny hoists her fiddle-leaf philodendron off the table, hugging it with one arm and circling her supply carton with the other. One trip. She must break away from him in one trip.

"Let me get the door for you." Saul springs up.

"Thanks." Jenny may be a fool to feel sorry for him. Saul may have all kinds of plans for when she is gone. Enraged enough to escape from him, she lunges past Saul, down the back steps. No need to look where she is going, the important thing is just to get out.

The door slams shut behind her. Over her head, rain rat-a-tats her philodendron leaves like a shower hitting plastic. Jenny sets the plant down next to her locked car, and races back to her kitchen.

The room is empty. No footsteps. No running water, Jenny hesitates at the bottom of the stairs. Saul is probably back in bed. They could tumble a few minutes in love. Snatching her keys off the radiator, Jenny presses the warm metal teeth into her palm and runs with them, silently, back out into the rain.

Into chiaroscuro, silvery and dark, like a night lit by mirrors. Always it is like this when she goes out by herself. Behind her in the house her family—husband, parents, children, all identical—lurks in wait. And as soon as Jenny gets away from them, weightlessness enters her. She inhales in a single deep breath the sodden, leafy, chilled, rotting, fertile, wet dog smell of autumn, and finds herself skipping toward the car, like a child on her way to school.

The gallery is a former dance studio on the third floor of the Allyn Building. Jenny climbs up. On the second floor, blurred figures shift behind starry glass door-panels. Wondering who these people are, and what they are doing, Jenny keeps trudging. On the gallery floor, the doors are dark, the stars in the glass panel like fake snowflakes, each one the same as the next. Jenny walks into Woman Space East. She switches on the lights.

When she came for her interview, a huge mirror covered the dance studio wall. Now the walls, like the floor, are covered with carpet that looks like rye bread. Jenny shoves her plant in a corner. The huge philodendron would be just right in one of those classy galleries that exhibits second-rate Roualts rather than great stuff by unknowns. This is no setting where Jenny belongs.

But until she finds out where she does belong, this is where Jenny is. She lets her cape fall to the floor and remembers it, in California, a silver puddle at Iris's feet. Jenny faked it then, she can fake it now. Picturing herself tall, svelte, in a gray flannel suit and heels, her golden hair perfect in a smooth french twist, she kicks aside her cape and gets to work.

Jenny pulls a table out of the back room. She surrounds the table with folding chairs. One for Cynthia Costello, one for Lois Krauss, one for Iris, and one for herself. Jenny, who has seen this sort of thing in the movies, is Secretary for a Board of Directors.

The coffee can she pierces, with the opener she was efficient enough to bring, sighs. Jenny had hoped for art, not business. She would rather Chair a Board than be its Secretary. Ripping open a bag of ice, she works a bottle of champagne down into the cubes. Jenny thought this time, she was leaving Saul for a good reason but in this stultifying luxury, it may be hard even to have fun.

Champagne glasses and party napkins help. So does the smell of coffee. And by the time Jenny spots a fuzzy face outside the starry glass, she is ready to celebrate. Her first job. New friends. And this super-elegant gallery for women. What could be better?

Lois Krauss bounds in.

"I thought I was in prime condition, but those stairs are wicked." Peeling off her sopping sweat suit, Lois matter-of-factly towels her smooth, muscular body.

Jenny concentrates on the tawny hair, cut close to Lois's head. "You must be freezing." All jocks exude sex without meaning it. Aaron does constantly. Jenny has only to treat Lois like she treats her son. "How about a nice hot cup of coffee?"

"Never touch the stuff. Hey Cindy." Shaking a dry shirt out of a plastic bag, Lois covers herself. "Those stairs wicked or what?"

"Definitely a challenge." Lois's best friend, Cindy Costello, leans back, delicately, against the door. Like Esther, a photographer, Cindy slides her camera bag off her shoulder. She unbuttons her princess coat, her plastic booties. Her fingers deliberate, her eyes solemn, Cindy Costello removes her outer garments like a little girl playing Big Lady.

Jenny is appalled. After playing Big Lady for the last twenty years, she is ready now for the real thing. And not jock either. But these women, neither of them much older than her daughter, obviously know less of really being Big Lady than she does.

Cindy fluffs up her hair.

"What a neat plant!" she says. "How'd it get here?"

"I brought it." Embarrassed by her participation in their gentrification of this gallery, Jenny mutters.

"It looks super." Cindy sits down. She presses her knees together tucking her feet under the seat.

"Would you like some champagne?" Jenny carefully twists the cork off the first champagne bottle she has ever opened herself.

"Not for me," Cindy says. "I have to work this afternoon." She unwraps a tuna fish on white.

"Me either." Lois spreads her hand over her glass.

Jenny stands, the open bottle in her hand, shocked. These women are unwilling to have fun.

The door swings back.

"I may faint." Olga Zarecki tears her poncho over her head. "It's a miracle I made it up here." She flings herself into a chair. "Almost four hours since I had my last fix. Quick." Olga claws at a foil-wrapped grinder. "I need junk food." She clamps the grinder into her mouth. Sauce oozes like lava over her fingers. She licks her fingers clean.

Gulping, Jenny tastes tomatoes. She pours Olga a glass of bubbly. Olga grins up at her.

Cindy stares at them. "Do you mind, Jenny, if we get started without Iris?"

"Why should I mind?" Blood rushes into Jenny's face. Cindy thinks she belongs to Iris just like the people who consider Jenny nothing but Saul's wife. "I'm ready to begin whenever you are." She must make them see. Here Jenny is no one's lover, or daughter, or wife, or mother, or sister, or friend. She is Jennifer Reuben Weiss, the best person this committee could possibly have hired to be Facilitator of Woman Space East.

"It's just that I do have to be at the capitol before two." Cindy dabs at her lips with a folded napkin.

"No problem." But confronting Cindy's prissiness, Jenny's lips go stiff.

Iris fills the doorway. "Greetings, oh Guardians of the Tower." Stripping off her trenchcoat, she drapes it over the radiator as Jenny imagines Iris swooping around with silver raincape wings flashing rays across every woman in the room. "What have I missed so far?" Iris pulls two Almond Joys out of her briefcase.

"We were just about to discuss our opening event." Cindy has notebook and pen ready. "Anyone have suggestions?"

"I do." Jenny smiles. Lois's tawny cowlick sprouts up like a dog's ear. Cindy is giving Jenny the rapt but phony attention a polite student gives teacher. Sitting down, Iris peers through her smudged, little girl glasses. And Olga tilts back the last of her champagne. "I think we should sponsor a Thanksgiving Parade and Turkey Show." Never mind their ritzy gallery. Jenny will show these young women how to do something raffish, something outré, something Hartford needs.

"With a Miss Turkey Contest, don't forget." Lois checks to be sure Cindy is taking this in.

"No, listen." Jenny shoves words at her. She will teach the woman. "A parade and turkey show will be fun."

"I never pass up a chance to eat cotton candy," Olga says.

"I'm serious," Jenny says.

"Me too." Olga holds a potato chip up to the light, then slips it between her lips.

"We can do female signs, doves, flowers, any kind of balloons," Jenny says. "I know a man in the balloon business." And she is willing, for sisterhood, to share her connections.

"I don't think we should involve men in Woman Space events." Iris squeezes a candy wrapper in her fist.

"Thanksgiving is in less than five weeks," Cindy says. "A parade would take months to organize."

"How about if we have just the Turkey Show then?" Jenny asks. "Cindy, you could get the *Courant* to print an announcement inviting women to submit all kinds of turkeys."

"How many kinds are there?" Lois avoids Cindy's eyes.

Cindy swallows a grin.

"Thousands." Jenny glares. "Gerald Ford, for example, is a turkey."

"Let's not start out taking political stands," Cindy says.

"We'd either get too few submissions, or too many," Iris says. "Do any of you have time to judge turkeys? I know I don't." She knows Jenny does.

"In five weeks, how many turkeys could there be?" Jenny's voice quavers. Iris and her gang want to stifle her, just as the family she left tried to stifle her. "Don't you want to try something new?"

"Juanita Conklin has done some pretty good batik turkeys," Olga says. "She might let us show some of them."

"Just think, Cindy. You work at the *Courant*." Jenny imagines Cindy casting aside conventions for the first time in her life. "You could get us front page coverage of a Turkey Show on Thanksgiving Day." Which might also be Jenny's big chance to make the front page.

"That could be a problem." Cindy glances at Lois. "We don't want to appear ridiculous."

"I think the idea deserves consideration," Olga says.

"Maybe next year," Cindy says. "Right now, I think most of us would like to do something simpler."

"We could have a woman's art exhibit and reception," Lois says. "A mixed media event." By her that is avant garde.

Cindy writes Lois's suggestion down.

"With wine and cheese." Olga abandons her commitment to Jenny.

"How will a wine and cheese reception differentiate us from any other gallery in town?" Jenny asks.

"We'll be showing women's art." For Iris, that is enough.

"Next spring we can discuss a turkey show," Cindy says.

"I thought your grant was only for this year." Jenny's voice wobbles again. Fifteen minutes ago she would have said 'our' grant. But not now, not after what they have done to her.

"Barring complications, we expect to be renewed," Lois says. "So I suppose that's it then, for today." Arching her back, Lois stretches her magnificent limbs.

Jenny keeps her legs crossed. She folds her arms over her breasts. Saul can never accuse her of having left him for her own pleasure, not with this mob.

"So we'll start off, then, with our own work?" Cindy is buttoning her princess coat.

"Great idea." Lois pretends it is not what they intended from the beginning.

Jenny stares out a window into a white sky. She does not even have a dentist appointment this week. Her hair does not need cutting. Time for art gapes in front of her.

"What about a coat rack?" Iris shakes out her trenchcoat. "Will you get one for the gallery before the next meeting, Jenny?"

"Sure." Jenny stands up and flattens her folding chair.

"And we need a phone," Cindy says. "Can you please see about having one installed?"

"Sure." Jenny flattens another chair.

"See you next week then," Olga says.

"Great meeting, Jenny. Thank you," Cindy says. "So long, Iris."

"Catch you guys later." Lois lopes out with her friends.

Jenny slams the last chair. No matter that she now has something impressive for her resumé; buying things and hanging around waiting for workmen, she has taken a job as glorified housewife for half what a cleaning woman gets. Jenny will have no time for art. She stares across the table.

"At least that was short." In her trenchcoat, Iris is a prison matron rattling keys in her pocket the way Jenny's sister rattles pits.

"I feel like it's still going on." As if Jenny's life repeats itself, over and over, in new disguises.

"You should've discussed that loony-tunes plan of yours with me before you sprang it on the committee," Iris says.

"I thought they'd want to hear my ideas."

"Not when they're off the wall."

"Women's art should get off walls and out into the community," Jenny says. "I thought that was the whole point."

"Not of this gallery," Iris says.

Nor of any other gallery. Or school. Or club. Or government. All her life Jenny has had great ideas no one wants. But Iris was supposed to find Jenny something strange, unique, and wonderful to do. Something that would bring her recognition. Instead, Iris found Jenny a slot, and the only recognition she can get here is by brandishing jagged edges that do not fit in.

"So, you expect me to check with you before I open my mouth," she says.

"Cool it, Jennifer." Iris heads for the door, gabardine flapping like elephant skin over her backside and thighs. "Sisterhood has its limitations."

"I can see that," Jenny says.

The door thuds.

Jenny swats crumbs off the table. Smearing away tears, she packs up her coffee things, her champagne bucket, her can opener, her glasses, their trash. These people are slobs just like her kids. They are worse even than her sister. Jenny will have no trouble kissing off this lot.

Including that Olga Zarecki who checks light through a potato chip. Olga is no photographer, she is a quiltmaker. What right has she to care about light? Jenny yanks her extension cord out of the socket.

Flinging her cape around her shoulders, she wraps herself in cold wings, jabs her arms out of the cape-slits, grabs her supply carton, snaps off the gallery lights and slams the door. Jenny is out on the street before she remembers her purse, with her keys, wallet, and identification, upstairs on the table in Woman Space.

The janitor lets her back in. Grabbing her bag, she dashes right out again.

On Thursday, Jenny goes back to the gallery to see about the phone. A week later she is there for another horrendous committee meeting, the next week another, week after week she is at the gallery for terrible meetings.

At the end of November, the gallery has its official opening which the Committee deems a smashing success. Jenny recognizes most of the women in the crowd from other similar events. Nothing new here.

In December they feature a ceramics show like the one the Jewish Community Center has had for ten years but smaller than the one the Wesleyan Potters have been doing for at least twenty. The Committee is delighted by a profit of three hundred dollars.

Jenny lies low. After the first week of January, she spends every morning at the gallery. No one bothers her. Using the back room for a studio, she paints watercolors for the first time since college. Some of them are pretty good. She enjoys collecting her salary checks. But it irritates Jenny when she has to interrupt her work to answer the gallery phone, or greet the few stalwarts who make it up the stairs.

The Committee devotes their January show to needlework. Naturally. Needlework is now as traditional in a feminist gallery as dioramas are in a nature museum. Olga Zarecki, coming in to hang her quilts and tapestries, thinks this show is a splendid idea. No matter that soft sculptures are no better than stuffed birds. No matter to Olga that, in them, Jenny smells dust.

She stops bringing her lunch to Committee meetings by February, too tense to break bread with these women, too angry to be civil even to Iris. Jenny makes an appointment with Harvey Berk at his Employment Agency, hoping, after three months, to leave Woman Space East the same way she left Saul. For a job.

But she hates the images on Harvey's walls. Paint, applied to canvas, looks like birch bark, weathered barn-siding, snow, anything but paint. A line drawing of the Hartford skyline is overlaid with standard primary color squares. Where there should be art, there is only technique. Yet this is the junk that sells, this is the bland crap that Jenny cannot accomplish even when she tries. Harvey's office is decorated like a motel for business travelers as if a total obliteration of personality is a prerequisite for success.

Turning her back on the room, Jenny pushes aside a vertical blind and looks out the window at the Civic Center Bar. HAPPY HOUR. The metal sign sways in a vicious gray wind as two corporate women, hobbled by straight skirts and heels, scurry in.

Jenny reseals the blind, slides down in her chair, stretches out her legs, stares at her lap. She loves these baggy gray corduroys over thermal underwear. In panty hose, her legs feel confused, abraded, like onions in mesh sacks. It seems unlikely that Harvey will know of an enclave in an insurance company or bank, where women can work in slacks. Stuffing her mittens into the pockets of Aaron's hand-me-down ski jacket, Jenny unzips.

"Sorry to keep you waiting, Jenny." Harvey Berk, né Berkowitz, emerges from his office. "Come on in." Done up like a Yankee in a herring-bone suit, Harvey wears a navy necktie dotted with bright green whales, and yet, under his memorized facade, Jenny always thought she detected a certain decency. Not today. Today Harvey is facade all the way through. "Have a seat." He stands behind his desk assessing her.

"Thanks." Jenny dives into the nearest chair, and folds her ski jacket over her breasts.

This sharp-eyed headhunter is not the Harvey Berk who leans on the piano singing golden oldies at neighborhood parties.

"What can I do for you?" He angles forward, a smiling professional who follows the manual's recommendation to look directly into an interviewee's eyes.

"You can get me a job." Jenny slides deep into the chair. "At least I think you can." She is afraid of this man who could have her locked into a room like this one.

"What sort of job do you have in mind?" he asks.

"What sorts are there?" Jenny gushes sweat. "I mean for someone like me."

"I thought you were in charge of that new gallery on Allyn." Harvey makes a finger church and thoughtfully taps his nose with the steeple.

"It's not working out." Jenny sheds her jacket. "I'd like to make a change." She cannot wait to tell her tormentors she has been hired to do a better job.

"Are you planning to pursue your interest in art?" The tan walls behind Harvey are threaded like a cocoon.

"If possible." Jenny cannot imagine a butterfly emerging in this place.

"Have you any graphics experience?" Harvey asks.

"Not really." Jenny is committed to self-expression, not mere design. "In fact I have almost no credentials."

"At least you have a job," Harvey says. "That makes securing another much easier." He does not worry if every rung of a ladder is the same as the one below and the one above.

"I was hoping to try something new." When Jenny was in college, boys were wearing the same button-down collars Harvey has on now. What does Harvey know about new?

"Do you have a salary range in mind?" he is asking.

"Not really. I'd just like to make more than the three thousand a year I'm getting now." Grinning, Jenny defies Harvey to reach behind him into one of his filing cabinets and come out with a single possibility.

"What would you describe as your marketable skills?" he asks.

"I have spent years as a housewife, and months at Woman Space East, helping other people do what they do better." Now it is Jenny's turn to do. She stares at Harvey hopelessly. "Housewives make great administrators." Not that Harvey, or any of the employers he would know, would believe that.

"I'm sure that's very true." Harvey makes no move toward a filing cabinet. "Maybe, Jenny, if you narrowed down your options a bit. For example, you might want to check the U.S. Government's Occupational Listings." Writing this down, Harvey hands the sheet of paper across the desk as if it were a prescription. "You know Miriam Frankel don't you?"

"Yes," Jenny says. Miriam Frankel is as jittery and conventional as a squirrel.

"She studied the occupational list, took some communications courses, contacted someone at Travelers and got them to create the perfect job for her."

"Ah." Jenny jams Harvey's prescription in Aaron's pocket.

"Once you're clear about what you want to do, I may be able to help you contact the right person, Jenny." Harvey presses his palms to the desk, splaying his elbows like grasshopper legs.

"Don't you want to see my resumé?" Jenny spent two days on it.

"Sure. Leave one with me if you have copies. You never know what might turn up."

"Here, take two."

"Thanks." Glancing at the type, Harvey slides Jenny's resumé into a cabinet drawer. Under what heading, she wonders? "So tell me, Jenny, how is Saul?" Harvey stands up. "And the children?" He smiles, returning to a golden oldie conversation.

"They're all fine." Jenny drags herself out of his chair.

"Aaron enjoying Hampshire?" Harvey guides her into the outer office. "Scott is crazy about UVM."

142

"Listen, Harvey." Standing in the doorway, Jenny raises her eyes into his. "I do appreciate your seeing me." Now no one can claim she did not try. It is not Jenny's fault there are no jobs for housewives, not Harvey's fault that this is the system he represents. "You've been a great help." Jenny offers him her hand in true gratitude.

"My pleasure." Harvey's hand presses back. "And whenever you're ready, Jenny, I mean it." He flattens his hand over the whale tie as if he is pledging allegiance. "Come see me again."

"I will." Nodding, Jenny turns away. It is worse than she thought. Harvey is sorry he cannot slide her, like a book in a shelf, into one of his jobs. She closes the door between them with a soft click.

And finds herself alone in a corridor lined with closed doors exactly like the one behind her.

Jenny races to the elevator. She rides down to the lobby alone. Alone, she rams her shoulder against a heavy glass door and bursts outside, running, butting her head against the wind, charging, like a football player, toward a goal.

Luke is in Florida with her parents. This is the night Saul teaches the Virginia Woolf Seminar Iris is taking. Jenny has no new job to prepare for. So she might as well tackle a project she has been planning for months. Stopping on her way home, Jenny rents a wallpaper steamer.

But Saul is not at the college. His car is in the garage. Outside lights are on, but the downstairs is dark. Jenny fumbles her way through the kitchen. The bedroom light glows into the upstairs hall.

"Halloo." Jenny hurls Aaron's jacket on a chair. "Saul?" She takes the stairs two at a time.

"Up here," he calls to her. "The dean canceled my class." The television clicks off. "Half of Trinity is down with flu." Saul lies on their bed.

Jenny sets the wallpaper steamer, a red mailbox festooned with a pink hose, right by the door. The damned man has no right to be so attractive, no right to look better than when she first married him. Jenny keeps her distance. Tonight, she is going to get rid of the red, flocked, bordello-print wallpaper in this room. The steamer tank lists warnings on its red side: Do not, do not, do not, or you will burn.

If not for this, than for her other sins. "I hope you don't expect me to make you dinner." She gives him no kiss. Jenny scoots into her closet. "I'm just planning to grab something later."

"I'll fix dinner for us both." The bedclothes rustle. "But it's early yet."

"Not for me." Jenny pries off her shoes, slides down her corduroys. "I've been meaning to do this for a long time." Stretching up, over her head, she pulls off her sweater and drapes it over the closet pole. "Tonight's the night."

"I'm with you there." Saul's shoes thump, one at a time, to the floor. "We don't often get an opportunity like this one." Is that his zipper? "House all to ourselves." Saul's voice caresses Jenny's skin.

"Stop it." Jenny wants to spread her nakedness all over his body. "Just stop it, Saul." She does not want to be aroused. Jenny throws herself into a denim shirt and overalls. "I have other things to do right now." She jimmies her feet into the shit-kickers he hates. "Why don't you got out, and get yourself something for dinner?" Jenny swaggers out of her closet, a regulation lesbian.

The lovelight in Saul's eyes blinks off.

"I'm not hungry right now." He zips his pants.

"Could you at least get out of the bedroom?" Jenny takes the steamer into the tub. Use cold water, the instructions say. Fill to three inches below neck. She turns the faucet on full force. No more automatic sex. No more pretending she is Saul's whore. Jenny twists the water off.

Using a toothbrush handle for a dipstick, she estimates three inches. Close enough. She screws the lid on tight. The tank pulls heavy at her arm. In the bedroom, Jenny drops the steamer right next to the bed.

"You with Iris today?" Saul asks.

"No." He has no reason to be jealous. Jenny and Iris do little these days beside fight. "I went to see Harvey Berk about a job." She told Saul this morning she had the appointment. If he really loved her, he would remember what she tells him.

"Harvey helpful?" he asks.

"No."

"Surprise, surprise. Harvey Berk is an idiot."

"Not really." At least Harvey has enough sense to know the world does not want Jenny. Only Saul wants her.

Jenny twists off her wedding ring and drops it—clink—on top of the jar of Eterna 27.

"You have anything in the freezer?" Hunched over the edge of the bed, Saul ties his laces into tight, angry bows.

"If you'll just let me get started, I'll come down later and make dinner," Jenny says.

144

"Forget it." Saul is on his way out the door. "Iris said she'd probably stop by around dinner-time. We'll cook something up."

"Fine." Jenny pulls the bureau away from the wall. Their wedding picture topples face down.

"You want me to help you?" Saul stands in the hall.

"No. You go down and wait for Iris." With her in the house, there can be no sex. Jenny is pleased.

Saul is leaving her alone.

The steamer gurgles. In the good old days when mommy was there to keep an eye on daddy, Jenny could play happily in her room. Now Jenny grabs the steamer plate by its wood handle. The plate hisses and spits. The hose is hot and filled with reptilian life. Avoiding it, Jenny presses the plate against the bottom of a wallpaper seam, and slides up. Edges curl behind her.

With one hand, Jenny steams; with the other, she tears. Red curlicues melt in fringe drippings down the wall. Flocking turns to scum. Jenny gets sanitary napkins and lines them up along the base board.

The doorbell rings.

"Iris is here," Saul calls up.

"Tell her, 'hi.'" Jenny goes on stripping the wall, hurling wide paper ribbons into the bathroom. Her hands turn red. She finds a nail clipper and scrapes, digs, gouges, picking off stubborn red barnacles. So what if she leaves scars? Scars can be repaired with Spackle. Jenny will not rest until there is nothing on these walls but plaster, ready to be transformed.

"Wish I had a camera." Iris sidles in, closing the door behind her. "You look as beautiful as a mid-wife delivering quadruplets." Her admiration, like sunshine, closes around Jenny.

"I think this is more an abortion." Backing away, Jenny stares first at the wall, then at her red palms, her arms red to the elbow. No more California interludes. She has no time for sunshine.

Tears wobble down the steam-covered mirror on the bathroom door. A photo of Saul, age three, skitters to the floor.

"Time for celebration," Iris says. "Abortions correct mistakes." She picks up a scroll of bordello print. "And in this case, I would say, hardly a moment too soon."

"I hope Saul sees it that way." Jenny stares at him, lying on the floor, his Mickey Mouse mask in hand.

· "Forget Saul. I've got great news." Iris thrusts her hands out as if she is about to toss Jenny the world. "Woman Space East not only got its grant renewed for next year. We got it doubled."

"*Mazel Tov.*" Jenny holds her steamer plate between them like a shield.

"Next year, your salary will go up to five thousand, six if you go for it," Iris says.

"The facilitator's salary, you mean."

"I don't think there'll be a problem about you staying on." Iris's eyes slide over the bed Jenny shares with Saul. "As long as you don't go out of your way to antagonize anyone."

"What if one of them antagonizes me?" Stamping the heavy boots, Jenny tries to free herself from wallpaper curls entwining her feet. "I've got work I want to do here." She kicks off the last curl.

"What's that supposed to mean?" Iris asks.

"I'm quitting the job as of June." The money buys Jenny nothing she could not have without it. She has paid for the Gallery Director label in time, too much time. So the words falling out of her mouth are as real as the paper on the floor. Jenny is leaving the gallery. "I wanted you to be the first to know."

"That's terrific, just terrific, Jennifer." Iris opens the door. A cold draft slides into the room. "Suddenly this place is a downer." Iris takes a last look at the bleeding wall, the stained Jenny. "Bedlam." She flings herself down the stairs.

Slamming the door, Jenny goes back to her friendly dragon, the steamer now drooling on the rug. Again, she presses the wall. Jenny reaches high, she reaches higher, the weight on her arm and shoulder heavier and heavier, the writhing hose a burden Jenny carries with pleasure. She wants to be exhausted, wants oblivion in this cleansing, steam heat that takes away every shred of bordello print, every trace of her stupid housewife self, every remnant of her Jenny-the-Executive illusions.

"You coming down, or should I bring dinner up?" Saul yells to her.

"No," Jenny shouts.

"Which?" he asks.

"Neither." Jenny wipes steam dripping from her eyebrows, out of her eyes. The boy with his MIckey Mouse mask swims on the rug. Saul's feet bound up the stairs. All over the room, there are red streaks, streamers, stains. "Stay out," Jenny screams.

"At least come down and keep me company while I eat." Saul opens the door. "Oh Christ."

"Out. Out." Scooping his photo off the floor, Jenny smashes it against the wall, next to, but not at him. "Get out."

146

"Look at the mess you've made!" Saul gawks at the pitted, torn, and bleeding wall, the clotted Kotex, his wild-eyed wife.

"Okay, so it's bad." When a boil bursts, gunk comes out. "But it's only temporary." Squatting, Jenny picks glass out of the rug. "I'll fix it up." She drops fragments on the sad-eyed boy, peering out of his broken window, his sorrow unaffected by what she is doing now. "You'll see."

"I'm afraid you're right." Saul squats beside her to gather glass.

Last spring, it was Jenny and Iris under the table, in Davey Jones Locker, picking up scattered pieces. Now, Jenny puts her hand on Saul's knee. She slides it up Saul's thigh. "Trust me," she says. "I'll make a nice place for us." Power surges through Jenny. No one is better at making something out of wreckage than she is. "You'll see. It will be great once I'm done."

Jenny stands up, with Saul beside her, taking stock of the rubble. Nothing remains here to be destroyed. And they are intact, Jenny and Saul, still together.

Chapter XII

NEW ANGLE
• *Mid-May* •

Esther is waiting in the parking lot, a bearded blonde hulk in tennis whites beside her. Jenny has never seen this one before. Saul eases the car to a stop. Jumping out, Jenny approaches her daughter. They kiss. They stand back. Each smiles a sly smile, recognizing, once again inside the other, a twin.

And yet outwardly they are so different. Her hair bulging like a pillow on either side of a red plastic barrette, Esther wears no eye color or lipstick. Jenny's face is painted with extreme care. Esther has on a yellow blouse, one side buttoned a step down from the other, a purple skirt, its hem drooping, and high, black, boy's basketball sneakers. Jenny is wearing a beige linen pants suit and dainty, red, spaghetti-strap sandals. She is swathed in a mist of *'L'air du temps'*. Esther exudes her own pleasant body odor.

The immaculate young man hovering in back of her is enormous.

"This is Peter." Esther waves a pair of rhinestone sunglasses at him. "I put him in charge of the keg."

"Pleased to meet you, Ms. Weiss." Extending his hand, Peter bends toward Esther's mother in awe. Jenny reciprocates. Peter has the kind of muscles she sees in her dreams. Leave it to Esther. "Professor Weiss." The young man's voice is reverent. Sunlight glistens in his beard. "Luke." Peter gives Esther's brother a companionable nudge. "So you're the infamous little bro."

"Where'd you get these?" Grabbing his sister's rhinestone

sunglasses, Luke slides them in front of his eyes. "Pretty swift."
He looks like an over-dressed raccoon.

"I found them at a garage sale," Esther says.

"How much?" Luke asks.

"A dollar."

"Cool." Luke bunches his lips in admiration. "I'll give you two."

"No way."

"Three then, but not another nickel."

"Hand them over." Esther holds out her palm like a priestess
expecting her due. And she gets it. Gaudy jewels flash in her hand.

Jenny feels herself grow taller. The younger women to whom
she has been looking for guidance are too old, too set in their ways.
Jenny's prophetess is more likely here, close to home.

"Where do you want this stuff, Ess?" Saul flips up the back of
the station wagon.

"In the Arts Center. That building right there," Esther says.
"Peter will show you. I have to go get ready." Now that her troops
have their assignment. "Check you guys later." Esther heads,
across the Wesleyan campus, for her dorm.

"How do you want to handle this, Jen?" Saul stares into the car
at the keg, the cake box, the ice chest, the suitcase, the duffel
bag, the pillow-case filled with cheeses, the laundry bag stuffed
with breads, the salamis tied in a bundle, and, over all, the tangled
mass of apple blossoms that remind Jenny of the torn wallpaper
spirals that reddened their bedroom.

She cleaned up that mess. Jenny will sort this one out as well.

"First, take everything out and set it here on the grass." She
begins, as always, with an assessment. "I'll hold the flowers."
Jenny peers out through the branches. "Saul, stack the cheeses on
the suitcase." She has it all figured out. Jenny used to think she
could fall back on being a call girl. Now, a call woman, her
emergency plan is catering. "We can manage most of this in one
trip." Concentrating on amassing her gorgeous spread, Jenny
blocks the main event out of her mind.

"Hi, Weiss family." Alva Giddings is running toward them,
waving a tiny suitcase. Dueling pistols? Fringes waggle on Alva's
lavender suede shirt, lavender the perfect color with her dark hair,
her pale skin, her flowing skirt. Alva's breasts waggle with her
fringes.

"How are you?" Jenny can see for herself. "You look great."
Alva always looks great, every detail of her self-presentation
perfect. As if air-hosed, Jenny's mouth dries. Her daughter never
looks perfect. Esther's one-woman photography show will proba-

bly be sloppy and embarrassing, buttoned all wrong. Jenny dives for the bread bag. "Let's go."

"Esther sent me to help." Alva eyes Peter, her fellow orderly.

"Lookin' good, cowgirl." Peter turns away from her as if Alva's perfection is banal. He is here for Esther.

Jenny and Saul and Luke are also here for Esther. At least Jenny's daughter has the sense to marshal a good-size work force. But that may not be enough.

Peter lifts the beer as if the keg were already empty.

"You all follow me." Cradling the silvery barrel in his arms, Esther's Hercules takes off across the grass.

"Lead on." Saul falls in line with the cake on top of the ice chest.

Each with food or flowers, the rest of them follow like votaries bringing offerings to a goddess.

Jenny is ready to believe that her fortunes are tied to her daughter. If Esther can just pull this event off, there is hope for Jenny as well.

"I'd say Esther's new acquisition has his feats of amazing strength down." Dropping back toward his mother, Luke nods up the line toward Peter. "Need I say more? Need I say more?"

"Hardly." Jenny pokes him with her sheaf of salamis.

Across the quad, a hairy-chested piper in dark trousers accompanies three dancing girls in moth-wing dresses, the girls chanting, their words unclear. Jenny thinks she hears the name Esther.

"Far out," Luke says.

"Not really," Saul says. "There's always considerable exhibitionism on a college campus around exam time."

Jenny forgot that in college, people can get away with acting crazy. No wonder Iris keeps going back to school.

"Some of the art history majors are into *tableaux vivants*," Alva says.

Imagining herself re-enacting a nymph in he woodlands painting in her own moth-wing dress, Jenny trails Luke up a concrete ramp, through massive glass doors, into a monumental lobby that smells of cement.

"This is it, folks." Peter gently sets the keg on end.

"The show's right in there." Alva kicks the pointy toe of her white cowgirl boot toward inside glass doors. Behind them, on a cinderblock wall, Esther's name in handsome white letters, Esther's show, concealed.

The lobby is an unadorned, cinderblock box. A long steel table stands in front of yet more glass doors, closing off a gallery where chrome framed pictures glint in shadows. A flight of concrete stairs goes down, not up. Shaking off doubts, Jenny gets to work. She has exactly thirty-five minutes to turn this art vault into a celebration of life.

"Can you please get water for these?" She hands Alva the flowers. "Luke, pass me that suitcase." Unsnapping the lid, Jenny takes out her favorite queen-size sheet.

"I've got this end," Saul says.

Between them birds of paradise and tropical flowers billow out over the steel table.

"Not as shabby as usual, Mother." Luke strolls over to watch Peter tap the keg.

Jenny removes plastic forks, knives, and spoons from the lingerie tray of the suitcase her father gave her mother for their silver wedding anniversary cruise.

"I'm taking my wife on her grand tour," Simon said, as if, when they came back, Anna would be educated.

And she was.

"There is nothing, today, to compare with the old Queen Elizabeth." Jenny's mother learned what to buy with her husband's wealth. "It was elegant." Anna would like no better life for her daughter.

But Jenny does not want to dedicate herself to collecting luxuries. But to what? Her future is a blank. A blank with Iris in it, the thought of her lover making Jenny ache like someone cramped after sitting too long in one place. Yet Jenny is moving, this reception her last project, her gallery job over in two weeks.

Standing next to her, Saul unwraps plates and napkins while Jenny unpacks cutting boards and serving bowls. If she does go into catering, he can help her. But if she chooses art, as something in her keeps pushing her to do, Jenny will be on her own.

Sliding the empty suitcase under the table, she dumps cole slaw into a steel bowl and feels, as if the slimy cabbage shreds come from her gut.

Salamis thud onto a carving board. Saul has cut the twine.

"This okay for the flowers?" Alva comes up from the basement bearing a fragrant cloud of apple blossoms erupting from a silver punchbowl.

"Perfect." Jenny immerses herself once again in the job at hand.

Saul is opening pickle jars.

Luke stacks rye breads, then helps himself to one of the oranges Jenny is pouring out of a sack into a basket.

And garlic and apple blossoms and orange and caraway and cabbage and the room's concrete stench merge, like a French woman's sweat, sex, and perfume. Jenny has done as much as she can with what she has.

"Mind if I sample, Ms. Weiss?" Peter reaches for a pickle.

"Call me Jenny, and sure, help yourself."

"We don't often get goodies like this down where I come from," Peter says.

"Where's that?" Jenny asks.

"Texas, Ma'am. Dallas."

Jenny imagines her only daughter wallowing with this man in pure black oil. And in the things oil buys. Peter's muscles bulge, stretching his whitissimo tennis shirt, with delicious possibilities.

Luke sneaks up behind them.

"In those pants, Mother, you're a walking tragedy."

"Which some of us finds more appealing than a slinking impertinence." Saul slides the huge sheet cake he ordered from an Italian bakery out of its box.

"Congratulations, Esther," his cake says in letters surrounded by daffodils. All very pretty, the yellow with Jenny's oranges and her green pickles, but what if the message should be "Condolences, Esther"? Esther's name stares out of the glass doors.

"Hand me that bag." Jenny has her own ideas for a proper dessert.

"How come you never buy Yodels for me?" Luke snatches one and another. Jenny says nothing, knowing, probably as well as anyone here, how it feels when the guest of honor is someone else. Always someone else.

"Hey guys. The visuals are fantastic." Alva stands in front of the entrance doors, staring at the feast. Dust motes shimmer, a halo around her hair.

"Get out of the way." Peter charges past her. "She's coming."

Crowned with flowers, Esther leads the pale nymphs, their satyr, and assorted others across the quad. Peter thrusts the Art Center doors open. Alva lifts from her tiny suitcase a miniature trumpet that she raises to her lips. Along her arms and across her back, lavender fringes quiver as Alva's shrill fanfare joins pipes and reedy voices from the crowd.

Esther is wearing a 'new look' garage sale cocktail dress. Waggling her turquoise peplum, she proceeds across the campus like a duck ahead of her brood, Jenny's daughter and her following.

Jenny reaches for Saul, clamping his hand as she does when they are on an airplane, moving down a runway, gathering speed. It seems impossible that this child of theirs can lift so much weight, clear the trees, fly.

Flashing a grin at her family, Esther enters the gallery. The crowd eddies behind her.

Jenny and Saul shuffle forward, around the wall that screens their daughter's work.

They stop.

A single, mammoth, open eye dominates the room.

"Great."

"Fabulous."

The crowd bursts into applause.

Jenny's lips tremble. How proud she is! Her daughter has made it up, the ground sliding from under her mother. Who is Jenny now that her work is done? Gulping down tears, Jenny lets go of Saul's hand.

"Do you see how she did it?" Saul moves close to the eye.

The pupil is a blackened hubcap, the iris a ring of color photos mounted flat against the white wall.

"Can you tell those are letters?" Linking arms with Jenny, Esther points at celluloid lashes.

"Sure." But Jenny is too overwhelmed to make sense out of words cut from negatives. Positives bombard her. Family photos and newspaper shots.

" 'Esther's I,' " Luke reads for her. "Pretty sweet."

"The piece is a *tour de force*," Saul says.

"What do you think of it?" Esther peers into Jenny's face.

"It's wonderful." Jenny does not have to pretend. Exalted, she feels like falling on her knees in prayer before the giant eye. ".Oh please, dear God," she would say, "Teach me to be like my daughter."

"What process did you use for the photo on the pupil?" Saul is examining the hubcap. The black is not all black but holds, like the Labrea tar pits, ghost shapes.

Jenny needs to know how to get that kind of resonance with paint. Rothko did it.

"I made a low contrast solarized print of an aerial shot of the campus." Those techniques, Esther learned here. "I knew you'd like that part, Saul." She stands next to her father, smiling. "It's like literary, you know, that stuff about through a glass darkly."

"Like yeah." Saul smirks.

"Where'd you get the aerial photo?" Luke asks.

"I took it, dildo. Where'd you think I got it?" Esther punches her brother's shoulder. "If you want, I'll get Peter to give you a ride in his plane later."

Both of her children in the air. Jenny turns away.

"How are you doing, Mrs. Weiss?" the satyr asks.

"Great, thanks." Jenny deciphers Rick, the vegetarian. "How are you? I didn't recognize you at first, Rick, in costume." How could Jenny forget? In a way, Rick took her virginity. Jenny is not sure who got Esther's. She is not even sure any more if that part of a person's life counts. Not in the face of art.

A fat black man wearing a dashiki is giving Esther a secret-society handshake.

"Your eye, Esther, it turned out truly bad," he says.

"Hey man, meet my mother. Jennifer, this is Mustapha."

"Esther has so many of your pictures on display." Mustapha shakes Jenny's hand conventionally. "I feel as if you are already known to me."

As if Jenny has already been. Yet someone, even a daughter, displaying her work holds out hope.

"This is Neal Griswold, my faculty advisor," Esther says.

Jenny's art could just possibly be as good as her daughter, as her daughter's art.

"You must be very pleased, Mrs. Weiss." Esther's teacher is a tense young man in a pink alligator shirt and khaki pants. "This is a very daring show but somewhat, I must admit, to my surprise, more or less successful in what Esther was attempting to do."

"That's as close as Neal gets to a compliment," Esther says.

"Neal is a critic of every photographer's work," Mustapha says.

"It's my job to teach." Neal frowns as if a severe expression and preppy clothes were necessary to distinguish this professor from his students. Neal would fit right in at Woman Space East. "But tell me, Mrs. Weiss, how do you respond to Esther's project?"

"I'm thrilled." Pleasure floods into Jenny. Whatever she does from now on does not matter. She will go down in history as the mother of a star.

"Check out the shot of you I used," Esther says.

Jenny finds her image in 'Esther's I.' Between Jimmy Carter and Anwar Sadat, and a picture of Luke, Saul, and Aaron on skis, Jenny is the Earth Mother. Esther took that picture last fall when Jenny was bringing plants into the house. That was the day Jenny told the children about Iris. But her daughter included no picture of Iris in her eye. She does not show Jenny as a Radical Lesbian Feminist. Or as an artist. Esther shows Jenny only as a mother.

154

"I just love it." Jenny stretches her lips over her teeth and hopes this passes for a smile.

"Come with me." Esther pulls her. "There's something else I want you to see. You too, Saul." Esther walks her parents through the crowd to the lobby.

Her mother follows the turquoise taffeta ruffles obediently, as if now she is her daughter's daughter.

Alva is presiding over the food table.

"I wish you'd speak to Peter," she says to Esther. "He's being what you would call a *shtunk*." Alva's lips frame Esther's word proudly. "He keeps grabbing pickles and he's got Luke doing it too."

"Tell them to save a few for us." Esther is taking Saul and Jenny down to a concrete basement. "Be right back." A dank hallway where they are alone with shadows. "Now tell me. Really." Esther confronts Jenny. "What do you think of my show?" Even after her triumph, fear stares out of Esther's eyes. Her mother's fear.

But that was before.

"Cross my heart and hope to die." Now Jenny is not scared, at least not for her daughter. "You made art."

Pleasure flares in them both. And in Saul.

"Your 'I' just tickles me." He gives Esther the goofy grin he has always reserved just for her.

For once, Jenny does not mind.

"But let's get to the good stuff," she says. "What's with this Peter?"

"He's just a friend." Esther bustles down the corridor to a closed door.

"What's his last name?" Jenny has heard of Texas Jews. Stanley Marcus, for example. She can see pages of Esther's photographs featured in the Nieman-Marcus Christmas Catalogue.

"Meeker. He's a Methodist. But not to worry, Jennifer, Peter's kind of an air-head." Fishing into her dress, Esther pulls out a chain that holds, not a cross or a Star of David, but a key. "We've had some great times together, but he's nobody I'd ever get serious about." The key chain dangles like a rosary from her hand. "And anyway, right now I'm too involved with my work to get serious about anyone." Esther has got religion. Opening the door, she leads her parents into her church. "Welcome to our studio."

Jenny brushes her finger-tips along a slate counter-top. Rubber gloves, blue like the ones she wears to wash dishes, lie next to a stack of pans. Esther makes pictures rise to the surface of papers in those pans. Up to now, her mother was content to make bubbles appear in pancakes.

A rubber apron looks ready to be lifted from ts hook. In this religion, the place of worship is as sustaining and practical as a kitchen. Jenny is ready to convert.

"Finishing up is kind of a bummer in its way," Esther is saying.

"You're only done for a while." Jenny flicks a faucet on for the pleasure of smooth metal in her fingers. "Give yourself time to enjoy your success." She even likes the rags in here, dried flat and bumpy, like cow flops stretched over the pipes. "Pretty soon a new project will occur to you."

"Actually I do have sort of a new series brewing." Esther smirks.

"This the dark room in here?" Saul disappears through an inner door.

"Wait till you see what they make us use for an enlarger." Esther disappears after him.

Jenny stays. She has not finished absorbing the possibilities where she is.

A wizened lilac bows from a mayonnaise jar on a window sill. Slightly out of focus, a photo of the same lilac, at the height of its bloom, is pinned to the window frame, the image blurred as if seen through tears. No need to cry. The flower, conventionally lovely in its youth, now holds dark sunlight, clinging even in death, to beauty.

Pearly lights glide down film strips that waver, drying, from a line. How many socks, bras, sheets and towels Jenny has hung out to dry! She sighs. But was it really such a waste? She was great in that job. Esther proved that today. Jenny will be great in the next one now that she knows she must work to catch light, work to make it last, work to make her own 'Jenny's I.'

For once in her life she has time, the years from now on all hers. Sucking in a deep breath of chemicals, dusty sunshine, and school, Jenny feels holy water gush into the parched ditches of her brain.

Chapter XIII

HIGHER EDUCATION
• *July* •

This is Jenny's third time out in the world on her own. Going to college, and last summer's flying of the coop, she squandered on a quick attachment first to Saul, then to Iris. This time Jenny is determined to go her six weeks at Rhode Island School of Design alone.

Lying in her bed, Jenny stretches her fingers to touch iron bars. She stretches her toes to touch iron bars. Taking a deep, salt breath, Jenny thinks of the woman across the hall, finished after only two days.

Jenny only saw her for an instant, her body crumpled on the floor of her room. But Jenny can imagine her fellow student on a stretcher, in an ambulance, at the hospital emergency room attended by a staff accustomed to RISD victims. Strangers are pumping the woman out.

People are saying it was an adverse reaction to diet pills. They are saying she overdosed on sleeping pills. The woman across the hall never came back to explain. Other students who were here that first week also disappeared. An alarm gargles next door in Georgette's room. So far, Jenny has survived.

She has already made it through half the summer session. Forcing herself up, out of bed, she checks the bourbon bottle on her bureau. Half full. Just as it should be. Turning away, she does not unscrew the top and take a swig. Jenny does not even seriously consider one quick belt for her birthday, the day of her print class critique. A year ago today, she was in California, the after-light of fireworks fresh inside her. Now, Jenny grabs her hot pot and shuffles down a blessedly empty hall to a bathroom that smells, as usual, as if Saul got there ahead of her.

Angular as an erector set construction, Priscilla Twitchell looms over a sink.

"Morning," Jenny mutters.

"Are you just waking up?" Priscilla is dressed and combed. "I've been up for hours trying to decide which print to give Jewell-Anne to critique."

"I don't have that problem. I've only got one." Jenny shivers as cold, gushing into the pot in her hand, seems to rise in her too.

"That's an advantage." Priscilla flaps her bony fingers so water specks hit Jenny's arm. "How clever! You brought a coffee pot with you." The tower's clear blue beacons look down on Jenny. "You wouldn't by any chance also have an emery board?" She pinches a paper towel from the dispenser. "I told Jewell-Anne I'd find her one." Priscilla's nails are straight, clipped, business-like.

"Sorry." Jenny has a box of emery boards in her room. "Can't help you."

"Oh well. We're going to this place in the Italian quarter for breakfast before class. Hopefully, divine cappuccino will make Jewell-Anne forget to sharpen her claws." Guffawing, Priscilla pauses at the open door. "Didn't I hear someone say yesterday that today is your birthday? Do have a happy." She leaves.

"Thanks." Hurrying to her room, Jenny glances down at the violet kimono Saul gave her for her birthday, pressing like a limp spinnaker against her legs. Jenny has only her own resources to depend on and right now they feel skimpy. "Oh wait." She snatches up her emery boards and dashes down the hall. "Wait, Priscilla. I forgot." Jenny catches up. "I do have emery boards with me." She deals them out, their grit sand between her teeth. Maybe Jenny is a fool to give weapons to the enemy. "How many do you want?" Jenny is what she is.

"That's fine." Priscilla waves them and strides off for her rendezvous with the teacher.

Back in her room, Jenny feels better. At least she was true to herself. And now the lines are clearly drawn: Jenny is the kind and generous one. Priscilla is the ass-kissing user. Surely, Jewell-Anne Drayton will know whose work is worth more.

Jenny is the last one to get to the studio. Under metallic white lights, Jewell-Anne stands watching the door, her face pale and puffy as a baking powder biscuit as if, over the years, it has absorbed punch after punch. And yet she is on her feet. Her haunches taut inside tight black jeans, her breasts bulging, under a nubby sweater, like well-kept muscles, her dark, lusterless hair tossed back out of the way, Jewell-Anne Drayton waits, just waits, for her chance to punch back.

As she reaches up to hang her raincape over a hook, without being able to do a thing about it, Jenny knows that, from behind, she must look like a punching bag. She pivots around. Jewell-Anne is grinning at her.

"Priscilla said you looked, earlier this morning, like you were not feeling well, Jennifer." There is on the teacher's grinning face, a fixed, fire-eyed joy. "I was afraid you might not get here for your critique." On either side of Jewell-Anne, an easel faces the class. One holds Priscilla's gray on gray cracked egg, the other is empty.

"Sorry I'm late." Jenny hurries to the front of the room, sliding her print out of a garbage bag. "Just as I was leaving, I got a long distance call." She tilts the brown and yellow Seder into place. "My daughter wanted to wish me a happy birthday." Jenny flashes her own high-powered grin. On this day, Jewell-Anne and everyone else must be made to see, Jenny deserves special consideration. Besides, teacher and student are both middle-aged, each has a daughter, and they are, if there is even a ghost of a God in heaven, both women of good will. In fact, potentially, Jewell-Anne and Jenny are soul mates.

The teacher mounts a high stool.

Jenny sinks into place at her usual drawing table, across the aisle from Waldo Cobb.

Meeting her eye, Waldo winks.

Jenny smiles inside and out. Yesterday, Waldo's shirt and matching knee socks were yellow. Today they are lime green, a lime green so bad it is good, like Waldo himself, the antithesis of Gucci.

Jewell-Anne is glaring at them.

"Who's to go first, Jennifer? You or Priscilla?" As she leans forward, a cross drops out of her neckline.

"I'd just as soon get it over with if that's okay." Jenny eyes the swaying crucifix, a ghastly omen. Jesus was Jewish. She is Jewish. Jews always get nailed up, all too frequently these days by the most fervent admirers of God's Jewish son.

"I'd rather wait." Priscilla chuckles.

"Any of you care to comment about Jennifer's print?" Jewell-Anne's dark eyes roll over each person in the room. "Well, I'm not at all surprised." She smirks at the class. "With a print like this, it's hard to know where to begin. The eye is simply assaulted." Jewell-Anne glows with jack-o-lantern ecstasy. "This type of thing is what I call a 'Three A.M. Special' because unprepared students often attempt prints like this late at night when images that make sense are hard to come by."

Clutching her seat, Jenny presses down a finger for each day she has worked on her print. Eleven. Jewell-Anne has seen her, in this studio, struggling with this Seder for eleven days.

"The only thing that is clear is the title." Jewell-Anne drags her finger across the word. 'Seder.' "Now anyone familiar with the art of the past cannot help but recall other works with similar themes. By this I mean the Last Supper, the text-book illustrations in Bible School, and the covers of old fashioned cookbooks. Jennifer's particularly trite restatement measures up to none of these forebears." Beyond glee, Jewell-Anne's smile, like a Moonie's, has the brilliant impenetrability of a fence made of diamonds.

"Excuse me." Daphne Cyr raises her hand. "I have a question." Black hairs spring from her armpit. "You sound as if there are okay subjects and not okay subjects." Daphne's eyes are gray blue as bruises. "Are you saying that a picture of a Seder is taboo?"

"Of course, I don't just mean Seders, but Christmas, Thanksgiving, Birthdays, any time figures around a table are supposed to suggest a sort of smug contentment." Picking up her cross, Jewell Anne scratches it along its chain, back and forth. "Inferior artists are for some reason, often attracted to this type of subject. Your Norman Rockwells and other greeting card illustrators, for example. I personally do not think a Seder, in representational form, is a promising subject. But, from the point of view of pure craftsmanship, I cannot help but admire Rockwell's work, sentimental though it may be. But here, I'm confronted with a mess. A picture that has no idea what it wants to be."

Jenny's Seder is a blur.

"So far as I can tell—" Jewell-Anne squints at it. "—there is no reason for a single element in this design. Colors are juxtaposed without regard to their interaction. It's almost as if the person who made this print doesn't care all that much for her own subject. Not that I blame Jennifer for that. If, in fact, such a scene existed in real life, I feel sorry for the people involved."

Waldo's sharp, pointy hand darts in the air like a bat's wing.

"Are you sure these are artistic judgments you're making, Jewell-Anne?" he asks. "What you're saying sounds pretty personal to me."

160

First Daphne, now Waldo, Jenny has friends here. Letting go of her seat, she folds her hands in her lap. Her fingers ache. She had not realized how hard she was holding on. Nine-thirty. This cannot go on much longer if Priscilla is to have her turn.

"I am talking exclusively in terms of art," Jewell-Anne says. "Art is an illusion, based on the skilled understanding of techniques. In the medium of silk-screen printing, this means that the drawing is the basis for the finished work. A bad drawing cannot be trans-formed into a good, or even legible print as Jenny's attempt clearly demonstrates."

"I don't know." Georgette shakes her huge, pale, gentle head slowly, from side to side. "I really like that see-through yellow for the light from the candles and the moon."

"But Georgette, if you were looking at a well-composed piece, instead of picking things out, you'd see a whole," Jewell-Anne insists. "This print has no integrity. Instead of being guided inevitably from dominant to subordinate, the eye is left to pick elements. The viewer confronting a picture like this would get more satisfaction looking out a window."

A damp brown darkness stops at the glass. In here, harsh light beats, it beats down.

"Sometimes, even the tritest composition has a fine detail," Jewell-Anne says. "Not this one. Hands like lobster claws. Heads like pears. A raucous ground that crowds the figures. A bone, for some peculiar reason, in the middle of what I take to be a table. With so much emphasis on details, the two circles of light appear almost accidental, as indeed, does the entire composition. Nothing is bal-anced. The table is not centered but appears haphazardly placed. There are spots where there is too much ink. There are spaces where there is insufficient ink. The registration is poor. The color choices are poor." Jewell-Anne's finger stabs at Jenny's work. "The figures are anatomically primitive, but without the absolute regularity that makes primitives appealing. Nor is there logical abstraction here. Nothing about these particular wine glasses, or any of the other forms, justifies a viewer's attention." She has started her recap.

Jenny leans back against the table behind her. Rain, drooling down the windows, makes outside a moiré frame for the images in this room. Jewell-Anne is the evil fairy who comes to the christening. She is Cinderella's ugly stepsister in the version where birds fly down and peck out the stepsisters' eyes. Jenny's lips twitch up at the corners. Luckily, she needs no birds to help her. After all, she is a bulldog's daughter. Jenny knows what to do when under attack. Stripped of fear, defenses in place, she waits.

"Someone with a watch," Jewell-Anne is saying, "isn't it about time for the break?"

"It's quarter past ten." Jenny's voice wafts calm and clear from her mouth.

"Let's stop then until ten-thirty." Jewell-Anne plops down off her stool. "Unless, Jennifer, you have any questions."

"Not a one," Jenny says.

"Jewell-Anne, you want anything from the snack bar?" Priscilla asks.

"We have time," Jewell-Anne says. "Let's just scoot on over there together."

Standing up, Jenny moves with slow ease. As if she were swimming, she makes her way to the bathroom. She hides out. She combs her hair. She walks back to the studio. She sits down in her usual seat.

"Do not pay one single grain of attention to anything that woman says." Waldo's face is wavery, as if Jenny is looking up at it from under water. "When you're dealing with first time, adjunct faculty there's no telling what you'll get." He returns to his seat.

Jewell-Anne is back. She is on her stool sipping coffee. Priscilla sits at her work table. She is sipping coffee too.

Jenny does the dead man's float.

"As you can see right away, this print does not assault the eye." Jewell-Anne begins. "This is not a 'Three A.M. Special.' This artist has taken the trouble to formulate a design that makes sense. Priscilla draws the viewer in with curved lines that are truly pleasing." Over the rim of her styrofoam cup, Jewell-Anne stares at Jenny.

Jenny stares back. Fixedly. As if she were waiting in the Hartford Hospital Emergency Room for one of her children to be stitched up while, instead of an overhead TV blaring a "Price is Right," Jewell-Anne keeps urging her studio audience to pick True, not False.

"Any comments?"

"I like Priscilla's fatally flawed, perfect egg shape conceptually." Jenny's voice floats—a ribbon—from her mouth as, being fair, she glides like a hawk above the people in this room.

"Might as well compare grits and gravy to a light bulb as to contrast these two prints," Waldo says. "Depends whether you want to eat or read."

"Never mind. We have two serigraphs here," Jewell-Anne says, "and this one has none of the soda pop dots that make poor screen cleaning obvious in the other one. In fact, nothing in this work could be improved on." She glows at her darling. "What you going to do for us next, Priscilla?"

"I never want to see another bowl of corn chowder as long as I live." Removing his meal from his tray, Waldo settles in at the lunch table.

"Chowder's better than rice medley," Daphne says.

"Back home we feed our hogs corn," Waldo says. "The humans get meat."

"Corn's probably healthier." Jenny speaks to reassure them, and herself, that she is not dead.

"I don't believe that for an instant," Waldo says.

"Can I join you guys?" Georgette asks.

"Sure." Daphne slides over.

Holding her tray over Jenny's head, Priscilla pauses at her classmates' table. "I just can't believe how lucky I was. That Jewell-Anne really inspires me."

"Me too, but I'm not sure to do what," Georgette says. "I'm down to my last two tranks."

"I hate to add to your sorrows, but rice medley is on the menu for tonight," Daphne says.

"That's it." Waldo shoves back, his pointy little hands hooked, like two guns, over his white plastic belt. "There's only so much I can take." He glares up at Priscilla.

"You're positively menacing, Waldo." Turning from him, she heads for Jewell-Anne.

"This morning was brutal," Georgette says.

"It may have been worse to see than to be." Jenny pushes herself up, out of her chair. Her Novocaine is wearing off, she is starting to ache.

"Why don't we all get out of here later?" Waldo asks.

"I think we should all take Jenny out," Daphne says, "for her birthday."

"Love it." Jenny slips away from them, between other tables to the coat hooks.

"Seven in the dorm lobby?" Daphne calls after her.

"Fine." No need for Jenny to button the raincape around her neck. Steam is rising from the sidewalk, the world, a Japanese print, still gorgeous.

Jenny lugs herself up the hill, into the dorm, up the stairs, down the hall, into her room. Locking the door, she plunges face down on the thin, delicious, lumpy comfort of her own iron bed. And she sobs.

And she sobs.

And she sobs.

Until she cannot squeeze out one more drop.

Jewell-Anne Drayton could be right. No one may ever want to look at, much less buy, a single piece of Jennifer's work. But unless she goes on making images, Jenny will never get to see the ones that interest her. She will never figure out what they are about. She will never understand those figures, huddled around their Seder-symbols, looking for clues to their destiny.

A cracked egg. Yes, Priscilla's work is competent. Typical. Fifty-seventh street. Jenny is maybe Broome Street, maybe the Matrix Gallery at the Athenaeum. Or maybe just a secret place only she, and a few friends, will get to see.

"You okay in there?" Georgette rumbles at the door.

"Yes," Jenny says, "I'm fine." She kicks off her sneakers, crawls under her blanket, licks at her mucus, and curls into sleep.

"Jenny?" Daphne is knocking.

"Yes?"

"Your husband's on the phone."

"Tell him I'll be right there." A tight veil of dried tears sticks to Jenny's cheeks.

"Will you be ready to go out for dinner at seven?" Daphne calls in. "We're meeting in the front hall."

"What time is it now?" Shadows lie like downed curtains across Jenny's floor.

"Quarter of."

"I'll be ready." Leaping up, Jenny splashes her cheeks with 'Youth Dew.' She tosses aside her skirt, yanks off her shirt, drops her long, rust cotton dress over her head, stuffs her feet into sandals, ties her sash, and fluffs her hair. Hoping that wherever they go they run in to Jewell-Anne, Jenny skips out and downstairs.

"Hi." She pants into the receiver.

"Sounds like I took you away from something," Saul says.

"That's okay. What's up?"

"I just wanted to wish you a happy birthday." Saul's voice is forlorn.

"You did that yesterday." His sadness smacks Jenny like an accusation. "I adore the kimono." How much she owes this man!

"How'd your class go today?" he asks.

"Not very well. Jewell-Anne hated my Seder print."

"That's too bad." Saul does not sound upset.

"First she said it was an assault to her eyes." Jenny wants him to know how awful it was. "Then she said it didn't have a single element worth looking at and if anyone liked anything in it, it was because they didn't want to see it as a whole and should look out the window. Then Jewell-Anne said Priscilla Twitchell, who does the teacher's pet routine to the hilt, had made a print that didn't assault the eyes. In fact, Priscilla's work was perfect in exactly the way mine wasn't." Jenny relaxes her hold on the receiver. As long as she is suffering, it is okay if she left her husband to come here.

"What else has been going on?" he asks.

Outside the booth's glass door Jenny's friends are waiting to comfort her after what she has been through. Waldo has on her favorite lavender shirt and sock combination. Orange elephants, linked trunk to tail, circle Georgette's hips. Daphne gazes at Jenny, her eyes soft as pansies.

"I have to go now." Jenny has a life now that does not include her husband.

"You want to talk to Iris?" Saul asks.

"Briefly." Jenny's new life has no room in it for a lover. Covering the receiver, she leans out the door. "Be right with you. Save me some of that." She points at the joint in Georgette's hand.

"Happy birthday, Jennifer," Iris is saying.

"Thanks." Jenny wonders what Iris and Saul are doing together. Maybe it is not marriage that is the problem, but coupling of any kind. Maybe Jenny is better off on her own.

"They teaching you anything up there?" Iris asks.

"Quite a lot, actually." Today Jenny learned she is a hard-core artist. "I never realized it, but I'm pretty tough." She touched for the first time her own resilience, not quite the fountain of youth, but as close as a person can get. And for this Jenny has Jewell-Anne Drayton to thank. Jerking her head back, Jenny laughs.

"I could have told you that," Iris says. "And I'm sure Saul also knows how tough you are. Here." She giggles. "I'll put him back on."

Iris and Saul want Jenny to know they are up to something. When she gets home, she will have to straighten this all out. While she is here, they can do what they want. Opening the door, Jenny waves her purse and nods. She is with her colleagues now.

"What's this I'm supposed to know?"

"Not a thing," Jenny says. "But listen, Saul, I do miss you." A lie except for sexually. "And I love you." The truth. "Tell Iris I love her too." Easy to do at a distance, and useful for reminding Saul, Jenny is not ever again going to be just his wife.

They both hang up.

"How does shellfish strike you?" Waldo favors Jenny with an unmistakably lustful grin.

"Great," Jenny says, "I love it." If she wants to she can always find someone likable to sleep in her bed. But there is no rule. If she wants to, Jenny can revert to her normal sexual reticence now that she knows exactly what it is she would be missing.

"I groove on steamed clams." Georgette passes Jenny the joint. "With garlic bread. And white wine."

"Mmn." Taking a hit, Jenny passes to Daphne.

"None for me. I'm driving."

"Excellent." Jenny sucks at the dope.

Now Saul and Iris shrink into distance. Waldo takes Jenny's arm. She smells whiskey on his breath, out of his skin, as if, in Providence, they are all together on a great tide of marijuana, whiskey, white wine, and human decency. And, with Jewell-Anne's splintered bottle fresh on her prow, Jenny slides serenely out to sea.

Chapter XIV

LOSING WEIGHT
• *September* •

After summer school, Jenny's house is a garden of possibilities. Images bombard her in Esther's room. Shells. Some people save only perfect specimens. But Jenny and her daughter always bring home from the beach shiny chips, smoothed mustard chunks, bony spirals, scallop fans chipped like country teeth to strew on bureaus, window sills, radiators, desks, as if their collections were washed up by ocean waves. As if Jenny, or her daughter, could keep the sea.

Or imprison it in paper. Taking her scrap bag off the bed, Jenny sets aside the bolt of purple velvet she has not yet figured out how to use, and pulls out strips of furry cloth, wool tweed, a plastic net onion bag, a slat broken from an orange crate. According to Minnie Mouse, twitching her gloves on the walls, Jenny has two hours.

That should be more than enough time for her first collagraphy assignment. Jenny is to hand print, using one particular texture, until she thinks of a use for the figures that result.

Crawling under the old ping-pong table she and Saul set up in here, she scurries to the bathroom for water. She stops in her room to take the phone off the hook. She hisses the cat out of Esther's room, and closes the door. Orange. Jenny will print suns.

She pours tempera into two paper cups, adding water to one, leaving the other thick. She will start with the net bag. He said the materials need not be absorbent. Bunched, plastic net will print one way, flat another. Jenny flips to the first page of her newsprint pad. She squeezes the net, dips it in paint, and dabs, producing a splotch. A dotted splotch.

She prints another, full strength. And another, diluted. She holds the fabric perfectly still, punching the paper as if she were the press she will eventually use. Presses do not twist. Jenny tries twisting.

Now her splotches have tendrils. Maybe she could print by hand. Moving across the paper, these blurs remind her of underwater plants, wavering in a current. Not that anyone else would look at them like that. Jenny tears off the page.

She goes back to untwisted spots. Gauzy stars. Snowflakes. Her fireworks, after all? Too dull. Yet these marks are something she has seen in her dream of real life. Rip.

Jenny does a page of isolated spots. Rip. A page of clumped spots. Rip. She makes spots the perimeter of a square. Rip. A triangle. Rip. She makes an ess out of spots for Saul, or Snake. Rip. She does a spot cluster, smearing down a line like the stem of a flower. Rip. Page after page, Jenny colors and rips, looking for shapes that belong to her.

Shaking off excess paint, she presses bunched spots in a circle. Rip. In a line. Rip. She tries random spots. Rip. With her eyes closed. Rip. Monotones. Rip. Dark and light. Rip. She pours colors into a line of paper cups and tries multicolor spots. Rip. Two colors. Rip. Three colors diluted, the poured areas like stained cells that will grow into something. But what?

The back doorbell rings.

Jenny looks to Minnie. After eleven. Jenny has been in here more than an hour; it feels like fifteen minutes. In forty-five minutes Saul will be home.

The bell rings again.

Meter readers give up after one ring, U.P.S. after two. Whoever this is must know she is in here. Probably collecting for cancer, leaning on the bell.

Let whoever it is lean. Jenny has not yet tried pressing the net printer flat. If she ends up using this stuff in her collage, flat will be easiest. Probably print out a grid. She drops the plastic scrap into a cup of blue paint.

Whoever is at the door keeps ringing as if this call is serious.

Papers slither off the bed, over the edge of the table as, dropping down, Jenny crawls to the door. In the hall she stretches, noticing for the first time that her back is stiff. Switching positions feels wonderful. And now she will know, even if she does not answer the door, who is out there, persisting.

168

Luke's room stinks from the dirty laundry scattered, like tomato-worm droppings, on the floor. Jenny tramples sweat pants, a sneaker, French vocabulary cards, her son's debris not unlike the mess his mother just left. From his window, Jenny sees a green beetle sniffing at the driveway. Iris's car.

The bell shrieks.

"Coming. I'm coming." Jenny hurtles down, furious. Avon ladies, Jehovah's Witnesses, these she can ignore. But love gives people power over her.

"What took you?" Iris has on her painter pants and a purple shirt instead of her going-to-work clothes.

"I was upstairs." Jenny jerks up the screen door hook. "Working on my collagraphy assignment." The hook dangles like her hopes. It took Jenny years to train Saul and the children not to interrupt her at work. Jenny does not have enough years left to train Iris.

Iris is coming in.

"You haven't gotten out today yet?" Iris folds herself around Jenny.

Jenny stands inert. For her this is not body time, not vacation.

"No." At summer school, alone, Jenny was all work. At home, with husband and lover, she is supposed to be all love. But Jenny is sick of adultery, sick of giving to love her days and nights.

"It's too fine to hang out here." Iris tosses her green knapsack on the table. "Let's picnic."

"I've got to finish my assignment," Jenny says.

"You can do that later." Opening the refrigerator, Iris lifts out the orange juice. "Want some?"

"No thanks." Jenny seethes. She was the one who told Iris to make herself at home here. Iris is the orphan who never had a family. Jenny should be glad Iris feels free to drink her juice. Yet Jenny wants Iris out. "Finish that up. I can get more." Jenny tries to cover up her selfishness.

"I thought we could go to Campbell's falls." Iris tosses back the last of the juice. Now Jenny will have to market. "We'll have it all to ourselves. We can swim without suits."

"I can't. I've got a drawing class this afternoon." With a model who, unlike Jenny, does not mind displaying her naked body. "How come you're not at work?"

"I went in Sunday so they gave me today off."

"Oh that's right." Jenny blushes. Sunday, tramping the Metacomet Trail with Saul and Luke, she did not miss Iris.

"I thought today, you and I could have a blast," Iris says.

"I wish," Jenny says. "Another time."

"When? I work during the week. Saul's got you weekends."

"Maybe I could stay over at your place Wednesday or Thursday night." Staring down at orange paint lining her cuticles, Jenny remembers wanting to be wanted. But she had planned to work on Saul's teaching nights. Jenny had planned to work all morning. Lifting her eyes, she collides with Iris's face. "How about some coffee?" Jenny strikes a match and lights a fire under the kettle.

"My period's due Wednesday." Iris flings herself into a chair. "I won't be in the mood to entertain. You better cut your class today." Jenny better or else?

"No. I really can't." Jenny hears her deliverer, the mailman. "Excuse me." In college, she cut classes, spent days drinking coffee, got away with as much as she could. But in art school, the teachers are saying things Jenny needs to know. She shuffles through the pack of mail, pulling out a card from Waldo.

The Big Apple is ready for me at last. O.K.Harris let me leave my slides with them. Can world fame be far, behind?
                                                              xx's
                                                              Waldo

Jenny chuckles, seeing Waldo in his pastel double-knits. She likes the man. And she likes the idea of someone in her league making it.

She goes back into the kitchen.

"A friend of mine just got slides accepted by a really important New York Gallery." Scooping instant and pouring boiling water, Jenny wonders if Waldo would interrupt his work to fix coffee for a friend. "He'll probably get a show there."

"If you intend to make it in the art world, you really should get out in the country to sketch on a day like today." Iris turns to Jenny glasses clouded over with steam.

"Please, stop telling me what to do." Jenny's heart races. Her lover, she now sees, looks like a mole. "If you'll just excuse me, I'd like to do a little more work on my assignment before lunch."

"Don't be so touchy." Iris pulls off her glasses, smearing the lenses with the end of her braid. "I can't help it if I don't understand what you're up to." Her naked eyes stare, dull and stunned as a starving child's. "Can you explain?"

Jenny flinches. She has no right to take time away from a needy Iris to do work that may never be any good. Jenny's mission is to make Iris happy. Instead, she feels Iris pulling her into her

170

perpetual discontent when the only solid Jenny has to hold onto is her work.

"I'm not sure there is an explanation." Jenny can only talk about techniques. "I'm just at the first stage. Eventually, I'll make a collage I can use to print with."

"If I were you, I'd stick with making plain collages." Now it is Iris who is trying to limit Jenny just as Saul used to do.

"I want to try something new." As long as Jenny is here, at home, they will all see her as a housewife. No matter how bad her gallery job was, going out to work put her in a higher category.

"That's crazy," Iris says. "A few of your collages were quite good. Why don't you work on them and become Queen of Collage?"

"That's not what I want to do right now." Jenny may be afraid of success. Her collages were starting to sell. Iris may be right. Oh how Jenny hates the woman!

"You have no idea what you want." Iris's skin has the color and greasy sheen of stale swiss cheese.

The thought appalls Jenny. Poor Iris. She needs a mother who loves her. Jenny prides herself on being a great mother. It is not collages that should engage her, but Iris.

"That's just the trouble," she says. "But I figure if I take enough courses, something better will occur to me." Jenny's dissatisfaction with Saul may have had nothing to do with his being a man, may have had nothing to do with Saul at all. After that first delicious shock of new skin, sex with Iris lost its luster. There has been, for Jenny, only sporadic ecstasy in lovemaking these past weeks, more often with Saul than with Iris, his body as shockingly delicious, after the summer school absence, as Iris's ever was.

"I think you'd be better off forgetting about going to school," Iris says.

"It's too late." Fear drops over Jenny, clinging to her like a web. Iris could be right. Jenny should devote herself to loving others. "But I already paid my tuition for the semester."

"Maybe you can get them to give it back," Iris says. "Get your doctor to write you an excuse."

"I'm not sure I want to," Jenny admits. She wants to learn to draw. She wants to learn the elements of good design. Jewell-Anne Drayton was right about the need for her to do that. And as for collagraphy and silk-screen printing, Jenny wants to know as many ways to make art as she can. "Even assuming I could." Her eyes flick over the kitchen clock. Quarter to twelve. In fifteen minutes, Saul will be home for lunch. Jenny just has time to go up and cover her paints. She might, after lunch, get in another hour before class.

"A day off would give you greater perspective on what you're doing," Iris is saying, "and perspective is something you obviously need."

"I'm sorry." Jenny must get back to her orange paint. "Not today." Her colors have more to tell her. "But you're welcome to stay here and have lunch."

"Why is it I feel like I'm being offered crumbs from your table?"

"I don't know." In truth, crumbs are all Jenny wants to part with right now. But if Iris will be patient—."Saul will be here." Maybe that will hold her.

"A triangle wasn't exactly what I had in mind for today." Pointing her tongue, Iris slides it around her lips.

"Sorry about that." Jenny frowns. Saul will be here any minute. She wants him to know that this morning, she worked. She wants to discuss with him possible meanings for her blotches. She is finished making Saul jealous, finished looking for what to be. Not a dedicated lesbian, Jenny is an artist. Can't Iris understand that?

"You know this whole thing is getting to be a drag." Flinging a hand onto her knapsack, Iris shoots up. "I think I deserve better."

"I know you do." But Jenny was already married when Iris took up with her.

"You're just not a real lot of fun," Iris says.

"I'm sorry," Jenny says.

"I need a lover who's a little more available," Iris says.

"I know you do." Tears rush into Jenny's eyes. She had so hoped to transform Iris into a joyous woman.

"A lover who's a little more attuned to what I need," Iris says.

"If you could just wait till Wednesday night," Jenny says.

Iris barks out a laugh. "And then, after that, how long will I have to wait? Till mid-semester break?"

"Let's not make this worse than it is," Jenny says.

"You would know it couldn't get any worse if you had any idea how I feel," Iris says. "I was looking forward to today."

"I'm trying. I do love you, you know." Arms out, Jenny glides toward Iris. "I didn't know the picnic meant so much to you."

"Forget it." Iris twists her knapsack, as if it were Jenny's inadequacy, between them. "Just forget the whole fucking thing." She sniffs. "I don't even feel like being with you now." Iris smacks her eyes into Jenny's. "You've ruined my whole day." Iris stands in the middle of Jenny's morning which lies, shattered, around them both. "I'm splitting. For good." Her eyes press hard against Jenny's, stone on stone. Iris means this. "I need a lover who enhances me, not a woman who makes me feel like I'm in her fucking way." If Jenny does not yield up her hours on demand, their connection is broken, ended as of today.

"So be it." Jenny is equally resolved. She wants a friend, not a blackmailer.

"You had your chance, Jennifer." Iris swings toward the door. "And you blew it." The screen closes between them.

Jenny stands, watching the bus that carried her here, to this new place, pull irrevocably away. Not even a whimper. More like pounds dropping off, Jenny's weekdays miraculously, marvelously open up to her. Lesbian. Bi-sexual. The labels turn out to mean nothing. Love is always possible. And so is adultery. But if Jenny is unfaithful, she cannot blame nature. With nervous relief, Jenny hears Iris's car door swat.

In five minutes, Saul will be home. Jenny grabs a roll of plastic wrap and races upstairs as if, instead of Iris, she is in love now with the splotched papers strewn around Esther's room. And, as always, love makes its demands.

Snatching at the newsprint, Jenny slaps it, page by page, into a pile on the bed. She yanks patches off the roll of plastic wrap, and stretches their pure light over her cups of color. Once again, she may have let the sea slip through her fingers, but this time Jenny has salvaged this spattered newsprint, heaped on her daughter's bed, like kelp in the sand.

Chapter XV

REVERSAL

• *November* •

Cut from her lover, Jenny still has no time for art. The hell with art. Jenny has more important work to do now. She drives, as she has been driving regularly for the last six weeks, from Hartford to White Plains, from her house in Connecticut to the Burke Rehabilitation Center in New York, as if the White Plains turnoff that takes her past Bloomingdale's and Saks—the stores she grew up with—is her route to home.

Jenny slows, easing the car over the first welt in the Burke driveway, the second, third, her last bump into the past. Here, she is Anna's little girl. Parking the car, Jenny checks herself in the mirror. ("Why are you the only one with messy hair?" her mother used to ask when she came to school.) Jenny combs her hair, smoothes on lipstick, takes a deep breath, and leaves the car, striding into the lobby as if she belongs here.

The guard, who usually stops her when she is early, is watching a maintenance man wax a floor already shiny as black ice. "CAUTION," the signs on sawhorses read. Jenny streaks past the signs to the stairs.

By the time the heavy fire door clicks shut behind her, she is up half a flight. Visiters are not allowed for another hour but her mother will be waiting.

Pushing the door, Jenny bursts into a flock of wheel chairs. "Hello." Anna's illness has taught her daughter to make eye contact with seated people.

"She's doing pretty good today, your mom." Eileen's white crested head sinks like a friendly vulture's between her shoulders. "She took a few steps."

"That's terrific." Jenny's knees wobble. The doctor has been saying her mother could walk, but up to now, Anna has not.

"They'd of had her do more but she said she was too tired. I told her, I says, 'It's good for you to get tired,' but you know your mom. She don't listen."

"How'd you make out today, Eileen?" Jenny asks.

"Halfway down the hall and back."

"Great." Jenny squeezes Eileen's bony shoulder and strides on, around the corner.

"Your mother's starting to get somewhere." Hy, who had his stroke the same day as Anna, with the same left side involvement, is already hobbling with a four-pronged cane. "She took a couple of steps."

"So I hear." Jenny rushes toward the nurses' station where her mother sits, waiting in her wheel chair, her brown eyes open and unmoving, her platinum hair fanning out from its white roots like the gold halo of a Byzantine Saint.

"You look positively ethereal." Kissing her mother's soft cheek, Jenny's lips remember sucking at Anna's breast.

"Really?" Anna's face collapses like a rubber mask. "I can't stand to look at myself in a mirror." Tears gush from her eyes, her mouth. "In just six weeks, I've turned into an old woman."

"Could be worse." Grabbing the wheel chair handles, Jenny steers for the elevator. "Only the dead are forever young." She jabs the words at her mother. Anna devoted her whole life to her husband and children. Now she must be paid back. "I hear you did very well today."

"It was terribly hard."

"But worth it," Jenny says.

"Easy for you to say."

"Don't you want to walk" Jenny asks.

"I don't know." Anna resists having to relearn what she once knew. "It's very hard."

"If you keep working at it, it will get easier and easier." Jenny pushes her mother as her mother used to push her.

"Make her wheel her own chair." Ahead of them, Hy looks back. "It's good exercise."

"He takes quite an interest in my progress." Anna motions for Jenny to come close. "Tell you the truth, I think Hy's sweet on me." A tiny smile cracks her marble face.

"Why not? You're very lovable. And listen, Hy can teach you a lot." Jenny wishes her mother were more like him. "You're not doing nearly as well as he is."

"He's not so great," Anna says. "There's no comparison between him and your father."

"Then why are you comparing them?" Jenny wishes her mother would stop measuring everyone against someone else, Jenny against her sister, Jenny's father against Saul. "I'm done pushing." done measuring her mother against Hy.

"Your father's the greatest." Anna shoves her chair forward. "Some smart dame will grab him if I don't get out of this place soon."

"Work hard so they'll spring you," Jenny says.

"Simon's been marvelous to me since this happened," Anna says.

"What did you expect?" Jenny's father has been a little too marvelous, taking over for her mother. It may not be coincidence that this, the first time Simon has stayed away overnight, is also the first day Anna walked. "Did you think he'd desert you?"

"I don't know." Stopping, Anna hauls the useless hand up over the side of the chair, dumping it like a dead fish across her lap. "Your father just can't seem to do enough for me."

"Maybe, right now, that's not so good for you."

"Simon's a wonderful guy," Anna says.

"That's not the point."

"No one could be more devoted than he is." Anna insists as if she needs to convince someone.

"What about you?" And Jenny who has devoted the last six weeks entirely to her mother? "Wouldn't you do whatever you could for Simon if the situation was reversed."

"God forbid. Of course I would. But men are different. I never knew before how your father loves me." Anna is again sobbing.

"Would he love you any less if you did for yourself?" Jenny tastes salt in her own mouth. For a while, Saul did love her less.

"Whatever I do, my husband is the most brilliant, the most wonderful—" Grief dissolves Anna's voice.

"Why does Simon's wonderfulness, his brilliance, make you cry?" Jenny asks.

"The doctor says my crying's a symptom." Anna now carries a towel for her tears. "All I know is, since this happened, Simon's been a god-send." But the godsend has not restored her to health. "Nothing is too much for him." Anna is bawling.

"Simon could probably use help. How about it, Anna?" Jenny asks.

"I'm trying." Snuffling, Anna droops over the left arm that lies, sweet and flaccid as a sleeping baby, across her thighs. "But you have no idea how tired I am."

"We'll just stay here until you feel rested." Jenny leans against the wall.

"You know, you're a real Simon Legree." Wearily, Anna again shoves at her chair wheel.

"You're doing great work." Jenny wraps her fingers around a railing on the wall. Her mother is not a doll to be pushed proudly in her carriage. Jenny must stand still while Anna slaps at the wheel and moves inch by inch down the hall.

"I'm trying." Grabbing the wall railing, Anna speeds up by pulling the chair.

"You're succeeding." Jenny lets out her breath. "So, how'd it feel to walk on your own two feet?" More exciting to Jenny than any of her children's first steps.

"It was absolutely exhausting," Anna says.

"Where is it written that it should be easy?" Reaching the elevator, Jenny lunges at the button.

"How come you didn't make me do that?" Anna's brown eyes brighten. "You starting to take pity on your poor old mother?"

"You wish." Next time, Jenny must control her need to get this over with.

The elevator doors ooze open.

"The therapist says I'm supposed to turn the chair around and go in backwards." Facing the elevator, Anna looks bewildered.

"Sounds like a good system." Jenny goes in and switches to HOLD.

"Hy told me to use my good foot."

"Then why don't you?" Jenny props herself in the corner.

"All right." Sighing, Anna kicks at the floor and backs the wheel chair into a wall.

"Take your time." Pinning her hands under her arms, Jenny remembers the good old days when she was stuck in the elevator with Luke and Aaron. Then she could sketch.

"This is harder than you think." Anna angles the chair toward the doorway.

"False. It's hard for me not to help you."

"I don't think I can manage it." Sagging, Anna stops at the threshold.

"Take a rest." Jenny clamps her arms tight, over her hands.

"You have no mercy." Anna kicks herself in.

"I'm saving it for when you really need mercy." Releasing HOLD, Jenny presses two and the box begins its descent, sinking very, very, slowly, as if everyone here has time, time, and more time, but this elevator is only for patients and their companions, only for them the new, dragging pace. The able-bodied run up and down stairs.

"Please, will you push me into the dining room?" Anna begs Jenny.

"For special." A treat Jenny will give to herself.

The elevator doors slowly, slowly open.

"Surprise!" Jenny's sister Barbara stands arm in arm with Anna's friend Ida Polovy. "We came to join you for supper."

But last night was Barbara's night. Tonight, Jenny was supposed to have her mother to herself.

"So how are you, sweetie lamb?" Barbara bounces a kiss off the top of Anna's head.

"The same." Only Anna's lips move.

"You look radiant, darling." Ida's lips glance off her friend's cheek like a butterfly off stone, and Ida stands back to assess. "What an improvement in just the week since I last saw you!"

"You really think so?" Anna's eyes plead.

"Cross my heart. I can't wait to go home and tell Oscar." Ida and Oscar have an apartment in Anna and Simon's Florida building. "He'll be thrilled." They also have a house in Scarsdale. "So tell me, what progress have you made, darling?"

"They had me walk today," Anna says.

"You mean you walked by yourself," Jenny says.

"I couldn't have moved an inch without the therapist telling me what to do," her mother says.

"Anna darling, the important thing is that this proves you can walk. *Mazel tov.*" Clapping her hands, Ida flashes from her wrist the gold profiles of grandchildren.

"That's right, that's right." Barbara beams.

"It was only four steps," Anna says.

"Four steps is absolutely fantastic." Barbara hoppity skips a four beat dance. "Absolutely fantastic." Something—pits probably—in her pocket knocks like distant castanets.

Jenny grins. She is not the only one responsible for her mother. Her sister lives close by.

"What a perfect homecoming present for father!" Barbara says.

"I don't know if I can do it again," Anna says. "I had to think about every movement. I'm exhausted."

"So tonight you'll sleep." Drained as she is, Jenny is driving back to Hartford tonight. She will be in class tomorrow morning. What she can do, her mother can also do. "Tomorrow you'll walk twice as far as you did today."

"Yes, yes. All right." Anna sighs.

"Don't forget, I've seen what you can do," Jenny says. "I'm just pushing you now for special." Into the patients' dining room, through a thicket of wheel chairs and walkers, Jenny and her sister make way, smiling and saying hello to old patients and new, while Ida chats about the weather, and their mother faces dead ahead.

Parking Anna's chair at an empty table, Jenny sets the brake. "I'll get your dinner."

Jenny threads her way to a kitchen where swishing clinking dishwashers are run by black, shower-capped workers who, flirting and bantering with each other, swirl about.

"Is my mother's tray ready?" Jenny calls to them.

"Right cheer."

"Thank you." And not just for the food. The kitchen people remind Jenny there is health.

"What'd they give me?" Anna asks.

Barbara swoops the plastic dome off the tray.

"Broiled chicken with string beans, and rice, and a salad, and chocolate pudding. Looks great."

"Looks are deceiving," Anna says. "The food here is lousy." Snatching a drumstick, she tears at it with her teeth. "All dried out."

"Want me to get you a little mayonnaise?" Ida asks.

"Want me to cut up the rest for you?" Barbara asks.

"Do whatever you want." Anna slams down the naked bone. Her chin shines with grease.

Barbara and Jenny glance at each other. This animal is their mother. Jenny stares at the edge of her tray, how it curves dark on the underside.

"*Gott sei dank*, nothing's wrong with your appetite, Anna darling," Ida says.

"Open the milk for me, Barbara." Anna spews chicken flecks. "Your *shtunk* of a sister doesn't like to do anything for me."

"You might try saying please," Jenny says.

"What about a straw please? Please." Like a chimpanzee, Anna draws her lips back over her teeth.

179

"Here." Jenny hands her a straw. "You can take the paper off yourself."

"Good idea," Barbara says.

"Aw shit." Anna nips, spits, works paper with the fingers of her good hand, millimeter by millimeter, down the stiff, plastic tube.

When Jenny was little she could hardly wait to have veiny, competent hands like her mother's. Now, Jenny has those hands, and skin loose as Roman shades drapes her mother's knuckles. There may not be time for Jenny to save Anna's life. There may not be time left for Jenny to get good enough for a museum show before her bones too are shrouded.

Anna has peeled the straw.

"Good going," Jenny says.

"Want me and Ida to wait for you to get your dinner, Jen?" Barbara asks.

"No. I'll stay here. You go first."

"I'm starving." Barbara shoots to her feet.

Ida follows her into the cafeteria.

Anna sucks echoes from her milk carton.

"Try the salad," Jenny suggests.

"I don't feel like it." Anna smears her mouth with pudding.

Not even a child, Jenny's mother is an infant, and incorrigible.

"Slow down or you'll be done before I even begin." Jenny knows Anna will want to go back upstairs as soon as she is tired of eating.

"I wouldn't know how to make a pudding this lousy if I tried." Anna clanks her spoon into the empty dish.

"You've got chocolate there and there." Jenny points to her own nose and chin.

Lifting her napkin bib, Anna swipes at her face.

"The left corner of your mouth," Jenny says.

"So I won't be Miss America." The crumpled bib flutters like a beard under Anna's chin. She does not care. Her last bargain, a pink organza De la Renta peasant dress with price-tags dangling like fishing lures from its ruffled neck (two hundred marked down from four fifty), hangs on her closet door at home.

Jenny vows she will never give up the vanity that sustains her. She worries that she will lose her vanity just as her mother has.

"I'll tell you this much, I couldn't serve food at home for these prices." Barbara duplicated her mother's meal. "All this for two-fifty."

"Excellent value." Ida sets her bowl of soup and two saltines on a napkin placemat. "You go ahead, Jenny darling. Get your supper. I'll keep mother company."

"What about 'sister'?" Jenny asks. "Will you stay here with her too." Or is it only 'mother' who needs a baby sitter?

"Sister and I will both stay." Ida waves a hand, flashing talons, wine dark as fresh blood. "Go. Take your time."

Jenny wishes she could. On the other side of a wall, the cafeteria is heaven. Not one of the hospital workers sitting in booths or at tables in this room is crippled. Jenny grabs an egg salad sandwich, an orange, two cups of coffee. At least on the Disease-in-the-Family-Diet, she is losing weight. Returning to the patients' dining room, Jenny slides her tray onto the table and sits down.

"That's a very nice orange for this time of year," Ida says.

"Want it?" Jenny is sorry she was angry at her mother's friend. Visiting Anna here cannot be easy for her.

"No, you have it, dear," Ida says.

"I knew you'd take the egg salad," Barbara says. "My sister used to live on egg salad."

Chewing the soft bread, the mayonnaisey yolk and smooth chunky whites, Jenny's mouth remembers the egg salad sandwiches her mother used to make.

"I want to go up now." Anna slaps her napkin bib on her salad. She releases her brake.

"Let Jenny finish," Barbara says.

"Bring it up with you, Jenny." Shoving her chair back from the table, Anna heads for the doorway.

"Sit here with us for just another minute, darling," Ida says.

"I sat enough already." Anna keeps pushing.

"She gets like this." Jenny stands up. "Here, you take the orange home for Oscar, Ida. I really don't feel like it."

Like a salmon battling its way up a water-fall, Anna is heedlessly colliding with wheel chairs, knocking down walkers, beating her way out of this room while Barbara hurries after her, apologizing, righting aluminum cages.

"I'll tell Oscar it's a present from you." Ida concentrates on the orange.

"Good idea." Balancing her coffees, Jenny hurries after her mother and sister.

"Tell Barbara I've got her purse." Ida tidies their table.

"I'm bringing Aunt Pearl tomorrow night." Barbara steers Anna to the elevator.

"Ida's coming with your pocketbook," Jenny says.

"Push the up button," Anna says.

"I'll be back to see you again next week, Anna darling." Ida's lips leave a pink hive on her friend's cheek. "Okay?"

"Fine." Anna stares at the elevator doors. "What's taking so long?"

"They're here now, sugar." Barbara bobs down for a kiss. "See you tomorrow."

"Drive carefully." Anna stares at the elevator doors. They are opening.

Barbara and Ida hurry over to the stairs.

Anna wheels herself into the elevator. Jenny follows. Very slowly, the doors bump together to close.

Now Jenny has her mother all to herself.

"That was nice, having company at dinner," she says.

Anna stares at the light over the door.

"Slowest goddamn elevator I ever saw," she says.

"Absolutely," Jenny agrees. "But what's your rush?" Where are either of them going at this rate?

"I suppose." Anna shrugs.

In her room, a spotlight shines on a rubber sheet and paper diapers spread across the mattress. Bales of paper diapers stand in a shadowy corner. A withered chrysanthemum shivers on the radiator.

"Your plant needs water," Jenny says.

"I've got more important things on my mind right now." Anna stops her chair in front of the bathroom. "Ring for the nurse."

"What for?" Jenny looks up at the wall clock above the television. "It's only quarter-past-six." The nurse will not let Anna go to bed before seven-thirty.

"Never mind. Just ring."

"Do it yourself."

"I have to pee."

"I'll take you," Jenny says.

"I don't want you to take me." Anna sits up tall in her wheel chair.

"It's silly to bother a nurse when I'm here," Jenny says.

"Do what I tell you," Anna says.

"Do it yourself." Jenny sinks down on her mother's bed.

Anna presses the call button and wheels herself back in front of the bathroom.

"The nurse won't let you lie on the bed."

"I'll get up when she comes," Jenny says.

"Go see if she's on her way."

"You just rang."

"Just go out and look."

"Fine." The hall is empty except for Eileen who sits watching lights flash over the door in the room next to Hy's. Maybe someone in there is dying. It must happen in this place all the time.

"The nurses are all busy right now." Jenny rushes back to her mother. "Want me to take you?"

"No. I can wait."

"Whatever you say." Jenny pulls her sketch pad and a pencil out of her shopping bag. Sitting in a plastic arm chair, she flips to a blank page.

"Now what?" Anna asks.

"I'm sketching your chrysanthemum."

"I wish you'd get rid of the damn thing," Anna says.

"I like it." A few lines suggest the foil-wrapped pot. "Besides, I've got a drawing class tomorrow." Jenny uses the side of her pencil to make heavy strokes for the stalks, draws quick lines with the point for the string, tied around the plant like a fence. "I'm supposed to hand in something for a critique."

"Take my advice. Forget it," Anna says. "Stay home and take care of your husband."

"And when he goes out?" Jenny outlines petals, darkening the tips into a wild halo like her mother's. "You want me to devote the rest of my life to cleaning house?" The mum leaves hang down like useless arms. Jenny shades the withered curves. "I'm not into shopping."

"Saul should stay home more," Anna says.

"He has a job to go to."

"You sure that's all?" Anna's eyes gleam with sudden intelligence. "Is everything all right with you two?"

"It wasn't," Jenny admits, "but it is now." The day of the stroke, it was Saul who thought to ask Anna if she was thirsty, Saul who got her juice. Jenny just stood with her father, neither of them looking at Anna's twisted mouth, the staring eye, the dead side of her body, or the tongue, poking at her lips. Jenny blinks back tears. She will never forget Saul's kindness. "In fact, I'm crazy about Saul these days."

"All the more reason to stay home and take care of him."

"Not really. He manages all right without me." Jenny assumes he is with Luke, not Iris or Angela. There is no need now for either of them to have affairs. "I've rented a studio so, when you're better, I'll be going out to work every day." The day before the stroke, Jenny moved her ping-pong table, easel, paint brushes, scrap bag, bookcase, and coffee pot into a loft across the hall from Woman Space East. Now she rips the flower off her pad and sketches the clock on her mother's wall.

"I don't see why you can't work at home," Anna says.

"At home, I feel like a housewife," Jenny says.

"Is being a housewife so terrible?" Anna asks.

"Not if that's what you want to be." For Jenny, it is the easy way out. "But I want to be an artist."

"I thought I wanted to go back to teaching after you were born," Anna says.

"How come you didn't?"

"Your father didn't think it made sense," Anna says.

"Did you ever regret listening to him?" All her life, Jenny has wanted to talk to her mother as if she were a friend. Flipping the cover over, she puts away her drawing pad. "Would you have been happier if you had gone back to teaching?"

"Not really."

"Simon wouldn't have left you if you chose to do your own thing, you know," Jenny says. "He's always adored you."

"Maybe so." Anna shrugs. "But I thought it was better to stay home, raise you, keep an eye on him."

"What about after Barbara and I were grown up?" Jenny asks.

"Especially then," Anna says.

"What's the problem in here?" A Jamaican nurse blows into the room. "You have to empty your bladder again, Anna?"

"Yes."

"You're supposed to try to hold it in." The nurse clicks the call button off.

She should have made Anna do that.

"I can't," Anna says.

"The doctor says for you to try," the nurse says.

"But I can't," Anna whines.

"Well then, let's go." The nurse spins Jenny's mother into the bathroom.

If Jenny were in charge, Anna would have to do what the doctors say. Jenny sips nasty cold coffee, styrofoam clamped between her teeth. If she has to come here every day to make her mother do what she should do for herself, Jenny will never again have time for art.

The toilet flushes, sucking loud, sucking long.

Anna glides out of the bathroom.

"I'd like to go to bed now please, nurse." Anna wants only to sleep.

"It's much too early. But you can start undressing. I'll come back later to put you in." The nurse pulls a curtain in front of the door and disappears.

"Shiftless and lazy every last one of them," Anna mutters.

"Look who's talking." Jenny sighs. The stroke that took away so much of her mother left Anna's racism intact. And Jenny is this woman's daughter.

"The therapist says I can undress myself," Anna says.

"Then why don't you?" Jenny asks.

"I don't know." Slumped in her wheelchair, Anna makes no move. "Too much effort I guess."

"Nothing will get easier if you don't practice." Six thirty-five. If Anna goes to bed early, maybe Jenny can get out of here by seven. "Why don't you start?" Thinking of her own bed at home—she could possibly be in it by nine—Jenny aches.

"You don't know how hard it is." Anna unbuttons the top button of her blouse.

"You did that very well," Jenny says.

"Buttons aren't too bad." Anna is already on her third. "Pretty easy, in fact."

"Today buttons. Tomorrow the world." Jenny picks up a letter from Aaron. "What did my son have to say?"

"The usual." Anna opens the last button. "He hopes I'll get better soon. All that crap."

"You don't think Aaron hopes you'll get better soon?" Jenny wishes she could turn on the television, but that might distract her mother.

"I don't know." Her blouse gaping to the waist, Anna sits, finished.

"Keep going," Jenny snaps to ward off her mother's sadness, seeping into her. "What are you supposed to do next?"

"The therapist says the bad arm should always go into a sleeve first, and always come out of a sleeve first." Anna presses the sleeve down over her shoulder. "That means I should start with my left arm."

"So far, so good." Sweating, Jenny slips off her own jacket.

"This morning, the nurse who gave me my shower said I have the back of a young girl." Anna stops working, as if a smooth back is enough to carry her.

"Try grabbing the end of your sleeve," Jenny says.

"Give me a hand with it," Anna says.

"First, let's see if you can do it yourself."

"I'll never get this off without help."

"Never is a long time. Keep trying. It's only been ten minutes. Maybe you could try using your teeth."

"When the therapist is there to show me exactly what to do every step of the way, I can do it," Anna says. "But without her, I can't."

"Once you get it past the elbow, it will go easier." Jenny once saw Saul grasp an eel's skin with a pliers in order to tear it off. Then too, she wanted to cry out, 'Stop! Leave the damn thing be!'

"Everything is difficult for me now." Anna yanks. Her sleeve stretches. She lets go. The sleeve crawls back up. "I'll never get this thing past my elbow."

"The therapist says you can," Jenny reminds her.

"What does she know?" Anna pushes the sleeve past her elbow. "Now what?"

"Down over your hand, I presume." Seven o'clock. If that blouse is not off by seven-thirty, Jenny will help. "You're doing beautifully so far."

"There." Anna's arm sags out of the left sleeve. "You have no idea how exhausting this is."

"Wrong." Jenny needs more coffee. She has never been more tired in her life. "But keep going. Do the other sleeve."

"How?" Anna stares at the hand lying curved in her lap.

"Try the teeth," Jenny says.

"Some of these teeth aren't my own, you know." Anna bites at her cuff.

"They'll do in a pinch. Look. It's working." The sleeve inches down her mother's arm. Jenny bounces on the bed. "You're doing it. You're doing it. That's great. It's off. Forty-three minutes today, tomorrow thirty-five. Anna, in a week you'll have your blouse off in fifteen minutes." If Jenny is here to make her mother do it.

"You certainly don't expect me to take off this bra by myself, do you?" Anna is already pushing the left strap down over her shoulder. Maybe now she really will go on doing things for herself.

"Why not?" Jenny asks.

"I'm much too tired." But Anna is still pushing her strap down.

"Keep going. You're getting to be an expert," Jenny says. "After that one's over your shoulder, try unbuckling the right strap. That's it." Anna is picking at the buckle. "When that's open, you can pull the whole thing down, turn it around, and work on the hooks." Tomorrow, Jenny will bring her mother front-opening nursing bras. Jenny will cut her drawing class, drop out of art school, devote herself to her mother's independence.

"Don't you think I already did enough for today?" Anna pulls the cloth strap up, out of its metal frame. "I'm exhausted."

"What's going on here?" Flinging back the curtain, Simon bustles into the room. "Come here, *bebbela*." Yanking Anna's wheel chair toward him, he kisses the face she raises.

"How was the trip?" Anna slumps back, inert.

"Ach, the usual nuisance. People can't seem to get the smallest things right. I have to go over everything myself." He turns to Jenny. "So, how'd you make out here without me?"

"Fine," Jenny says. "Anna did a lot for herself."

"Don't you believe it." Anna's mouth twists. "I missed you every second of every minute of every hour of the day you were away."

"She's in the middle of undressing herself now," Jenny says. "The blouse took her forty-five minutes but she did it with no help at all."

"Here." Simon unhooks Anna's bra. "Let me give you a hand with that, *bebbela*."

"She's supposed to undress herself." All Jenny's work undone the minute her father gets here. "The therapist said."

"Ach therapist, shmerapist, what do they know? Nobody these days does anything right." Squeezing Anna's cheeks between his palms, Simon shakes her head. "What else can I do for you, *bebbela*?" He does not just call her little baby, he insists on it.

"Get me ready for bed." Anna commands him.

"It's bad to do these things for her even if she asks you to," Jenny says. "Anna's supposed to take off her own clothes. She'll never learn if you keep doing it."

"She will, she will." Tossing the bra in a drawer, Simon darts into the closet. "All in good time."

"The blue one." Anna makes no move to cover the breasts hanging like spent balloons in her lap.

Jenny's revulsion is tempered with pleasure. She is not the only one; her mother too has a body.

"Saul and the children are all right, I trust." Simon slips a blue nightgown over Anna's head.

"Fine," Jenny says.

"Ida was here and found me greatly improved," Anna says.

"Shows how much Ida knows." Simon eases the nightgown over Anna's arms. "When someone's already as gorgeous as you are, *bebbela*, there is no possibility for improvement. Tell your mother, Jenny." He smiles at her.

"Nobody's perfect." Jenny glares at him.

"Ida thought I looked much better," Anna says. "You notice any progress since you've been gone?"

"Only one day and you always look beautiful to me." Simon smoothes down her hair. "You're much too good for me."

"Nothing's too good for you. Nothing." Anna begins sobbing.

"Now stop that. Stop that." Simon thrusts a handkerchief at her.

"She walked today." Jenny wants him to know how much her mother can do without him.

"Four steps," Anna says," and the juice wasn't worth the squeeze." Tears shine like sweat on her cheeks.

"That's wonderful, *bebbela*, wonderful." Dropping to one knee, Simon slips off her shoes and socks.

"She's supposed to do that herself," Jenny says.

"You know what, darling?" Hoisting himself up off the floor, Simon juts his jaw out at Jenny. "It was awfully nice of you to come down to help out while I was away." He stands, a guard dog in front of his wife. "I appreciate it, and I'm sure your mother does too, but now, why don't you go home? Take care of your son, your husband. After all, you have a long drive ahead of you."

"Barbara was here too," Anna says, "but I wish you wouldn't leave me like that, Simon."

"So who's leaving you? I just got back." Simon checks through Anna's mail. "What did Harry have to say?"

"Not much," Anna says. "Please, darling, help me into bed."

"Right away, *bebbela*." Dropping the letters, Simon hurries over to Anna. He slaps up her foot rest. "Weight on the right side." He bends his back under her.

"She's not supposed to go to bed this early," Jenny says.

"If she's tired, she should rest."

"I guess I will leave." Jenny has proved her Mother can do things for herself, but Anna will not.

"When you coming to see me again, Legree?" Anna grins at Jenny over Simon's shoulder.

"Not for a while." Once, Jenny had to hate her parents in order to leave them. Now, she leaves them together with relief. "I have a ton of work to catch up on."

"That's fine. In a few weeks, I'll be taking your mother home." Simon eases Anna down onto the bed. "Why don't you wait and visit us there? I have an idea that once I get my *bebbela* home, she'll be all right."

"That would be nice." Jenny kisses her father's cheek, his

stubble rasping her lips. "Meanwhile, take it easy, Simon." Rolling up her chrysanthemum drawing, Jenny pokes it into her bag.

"Just give me a hand here with your mother before you go, please."

"Sure." Jenny moves to the opposite side of the bed.

"One—" Simon says, "two—three!"

Together, Jenny and her father drag Anna's body up. They stand back. They look at each other, Simon's eyes glittering with tears as if Jenny's mother is already dead.

Turning away, Jenny punches her arms into her jacket sleeves.

"Button up before you go out," Anna says. "Ida said it's plenty cold."

"Yes, winter's in the air." Jenny kisses her mother's warm cheek. "Take care. I love you." But how little after all, that counts. Love will not make Jenny's mother better. "You too, Simon." Love will not make Jenny's father any more like her than he already is. "I love you despite our differences."

"I know. Drive carefully," Simon says.

Jenny plunges out of her mother's room, down the hall, the stairs, out of the building, into her car.

Pulling her drawing out of her bag, she grabs her wallet and takes out three quarters and three dimes, one for each of the tolls on the way home. She fastens her seat belt. There is nothing more Jenny can do to make the trip easier or safer.

She turns on the engine. Clutching the steering wheel, she drives, deliberately, over the bumps, into the old, the black clarity. Disheveled lights strike her with their brilliance. Jenny reaches the familiar parkway and her fingers loosen. Her body settles around her like a down comforter.

From now on, Jenny is the mother of her mother, the mother of herself. Like the rest of her children, she and Anna must fly or fall. Beside Jenny on the seat, her dead chrysanthemum picture curls like an open hand made of paper.

Chapter XVI

PARTIAL COUNT
• *February Second* •

Lying in her bed, the comforter drawn up under her chin, her head propped against the head-board, Jenny stares out the window. Though it cannot be much after four o'clock, silver rain needles are driving through darkness, sewing winter down, nailing her deeper and deeper into a sightless chasm. Already she lies blind in soft earth. Already much of her is gone.

First her daughter took off for college. Then her son. Jenny stupidly let her lover go. Her parents are in Florida, sunk in a gold chasm of their own. Jenny's last child is in school, preparing to go to college. Her husband is at one of his meetings. This time he may never come back.

Saul let Jenny get cancer. He did not keep the doctor from taking away her breast. Saul says the decision to have surgery was her own.

What decision? To die now or later, what difference? How long can a one-breasted woman keep a man? The bedroom walls Jenny painted sunshine yellow have turned greenish, like someone about to vomit. Near her dressing table, shadows crouch ready to spread.

Last night, she dreamed she was at a funeral. Her mother kept forcing her to look into the coffin. Jenny tried to run away. She tried to hide behind her sister, but Barbara was dancing too fast. X-rays, rising out of the coffin, were dissolving Jenny. Her breast was already gone. Jenny woke, screams clogging her throat.

"You sleeping, sugar?" Gliding the door open, Barbara creeps in.

"Sort of." Jenny's sister taught her everything she knows about fake sleeping. Jenny could never fool Barbara.

"That's good," Barbara says.

Light brays at Jenny's eyes.

"Could you please turn that off?"

"You'll get used to it in a minute. Guess what I saw when I went out to get your mail?" Barbara lays a sodden packet of letters, catalogues, and an *Art News* on Jenny's belly.

"You saw rain." The mail rises and falls as Jenny breathes.

"That too, but guess what else."

"I don't feel like guessing." Jenny looks out the window at the silver light.

"There are snowdrops up out of the ground, right next to your front stoop," Barbara says. "The groundhog is right. Today's the first day of spring."

"If you say so," Jenny says. "Would you turn off the light when you go back down, please?"

"Don't you want to look at your mail?" Barbara asks.

"Not now." Jenny does not want to move her mind, or her mouth, around words.

"I'm cooking you a chicken for dinner," Barbara says. "Luke says you love chicken."

That was in the old days. A week ago.

"I'm too tired now to want much of anything." Jenny is exhausted, lying here, wonderfully relaxed, floating miles below her old worries, her old exertions, her old appetites, and her sister, above Jenny in an irrelevant world. "Please, just let me sleep."

"Sure, sugar. See you later." Returning the room to darkness, Barbara steals out.

Jenny rolls over onto her good side. The mail slides off into the curve of her body, like boats beached by a hurricane.

Even in this gloom, Olga's writing is clear, bold, black. Probably just a get well card. Her sister has lined up ranks of get well cards on the bureau, like turrets in the Maginot Line. Nothing can defend Jenny against death. Not even a card from Olga Zaretsky.

("What did my son have to say?" Jenny asked her mother.

"The usual." Anna was opening the last button. "He hopes I'll get better soon. All that crap.")

Jenny is damned if she is going to be like Anna. Snaking her good arm out into the cold, she grabs Olga's letter. On Woman Space stationery.

Dear Jenny,

Can you possibly do a one woman show for us to open the second Sunday in May? As usual, we're a little late getting our act together, but we hope this still gives you enough time. Let me know, please, before the tenth. That's when we're having our next committee meeting. Yes, those lovely get togethers are still going on. Anyway, we all hope you can help us out.

Optimistically,

Olga

Out of the question of course. Staring at the window, Jenny's eyes swell with tears. How she would have adored the idea of her own show a week ago! But now Jenny pictures herself in May, bald, emaciated, dead. She must turn Olga down. Rain, turning to sleet, picks at the glass.

Woman Space does not really need Jenny. There are hundreds of other artists in Hartford. No one needs Jenny. Her children have their own lives. All she ever had for Saul was her body, and her body is not good any more. Jenny is too old to become a great artist, too sick now to be even a lesser one.

"Mom?" Luke knocks while walking in. The light flares on. "Okay if I come in?" He stands at the foot of her bed.

"Not really." Jenny feels a twinge in the place where her breast used to be. Years ago, that breast filled with milk at the sound of Luke's voice.

"Can I watch Mary Tyler Moore in here?" he asks.

It is a show they both used to like.

"I'd rather not." Now, Jenny likes nothing and no one.

"Want me to go practice?" Luke asks.

"That's up to you."

"Since when?"

"Since I got cancer." Not after all a lump, but a dimple. Jenny called the doctor so he could tell her a dimple was okay.

"I thought they trashed your cancer," Luke says.

"That's what they say but—." It is Jenny they trashed. They threw her breast in the garbage. Jenny imagines a stray dog, gnawing at her flesh in some gutter, her cancer roaming in the street, the sewers.

"Hey cool. Who sent you this?" Luke flashes a photo of a sow in sunglasses.

"That must be Waldo's,".Jenny says. "Give it here."

"What's the magic word?"

"Please." How little sympathy Jenny had for her mother when

Anna bared her teeth over the word! "Please, you little twirp." Jenny thrusts her good arm out into the cold air. "Or else." She makes a fist.

"No need to threaten violence." Dropping the card beside her, Luke heads out the door, switching off the light.

"Turn that on," Jenny yells.

"No sweat. Just testing," Luke says. "Aunt Barbara told me you were up here half dead."

"Just go practice," Jenny says. Him on the clarinet, her for the grave, after she sees what Waldo has to say.

He wants her to come to his opening at O.K. Harris on March seventh. Jenny imagines herself in another month, pale and lean, with interesting shadows pooling in her hollow cheeks. That would be one hell of a last personal appearance. She really should get herself to Waldo's opening.

O.K. Harris is Big Time. Jenny will mingle with Names in the Art World, with Critics. Who knows what could come of it? Waldo deserves the best. Jenny deserves nothing. All she has to show for herself is maybe one first class print, a collage, and, if she is being generous, a decent collagraph.

A tear seeps across her temple. If Woman Space East is ready to show her work, Jenny's work cannot be very original. Not unless original is in now. Picking up *Art News*, Jenny flaps pages. Conceptual is the ticket. Beuys has moved in with a coyote for three days. Laurie Anderson is performing. Jenny's stuff is nothing like this. But Woman Space must be desperate for anyone, anyone at all. Or else they heard about Jenny's cancer and feel sorry for her.

Barbara plotzes into the room.

"You know you're really very lucky." She lowers herself into the armchair next to the bed. The cushion gasps. "You not only have a terrific son, you're going to live to see him grow up."

"So they say." Jenny kept telling her mother she was lucky too. Now, like Anna, Jenny redefines luck. Luck is not having to watch Luke grow old. Luck is not living to watch people she loves suffer. Luck is lying here in easeful peace.

"God led you to catch it before it spread," Barbara says. "My friend, Marcie Plotkin, had to have a radical, but no recurrence, praised be He." If only Barbara would go Catholic and cross herself instead of smacking her chest, flesh on flesh. "Still, Marcie wasn't as fortunate as you are." If only Barbara would go away and leave Jenny alone. "She'll always need to wear special bathing suits but since you had a simple, you won't have that problem. Nothing will show."

"Great." Jenny will not have to wear a bathing suit if she is under heavy sedation this summer. Her doctor may prescribe marijuana for the pain. She laughs.

"There's nothing funny about it." Barbara drops her leg across the bed. "God made His countenance to shine on you. Blessed be His name." The other leg. "After a radical, a lot of women's arms swell up." Barbara's legs lie like liverwursts across Jenny's bed. "You should be grateful, sugar, you're lucky."

"So you keep telling me." Turning her head, Jenny hears her heart beating in her pillow, pumping cancer cells through her body like Nazis pumping gas. All her life she suspected that Nazis would get her. One way or another. Once, at a dinner party, a doctor told her breast cancer can show up years later anywhere. He had seen it in patients' brains and pancreases. He said there is no such thing as a complete recovery from breast cancer. After a simple mastectomy, Jenny is doomed. Simple. No more suspense. She can lie back and enjoy certainty if her sister will only get out.

"You think you're going to want an implant?" Barbara asks. "That's what my friend Toby Mintz decided on."

"How'd it turn out?" Jenny, who has always had a weakness for case histories, cannot stop herself from asking.

"Fantastic," Barbara says.

"How long did she have to wait after her mastectomy?"

"I think about six months." Barbara is visiting Jenny at home just as she visited Anna at Burke. "Once the healing process is done."

"I would think it would be weird, having a bag of water sewn up inside you." Since their mother's stroke, Jenny talks to her sister differently, as if illness breeds, or rekindles, intimacy.

"I don't see why," Barbara says. "As long as we've got bladders and kidneys in us, why not one more bag?"

"That's true." Jenny's other breast does feel a lot like a skin-covered juice pouch.

"You know regular surgeons don't do implants," Barbara says. "You have to go to a plastic surgeon. Toby says that's an experience in itself."

"Why? What are they like?"

"She says hers had flowing fountains in the waiting room and Muzak. She said it was like going to a jet set hairdresser. He even showed her pictures so she could choose the style she wanted."

"Why didn't he just match up the new one with the one she had?" Jenny asks.

"He said that while she was having it done she might as well let

194

him fix her up to look better." Barbara juts out her chest. "God knows I could use help, a lift, as they say." Caving in, she tucks her hair around her ear, and, for a moment, Barbara looks like a girl. "But listen, you want me to get you the name of a good doctor in New York, or would you rather have it done here?"

"New York, by all means." Jenny rather likes the idea of a New York breast. "But this is ridiculous." Six months from now, she will have more important things on her mind. This summer, Jenny could have a show of her own. "Didn't you say something about chicken?" Another carcass to taunt Jenny with past failure. Only death can save her from a show of her own.

"Absolutely." Barbara heaves herself to her feet. "Back in a jiffy."

"No rush." Jenny snuggles down under her comforter. If Saul were here to cook, she would enjoy eating her meals in bed. She would enjoy exploiting her husband just as her mother enjoys exploiting her father. Pushing herself up in the bed, Jenny catches her reflection in the dressing table mirror. Ghastly.

The doorbell is ringing.

"Who is that?" Jenny calls out.

"Just a minute." Luke has it. He is talking to someone, a man. Luke stomps up the stairs. "Special delivery." He frisbees a manila envelope at Jenny.

Jenny lifts her arm, the sudden movement yanking her skin. "Please."

"From Esther," Luke says.

"Next time, hand it to me." Jenny squeezes back into herself.

"Yes, your holiness." Luke veers around.

"Wait a minute. Grab me my mirror, my comb," Jenny says, "and my cosmetic bag in the drawer, and don't throw anything, please."

"Expecting company?"

"Your father should be home soon." Ripping open the envelope from Esther, Jenny slides a photo of her daughter onto her thighs.

"A preview of the real me," it says on the back. "The rest arriving some time Friday. xx's, Ess."

Jenny's cancer is bringing her daughter home.

"Not too shabby." Luke snatches his sister's picture up to the light.

Barbara comes in with Jenny's tray.

"How about a sit-up pillow, there, behind your mother's back?"

"Looks great!" Jenny lies.

Stewed chicken. Jenny's sister stews everything. Kosher

chicken. The metal tag, with its blue Star of David, pinches the fowl's gray skin. Hairs sprout from the wing.

"Be sure you drink every drop of that broth," Barbara says. "It's no myth about chicken soup's restorative power you know. Tests proved it."

"Fine." Jenny will deal with this food as soon as her sister gets out. "You go eat." Red Jello wiggles like a breast on her tray.

"Call me if you need anything else, sugar." Barbara hurries down to her own meal.

"Want the telly on?" Luke lingers.

"With the sound off," Jenny says.

"You care what channel?" Luke peers at garish figures that move, like fish in a tank, across the screen.

"That's fine." Jenny peels the skin off her chicken leg. "And please, go get me a glass of wine."

"I thought cancer's supposed to kill your appetite," Luke says.

"Maybe I'm in remission." Jenny waves him away.

The cat jumps up next to her. Jenny feeds him her chicken skin. She dips a chunk of bread into her soup and stuffs it in her mouth. Grease dribbles down her chin. Tearing meat from the bones, Jenny feeds the cat. Jimmy Carter gloats. With no audio, he is cheerful company.

"Miss Ward wants to know what day next week you can come in for a conference." Chomping on a red delicious, Luke hands Jenny her glass of wine.

"Can I have a bite?" she asks.

"Be my guest." Luke tosses the apple. "Take the rest."

Jenny has the glass in her good hand. She thrusts out the bad one and it works. Wincing, she grips the apple.

"Hey, how about that?" Jenny caught with her bad hand. Maybe the Amazons were right about cutting off a breast.

"Ready for the Major Leagues," Luke says.

"Hear, hear." Jenny bites the fresh cold apple and tastes, as if for the first time, the intensity of life.

"Quick. Pick a conference date," Luke says. "I have to take a wicked piss."

"Tell Miss Ward I can't come, and flush this Jello down the toilet," Jenny says.

"She'll need an excuse." Luke disappears into the bathroom. "Everybody else's mother is already scheduled."

"Tell her I've got cancer." Jenny is not going to fill up her remaining days with the teacher's conferences, dentist appoint-

196

ments, rush hours that eat up a life. "Tell her to send me a written report."

"She can't. Miss Ward's illiterate." Strolling back into the room, Luke leans over the bed and gazes at himself in Jenny's magnifying mirror. "Well what have we here, my good man?" He yanks down his T-shirt neck. "My very first chest hair."

"Congratulations." Jenny tears her comb through her hair.

"What for? It's just one step closer to the big D, that's all," Luke says.

"Don't be morbid."

"Sorry about that. Must of got it from the neighbors." Luke swings out of Jenny's room.

Propping her mirror on her knees, Jenny examines her face. Definitely needs work.

"Oh good." Barbara fills the doorway. "You're in the clean plate club."

"Could you please hand me that bottle of skin freshener?" Jenny asks.

"Sure. Want some more chicken?" Barbara asks.

"No thanks." Jenny bathes her face, rouges her cheeks.

"How about a cookie?" Barbara asks.

"Nothing, thank you."

"I'll go hard boil some eggs for tomorrow so you can have egg salad." It is like old times, Barbara filling in for Anna, mothering her baby sister, fixing Jenny's favorite foods.

The phone rings.

"Want me to get that?" Barbara asks.

"Why should you?" Stretching her arm for the phone, Jenny makes clear now that pain or no she is grown up now, Barbara too, both of them middle-aged women who must take care of themselves. "Hello."

"I just heard." It is Mimi.

"I thought you were in Japan." Jenny has been longing for her best friend.

"I am. In Kyoto to be exact. Are you all right?"

"Yes. How did the news get over there?" Jenny asks.

"Your mother ran into my mother in Florida and of course Dolores couldn't wait to cable me. I'd fly home but as you know, I can't stand sick people. I could however, in your case, make an exception. How bad is it?"

"The surgeon swears up and down I'm clean." Hearing herself say this, Jenny thinks it may be true. Cancer may be in her past.

"Good. I still need you," Mimi says.

"I've been asked to do a one woman show at the gallery where I used to work," Jenny says. "In May."

"I'll be there," Mimi says.

"You're on." Jenny throws back her comforter. Now that she has promised Mimi, she must tell Olga yes. A chill riffles her skin.

"I'm dying to get back," Mimi says. "Dolores tells me the baby has taken his first step."

"Great." Recovering herself, Jenny goes over what she has. Her Seder print, of course, and the two self-portraits, plus the drawing of her and Esther, and at least one collage. Jenny has the nucleus of a show. "But look, this is costing you a fortune, we can talk when you get home." She hears Saul on the stairs.

"I'll be home in ten days," Mimi says. "Either I'll come up, or you'll come down."

"Fine." Hanging up, Jenny tries to look wan since Saul had no business to leave her, on her deathbed.

"You look very appealing." Bending over, he slides his tongue into Jenny's mouth.

Even cancer cannot quell her lust for this man who smells like earth and iron. Shifting yet solid, Saul is Jenny's ground.

"Stop." She pushes him away.

"Here." Saul pulls a cornucopia of freesias out from behind his back.

"That's not fair," Jenny says. "You know I'll do anything for freesias."

"That's the general idea," Saul says.

"I just had surgery." Jenny is not interested in grabbing his damn lifeline.

"That was eight days ago."

"It takes time."

"Whenever you're ready." Saul stretches out beside her, damp, cool, inviting.

"How was your meeting?" Jenny reminds herself that he chose to leave her.

"Pretty productive. How were things here?"

"You know my sister can't cook." No need for Jenny to tell Saul she had a good time with Barbara. "What did you have for dinner?"

"A Lucullan Feast." Saul winds an arm around her. "Namely a cup of clam chowder." He cradles Jenny's head on his chest. "And a tuna fish sandwich." He strokes her hair. "Nothing you would not have approved of." His lips touch her ear.

"Glad to hear it." Quickly, Jenny checks Saul's face and finds that rather than making fun, he is paying her the serious attention he usually gives only to books. Jenny begins to like her new role of Cancer Victim.

"The doctor did say I could live to be a hundred, you know." Fair is fair. Jenny cannot help working her hand up under his sweater.

Saul gropes for her remaining breast.

"You know Saul, you have a one track mind." Under the bandage, Jenny's body tingles as if her other breast is still there.

"Break it up, you two." Luke kicks the door back against the wall.

"Come right in, Ed." Jenny flops back, away from Saul.

"Ed?" Luke falls for it. "Has the disease eaten my very name from the woman's brain?"

"Ed as in Eddy Puss," Jenny says. "I would obviously like to be alone with your father right now."

"First tell me when I can sign you up for a conference with Miss Ward," Luke says.

"What's this? Blackmail?" Jenny asks. "If I don't waste my time on your illiterate teacher, you'll play duenna?"

"Do you know what it feels like to be the only one whose mother doesn't show up?" Luke hangs form the door frame.

"All right." Jenny sighs. She is not dead. "But make it for early morning or late afternoon." Jenny has two weeks of drawing and collagraphy assignments to make up. A show to prepare.

"Now get out of here." Saul shuts the door after Luke and returns to the bed.

Jenny unbuckles his belt.

"Take off those pants." She helps him.

Saul cannot pretend indifference as Jenny can. As soon as she pushes down his underpants, his cock springs up. Jenny takes it in her hand. Soft and enduring as rose petals, his privates always call up in her a tender interest, plus a kind of maternal pity for someone whose treasures can never be tucked safely away. Saul trusts her to hold him, he lets her see how much he loves her palm rubbing his warm, suede skin. Jenny's insides water like a hungry mouth.

Downstairs, Luke shrieks clarinet gospel. Barbara is singing hymns.

Jenny has always fantasized having sex in public. This may be as close as she ever gets.

"You don't mind making love with a mutilated woman?" she asks.

"I look forward to it." Saul's breath is hot in her ear.

Giggling, Jenny pulls her nightgown up around her waist and wriggles against Saul's thigh, his belly, his hot cock. Heat smolders under Jenny's skin. It has been days since she felt Saul's naked body. Now she is outlined in fire, and the outline melts, and inside is outside, and Saul and Jenny are what they are doing, a single hot breathing surging in a dark sea, in the delicate oscillating fish, in wherever they are.

Saul lies, his weight soft on Jenny. She strokes his satin shoulder, love pouring through her palm.

"Am I too heavy for you?" Saul shifts his body.

"No." Jenny holds him. "Stay." The glue that sticks them together is still wet.

Luke knuckles their door.

"You guys want to watch 'The Ascent of Man'?"

"In just a minute." Saul scrambles off the bed and to his feet. "Be right with you." He throws on his sweater, his pants.

Jenny draws the sheet up under her chin.

"You can come in now," she says.

"It's already started." Glowering at the bed, Luke dashes for the television.

"If we miss a little, we'll survive." Jenny touches her bandages.

Jacob Bronowski floats into the television screen. Dying of cancer, he had time to finish this series, and now, wearing the greaser's black leather jacket Jenny has come to love, Bronowski's ghost is delighting in the inventive designs and intricacies of Moorish filigrees and tiles in the Alhambra.

Jenny's visions would make that Moslem stuff look sick. She has profound emotions to express. And she may still have time to produce images for Bronowski's ilk. How she would love that!

"Shut your eyes, Luke." Jenny pushes herself up, off the bed.

The scent of freesias trails her into the bathroom. Jenny closes it out. Surrounded by white tile, she turns on the overhead light, Jenny turns on lights flanking the mirror above the sink. She stands in the center of light that echoes off every white surface in this unyielding room.

When the surgeon first took off the bandages in the hospital, he said Jenny could take off the new ones and replace them whenever she wanted to wash. Jenny was planning to let the undertaker worry about washing her. Instead, she lifts her nightgown over her head, compressing a scream. The awful tightness is her fault. Jenny must exercise. No more acting like her mother.

Jenny opens her eyes. In the same full-length mirror where she first saw the dimple, she now sees a white pad taped to her like first base. Jenny presses it. Hard, tender, not painful. Swallowing her breath, she lifts a corner of the tape, peeling it, little by little as her skin pleads with her to stop. Jenny keeps pulling. slowly. The gauze comes off with the tape. Lifting the pad, Jenny lets her breath out.

There is no hole, not even a hollow. A dark red, puckered seam crosses the right side of her chest like a dry riverbed. The skin around this scar is splotched yellow, gray, and blue. After being covered so long, it smells like belly button.

Opening her fist, Jenny covers the place with her hand. As a child she felt this same flatness. Dropping her hand, Jenny confronts in the mirror half a little girl with a cracked, wrinkly, overlay of a woman's experience. Tears spurt up and out of her eyes like steam from the top of a pressure cooker. The person facing Jenny is no stranger.

Jenny leans back against the cold porcelain sink. She laughs. She fingers her new seam as if it sews up a treasure. In front of her, across a tile wall blank and inevitable as her own death, her reflection glimmers. And Jenny adds to the old *Courant* articles in her mental file of disasters, this new, pale, hard, gleaming image of a survivor.

Chapter XVII

FULL COUNT
• *Mother's Day* •

This is it. After today, everyone will know what Jenny is capable of doing. This and no more, at least not yet. Jenny leans against a table in front of the gallery windows, surveying her show. Clustered on the walls, crowded on pedestals, Jenny's pictures, constructions and assemblages, transform Woman Space until it is almost as thickly personal as her kitchen, every piece here a chip of Jenny's life.

The worst of it is her work has a primitive dashed-off look. That is what makes it accessible and funny. But no one will know or care how hard Jenny struggled to make art like a child's. No one, least of all Jenny, will know if it was worth the effort to get this stuff out.

"Ready"—Jenny's collage of herself, Luke, and Aaron on a white ground surrounded by a broad black mat on which she pasted news photos of a nuclear blast, a gun, a knife, a Nazi flag, a postcard picture of an electric chair, and Goya's Witches Sabbath, plus her own drawings of a devil, a snake, a skull and crossbones—is pretty effective. Stuck on their square white island, the people look safely trapped. So far, okay.

"Set" is a triumph. Jenny wishes Jewell-Anne Drayton would show up today to see not one misplaced dot. Jenny printed each figure to overlap precisely one half inch along the next. The background stripes clinch the fact that this is perfect registration. Nothing unintentional, Jenny made all the figures huge except for herself, a small woman like the catch in a chain of giant links. So much for Jewell-Anne. Jenny's Seder has the monumentality of Stonehenge. At least that is what Jenny hopes it has.

Sliding her overall strap up over her shoulder, she checks her next piece. "Round One" is, Jenny must admit, a regression. She learned to make papier mâché as a girl. Jenny shellacked this papier mâché roast chicken's skin as glossy brown as a picture in a woman's magazine. Display art.

Her "Round Two" is either a disaster or a tour de force. God, how Jenny wishes she could believe again and pray! Peering into her papier mâché chicken carcass, through a shredded 'meat' fringe, she can hardly see the tiny figure of a woman caged inside. What if no one sees her? What if everyone thinks Rounds One and Two are about food?

And will anyone understand what "Round Three"—a mirror with a smile painted on it—has to do with chickens? Maybe Jenny should have made Iris into a big white bus with red crosses, a unique ambulance. Jenny stands behind the tape line she pinned to the rug; the painted smile covers her mouth. But what about people whose mouths are at different heights? Will they know enough to move themselves into the right position? Or is this image of Jenny's too personal?

Jenny veers toward the windows. Late spring sun slaps her face. She could not have a better day for her opening, yet Jenny's hands feel as if they have been in a refrigerator.

Maybe no one but her family will come. Nothing could be worse than making a fool of herself in front of her family. After all, strangers are strangers. They can think what they like.

Here at the gallery this morning, Esther said the show is terrific. Even Luke said "Seeing Stars" is cool. But all Jenny did for that was superimpose a picture of herself on a photo of the earth seen from the moon so it appears that she is flying in space, the fuzzy stars and weightless body more her California interlude than any of the razzle-dazzle fireworks Jenny kept trying to recreate. Still, Esther took the picture of her. The cosmos belongs to N.A.S.A. Jenny can take credit only for the idea. That may not be enough.

Breathing on her fingers, Jenny cannot warm them.

Those who dislike "Round Three" will also hate "Nursing Wounds," her mirror with a frown.

And she can hear her sister right now commenting on "Re-Match."

"You call this art?" Barbara would point at the apron with boxing gloves ties to its strings.

"Conceptual art," Jenny mutters.

Talking to herself is not a good sign.

"This is another example of conceptual art." Pretending to be a docent, Jenny airily waves a hand at "Updating the Rules." No doubt about it, that T-shirt stuck with buttons of Jenny's own making—CHAUVINIST PIGS MAKE GOOD HAMS, SISTER-HOOD FOREVER, BETTER LAVENDER THAN DEAD, OPPRES-SION KILLS, and more a breast plate than a button, UP AGAINST THE ESTABLISHMENT MOTHER—is a brilliantly executed, witty idea. Poor Saul. What a pain Jenny was during her militant phase!

And what a stiff as a girl! Her high school yearbook picture, "Tactical Review," silk-screened in sepia, says it all.

"Back to Basics" may not say anything. It took Jenny months to figure out that she wanted to frame blank newsprint with bordello wallpaper on the sides, the words Woman Space on top, and on the bottom, the heading Classifieds. But now she sees she should have attached a pencil, let viewers participate in making art. No one will want to look at that blank space. Jenny has nothing new to say.

"New Angles"—Esther propping her mother up as if Jenny were the front of an easel—is very like the old advertisement: "You can rely on Klopman." Lifting her drawing off the wall, Jenny stands back to assess. Empty Space with Hook is worse. No matter how derivative "New Angles" is, it must stay. She hangs it back in place.

Jenny cannot, at this point, change anything. Her self-portrait grins at her. Shading purples for a black eye, and sketching herself with a jack-o'lantern grin was fun to do and funny to look at but now Jenny cowers before "Higher Education." It looks more like a character from "Hee Haw" than like herself. If Jenny is to be a great artist, she must learn better to nail down the essence of her feelings about what she sees.

She does have talent. Jenny lingers in front of her only collagraph, "Losing Weight." Until this image rose up in her, she thought she had chosen Saul over Iris. But Jenny's picture shows a balance scale, paint cans heavy on one side, an iris draped light on the other. As soon as this came out of her, Jenny knew it was right. Iris never had a chance against Saul.

However, had Jenny realized that layers of plastic net would print such great iris petals, she might better have left the paint out and committed herself to all flowers. She could have included her dead chrysanthemum, done a series of flower prints from birth to death to embody her view of the life process. Instead, Jenny used the particulars of her own experience. Now, seeing those particulars spread out for public viewing, she thinks she may have made a mistake. These images belong to someone else.

"Reversal," Jenny's next to last piece, has the same figures as "Set," her next to first piece. But this time, the figures are explicit: Jenny is Jenny, her sister is Barbara, both of them huge, silk-screened photos, their children medium size, their parents tiny, a double clasp linking the new chain.

In front of "Reversal," Jenny cringes like a guilty child. Anna and Simon will resent being shown with their children and grandchildren crowding them out. Tears melt Jenny's eyes. Once her parents told her what to do. Now, obeying the dictates of her art, Jenny wishes she had some other outside authority to turn to. Her sister has picked Religion. Jenny has only art. It may be that she has done every piece in this gallery to explain herself only to herself.

In "Partial Count" she finally found a use for her purple velvet. It lines a tiny white coffin, the cloth a hammock supporting a doll with one eye glued shut as if it is a winking, only half-dead corpse. Jenny grins at the doll.

Whatever anyone else thinks, she is satisfied. Mounted on, or in front of, the rye bread walls whose blandness once so offended her, Jenny's work has the shiny perfection of sliced tomatoes. This is polished, professional art. If it had been done by a stranger, Jenny would still enjoy it. Light gleams from her pieces as it used to gleam from Iris. Smiling, Jenny locks the door and skips across the hall to dress.

In her studio, the air smells of bananas, a whole crate of them, ripened to speckled perfection. Every thing is coming out right today. Certainty, like a cape, settles over Jenny. She has done as much as she can, probably enough.

Kicking off her sneakers, Jenny strips off her overalls and shirt and clambers onto the radiator. Her rust colored cotton blouse hangs from a handle high up on a window. As Jenny reaches for it, her fake breast does not follow the movement of her arm. Yet that breast will make some mouths water just as her papier mâché chicken will make some mouths water. And soon Jenny will have an implant and be almost good as new. Giving herself up to what has become a habitual moment of meditation, Jenny imagines cancer-eaters coursing through her body in a thorough search and destroy mission. Then, blouse in hand, she stares down at the floor.

How far up she is! She used to feel, in this studio, like a dwarf. Now, easing herself down, Jenny fits in. Her sandals are her sandals. The mother's day earrings Luke gave her this morning dangle from Jenny's ears. Her skirt and blouse, folded over her body with the old seductiveness, is unaware that now Jenny is bigger than she was.

She is more like her grandmother. Grandma lugged a trunk full of oranges from Odessa. Jenny drags her crate of bananas across the hall, into the gallery where she lays out the fruit in yellow waves on the table in front of the windows.

"Where do you want these?" Saul stands in the doorway, hugging her price-lists in one arm and an astonishing explosion of lilacs in the other.

"Over there," Jenny says.

"Flowers there too?" Saul avoids looking at the walls, as if the sight of Jenny's work might hurt his eyes.

"No. I'll take them." Jenny makes room for the lilac geyser in the center of the banana surf. "Where'd they come from? They're gorgeous."

"Esther showed up with them." Squaring his shoulders, Saul strolls over to the chicken carcass.

Jenny meant for him to begin at the beginning with "Ready." Saul is bent over, peering inside her chicken carcass. Jenny meant for Iris to be her lover, or at least her friend, for life. Yet the lilacs come from Esther who, ahead of her mother, knows how much this opening means to Jenny. And the lavender flowers remind Jenny of Iris who taught her that lavender is the red-white-and blue of the gay.

"You've pulled it off, Jen." Saul turns to her a face bright with relief.

Jenny sways, swishing her skirt along her thighs. Her show is all right. And so is she. There on the wall, and here swathed in rust-colored cotton, Jenny is oddly at one.

"Happy mother's day." Aaron sweeps in and whisks a cloth off a mountain of onion sandwiches, each one ruffled in minced parsley.

"It must've taken you hours to make that many." Jenny plucks one off the top and pops it into her mouth. "Heaven."

"You should thank me." Luke comes in with stereo speakers and a turntable. "That scuzzball made me do all the work."

"What do you think I gave you my 'Talking Heads' for?" Swooping the sandwiches away from Jenny, Aaron veils the platter and sets it on a speaker. "We must save some for the company." Aaron feeds his mother her own line.

Jenny moves to the mirror. People will be here soon and she has yet to paint her face. The mirrored smile under her chin like a collar, she pinks her cheeks and nose, colors her eyelids, outlines her eyes, readying herself as carefully as she did the night she met Iris.

"Hey, this one's pretty tough." Aaron is gazing into the doll coffin. "What's it represent?"

"If your mother knew how to express her meanings in words, she would be a writer, not an image maker," Saul says.

"I like the way the purple velvet goes with the pink plastic skin," Jenny says to prove that she can too explain her work in words.

"How come you guys left all the heavy stuff for me?" Esther tramps in holding a carton of champagne, bags of plastic glasses hanging from her fingers like fat icicles.

"I'd have carried that if you'd asked me." Saul rushes to take the carton from his daughter.

It has been two years and still Jenny has not convinced him that women do not need the help of men. And no wonder. Luke is setting up the stereo. Aaron is icing the champagne. Queen of the bees, all Jenny is doing is making herself up.

"Am I early?" Her chest heaving, Barbara staggers into the gallery.

"You're the first." Jenny screws the top on her mascara. Tight. "Welcome."

"The folks sent you this." Barbara holds out to her sister mums and ferns in the shape of a giant banana split. "Read the card."

"With you in spirit if not in reality. Your proud parent." Tears muffle Jenny's voice, blur the bronze flowers. She does not want a mother and father who do not even realize, with their eternal chrysanthemums, that this is spring. Jenny wants Simon and Anna, a buffer between her and disaster. She sets their flowers below the doll coffin.

"I'll have to tell them how perfect it looks." Reminding herself that the last thing she wants is for her parents to see her work, Jenny hooks her tears before her eye make-up streaks.

"I'll tell them. This is quite something." Barbara stands, a hand on each hip, in front of "Reversal."

Jenny freezes.

Her sister must recognize the people at that Seder. She must see the striped wallpaper, must know her dining room reminds Jenny of a prison. Barbara will tell their parents that Jenny used her family without permission.

Aaron rushes between his mother and his aunt.

"Since when is Mr. Berkowitz into art?" He jerks a thumb at the doorway.

"Harvey, how wonderful you could come!" Assuming her public stance, Jenny glides toward Harvey like a dancer. Luke has music playing. Maybe Barbara will waltz back to New York without telling Jenny what she thinks. Maybe she will have a fatal accident on the way home. "I'm really glad to see you."

"It's good to be here." Harvey wears patchwork slacks, a shocking pink T-shirt, a sincere smile. "Your work's very impressive, very inventive." In the old days Harvey would have leaned down and kissed Jenny, or, at the very least, put out his hand for her to shake. Now he stands back, on his face the poor-cancer-victim look Jenny has learned to recognize.

"You were right not to find me a job." Jenny flings the fact at him like a glove. "As you said, the best jobs are the ones you create for yourself." She is still irked that Harvey could find no slot for her, still not sure she will know, with no one to tell her, day after day, what she must do.

"I hope no one else listens." Harvey chuckles professionally. "If everyone was to invent his own job, I'd soon be out of work placing people."

"Would that really be so terrible?" Jenny asks.

"Believe it or not, that's a question I pose to myself from time to time." Harvey's eyes suddenly swim into hers. "But I still haven't come up with a good answer." His eyes gleam with wet.

"I wish I could help you." How Jewish Jenny is! Even in the midst of her triumph she feels for Harvey's grief.

"You make it sound serious. I'm really fine." Harvey, his teeth sharp as the metal edging Jenny sets around her garden to keep out weeds, slides his smile back on.

"Excuse me." Jenny whirls away, toward Waldo, dressed today in daffodil yellow.

"I'm so glad you could make it." Kissing his cheek, Jenny smells the odor of old bourbon.

"Couldn't keep me away from it," Waldo says.

"I particularly want you to see this one." Jenny leads Waldo over to her Seder print. "Look familiar?"

"You do remember I said all along you had greatness in you." Waldo's New York show was anything but great. His opinion cannot be taken seriously.

"How could I forget?" Jenny waves to Olga Zarecki. "It's the nicest thing anyone's ever said to me."

"I may never eat another Twinkie as long as I live." Olga holds an onion sandwich up as if it were a prize. "All my life I thought

Twinkies were as near perfect as food gets." She thrusts the whole sandwich into her mouth.

"Waldo Cobb, Olga Zarecki," Jenny says.

"I do love a woman with a good appetite," Waldo says.

Esther bobs up behind Jenny.

"Be warned. Your ex-boss is here with her camera."

"That's great," Jenny says.

"And I suppose Iris will show up too?" Esther examines her mother's eyes like a doctor searching for a subtle symptom of disease.

"If she does, she does, but she won't." Though Jenny can go no place in Hartford without bumping into someone she knows, in the last ten months she has not once run into Iris. Iris may not even know about the mastectomy. Beside their affection for Saul, Jenny and Iris never did have much in common.

And yet Iris's shoulders, her eider-down breasts, her waist and buns, and the certainty of those mergers with Jenny in the night are as fixed in Jenny as a ring inside a tree, her year with Iris a dark distortion heightening the serene, honey circles of her usual life. It is Iris who brought Jenny here; Iris, Esther, Anna, and cancer that taught Jenny how to milk time.

"That's cool with me," Esther says.

"Me too, I guess." Jenny, with "Cheek to Cheek" playing in the background, approaches her old enemy swaying like Ginger Rogers nearing Fred Astaire. "It's been my ambition to make the *Courant*." Jenny does not insist on the front page, not yet.

"The gallery can use the publicity," Cynthia says.

"Say 'Orgasm'," Esther shouts.

Jenny laughs. After the flash, polka dots float in the air. Mimi is here, wafting along the wall, her eyes on Jenny's work.

Jenny drifts up to her. "Like it?"

"I've seen far worse exhibits at the Whitney." Kissing Jenny, Mimi enfolds her, as Jenny's mother once did, in 'Joy.' "This is fun stuff." Mimi does a little dance step, gold chains on her shoes twinkling. "You've even got my most favorite music."

"Luke's responsible for that." Jenny tries not to mind but her work is meant to be more than fun, and it is not the music she wants people to like.

"I knew you guys would get off on golden oldies," Luke says.

"What are your plans for this summer, Luke?" Mimi takes two champagnes from Aaron's tray. "Tell you why I ask." She gives a glass to Luke. "The baby-sitter who was supposed to go with us to Bermuda has, it now seems, to go to summer school."

"I've never been to Bermuda." Holding his champagne to his lips, Luke looks up at Mimi as if she were his fairy godmother.

Jenny drifts off, a bubble touching for a moment this friend, that relative in a community she once sought in sisterhood. But ready-made was too easy. This is the afterglow of Jenny's work.

"Eat that before it disappears." Aaron shoves at her a platter holding the last onion sandwich.

"You want I should die an old maid?" Thanks to the women's movement, Jenny's children know nothing of the concept. "Oh God, that's delicious."

"I can't believe what a bunch of pig-outs your buddies are," Aaron says.

"Some man in yellow double-knits wants to buy 'Set'," Esther says.

"Ask your father if he brought the box of stars with him and if he did, stick one on the 'Set' label." Jenny scoots over to Waldo. "My first sale. I'm really flattered." Actually sheepish. Jenny owns none of Waldo's prints.

"I regard my purchase as an excellent investment." Waldo's voice slips, like a massage, over her body.

"An investment in art, I trust," Jenny says.

"What else is there?" Waldo winks.

"How about my quilts?" Olga's lips make sticky little banana noises. "Want to see some of them later?"

"Sounds most enticing," Waldo says.

"Watch out for this old fox." Jenny grins at them both the euphoria she is feeling.

"So." Barbara thunders up. "Before I go, there's something I must tell you."

"Sure. Go ahead." So much for euphoria. As if caught in a cloudburst, Jenny is cold and flat.

"Emily's making me a grandmother," Barbara says.

"That's marvelous." Jenny takes her sister's arm, Barbara's flesh warm and soft as the baby to come. "When?"

"November. Around Thanksgiving."

"I envy you." Jenny means this.

"What can I say, sugar? We envy each other, always have and probably always will." Barbara waves at the show. "I could never do anything this ambitious."

"Sure you could. Take time for yourself. Don't let them make you babysit," Jenny says.

"God willing." Barbara lifts her eyes to fluorescent lights.

"God?" Jenny asks. "This is my show and He isn't invited."

"No such of a thing," Barbara says. "Invited or not, God is everywhere."

Luke slinks up behind Jenny.

"Most of them are saying it's a kick-ass show," he says.

"Keep listening. Later, you'll give me details." Most of them like her stuff, not all. Jenny tries to spot the holdouts.

"What did I tell you?" Esther flashes her a high intensity smile. "You're a hit, Jennifer."

"So when will we get to see some of your work in New York?" Barbara asks, the question a winch twisting Jenny's belly into a neat coil.

"Maybe never." Jenny has not even conquered all of Hartford. Behind her sister, she sees Saul watching her. "Maybe in a year or two." Waldo did it. Jenny must let Saul know what to expect next.

"Take care, sugar," Barbara says. "I'm off."

"You're not staying for dinner?"

"I want to get back to the city before dark."

Already the golden light outside is turning silver, and the crowd inside is flowing away. Jenny kisses Mimi goodbye. Luke dismantles the stereo. Olga is taking Waldo out for pizza. Esther and Aaron pass a champagne bottle back and forth, tilting their heads and drinking as if from an angel's trumpet. And Jenny's show seeps, vague and indelible as the smell of bananas and lilacs, into memory.

Saul waves a sad hand at the table.

"What do you want me to do with these bananas?" he asks.

"Bring them home."

"They're almost round the bend."

"That's when they're at their best." Jenny's eyes take his. "Throwing good away isn't my style." What if his youth is gone? So is hers. Nothing for it but to adore him.

As for herself, too empty to pack up the remains of her opening, Jenny is suffering as if from jet lag. Languidly, she looks around at banana peels and paintings. The gallery is not lurching, she is not stuck. Yet Womanspace could be for her an elevator going up. Two years ago, Jenny would have known what to do. But this is now.

ACKNOWLEDGMENTS

I had a lot of help with this novel. Anne Bassinger and Natalie Bassette started me writing. Mary Nash said I had talent. Hilma Wolitzer recognized my passionate commitment to this story. Richard Ford heard a voice. Louis Peterson gave me an "A." Tobias Wolff said my work was good enough to revise. Barbara Greenberg saw in me a novelist. Louise Glück taught me to distinguish my dross from ore. David Huddle understood better than I what I was trying to say, and he made me feel it worth the trouble to say it. Timothy Seldes caused me to confront my own plot. Jehan Agrama went through each chapter asking why Jenny did what she did; answering was like following a thread through a maze. Linda M. Nelson and Jeene DeVane encouraged me to roll that thread around my finger. Erik Bendix, John Calandrillo, Lee Meitzen Grue, Diane B.D. Hockstader, Adam, Amy, Max, and Seth Leventhal, Stephen and Virginia Minot, Warren C. Miller, Joseph Ornato, Gloria Safier, Laurel Speer, Janet Sullivan, and the members of the West End Writers' Collective (most especially Pamela Casey and Suzanne M. Levine) are critics who told me what was wrong with my writing, not what is wrong with me. Hortense Spillers took me seriously from the beginning. Dianne McKinley Hunter believed in my ability when it was inchoate. Bill Knott grooved on what is right about my writing as does Elizabeth Anne Grant Cox. Myrna Shelton stopped me from rushing at the end. Frank Conroy trained me to be my own editor. Anne Bernays jabbed the first three chapters with her needle and left the rest for dead. Dan and Anita Lahn kept guiding me toward publication. The Ossabaw Island Project and the Millay Arts Colony granted me working time. Over the years, John Calandrillo, Jill Diskan, Roy Orbel, Joseph Ornato, and Anne Robb made writing space available to me. Channa Eberhart and Carol Lane typed whole drafts. Being in contact with these people has been my good fortune. To all of them I give thanks.